Nick Tyrone is a writer and political commentator who has written for the *New Statesman*, *Daily Telegraph*, *Independent* and *Daily Express*. He has also appeared on *BBC News*, *Good Morning Britain*, *Sky News*, *Al Jeezera* and *Intelligence Squared*. In 2017, he wrote the book *Apocalypse Delayed: Why the Left is Still in Trouble* about the future of UK politics.

Nick lives in London with his family.

www.nicktyrone.com
 @NicholasTyrone

Politics
is
Murder

NICK TYRONE

ACCENT

First published in 2020 by
HEADLINE PUBLISHING GROUP

2

Cataloguing in Publication Data is available from the British Library

ISBN 978 1 7861 5778 2

Typeset in 10.5/13.75pt Bembo Std by Jouve (UK), Milton Keynes

Printed and bound in Great Britain by Clays Ltd, Elcograf S.p.A.

HEADLINE PUBLISHING GROUP
An Hachette UK Company
Carmelite House
50 Victoria Embankment
London
EC4Y 0DZ

www.headline.co.uk
www.hachette.co.uk

To my wife, Polly

Chapter One

The worst part of my job is having to sort out these boring morning events. This one is typical: the Associate Directors cook up a terrible idea which they convince Reginald is wonderful. Then, they figure out the only way it will fly is by inviting a minister to speak on the tedious topic they have chosen. At this point they turn to me and ask, as the only person who works at Eligium who has any worthwhile political contacts (apart from Freddie, who cannot reasonably be asked to do anything which would resemble work), if I will suggest a minister for the event and then convince them to come. I execute this task – and then end up here at eight in the morning, in some poky room at the arse end of Westminster, alone, holding the bag.

As I'm putting out the cups at the rear end of the room, Tom turns up.

'Aren't you supposed to be back at the ranch answering the phone?' I ask him, hiding the fact that I'm happy to see him.

'No one calls the office this time of day, unless it's Chad Cooper. I figured you'd be by yourself and could use the help.'

Tom is the office dogsbody, doing jobs that are vital yet no one else is willing to bother with. He is 6'2, 6'3, in good shape but without being overly, off-puttingly muscular, with a face that is gorgeous but not in a mawkish, pretty-boy kind of way. I fancy him, but he's too young for me and besides, I would never foul my own nest.

1

About three minutes after Tom arrives, Charlie's Angels appear. These are the three junior researchers, Kate, Aashi, and Violet, given their collective nickname by the male staff of Eligium as they do everything I tell them and although Reginald is technically their line manager, pretty much work for me.

'Got here as quickly as we could, Charlotte,' Kate says, her heavy breathing showing she is telling the truth. I had texted the three of them when it became clear the Associate Directors weren't going to be around to help me set up the room.

'What can we do?' Aashi asks, as ever the teacher's pet. I point each of them in a respective direction and within fifteen minutes the whole room is up and running, ready for the Secretary of State for Emergencies and Contingencies, Geoffrey Bryant, to turn up and put a room full of twenty-three wonks to sleep with whatever twaddle he's planning to unleash.

Bryant is classic cabinet fodder; the type of person who will never contradict the Prime Minister, simply because they are incapable of forming their own opinion on anything. The department he leads is a joke, created last year as a PR exercise in the wake of several bad floods in the north-east of England. It is often referred to within the Westminster bubble as The Ministry of Silly Walks. It doesn't hurt that Bryant resembles a poor man's John Cleese, very tall with exaggeratedly long limbs that make him look a little like a cartoon character.

I walk out into the hallway when I think I hear Bryant's entourage arriving. Instead, it's Chad Cooper.

'Thought I'd come here instead of to the office and see if you needed any assistance,' he says. Chad Cooper is the most annoying person I've ever encountered in Westminster – and that is saying something profound. He is short, fat, bald, and speaks with an affected accent, apparently the result of a childhood which took him back and forth between America and Britain several times. The fact that we share youths marred by constant upheaval should bond us; Cooper's enervating presence cancels this out.

About a year ago, after a lot of badgering from Cooper, Reginald made him a 'Senior Fellow' of the think tank; an unpaid, honorary position. Reginald figured making this gesture would cause Cooper, who had taken to emailing or calling him twice a day, to leave us all alone. Unfortunately, giving Cooper the title he was after had the reverse effect and made the problem dramatically worse. Cooper took being put on the website as a Senior Fellow as licence to enter the office anytime he wished and just generally pretend he works for the think tank. He even had Eligium-branded business cards printed up at his own expense.

I set Cooper to work cleaning the cobwebs out of the toilets. A moment after he dashes off with some rubber gloves and a cloth, Bryant and his crew turn up.

'Hello, Charlotte!' Geoffrey says, grabbing my shoulders a little too firmly and giving me a large smooch on the cheek. 'Where do you want me?'

I take the Minister over to the podium and tell him that after I do the introductions, he has a twenty-minute slot.

'But no one's here yet!' he says to me like a five-year-old boy who has just been deprived of ice cream.

'That's because we don't open the door for another ten minutes, Geoffrey,' I say. He looks at his watch, confused (or at least, more confused than usual) and, annoyed that he is slightly early, wanders to the back of the room to get himself a coffee.

As the Secretary of State for Silly Walks saunters off to get some caffeine, Reginald runs into the room a sweaty, panting mess, having clearly run to try and get here before Bryant's arrival.

'Where's the minister?' Reginald just manages to ask me. I point him toward Geoffrey, who is still attempting to figure out how the coffee machine works. Instead of taking a moment to compose himself, Reginald instantly runs up to the minister, tripping a little when he gets to Bryant so that he has to crudely grab hold of the Secretary of State to steady himself.

'Reginald Beavers. I mean, Meavers! Reginald Meavers! I am so very, very happy that you are speaking at an Eligium event, Minister. Extremely, frightfully exuberant that you are here with us today. Really, really am. Today of all days, today being a day you are here with us to speak about things you wish to speak about. I would be ever so grateful as to buy you lunch on an occasion of your choosing.'

Even pond life like Bryant is going to react negatively to such a pitch.

'You work at the think tank Charlotte runs, do you?' he asks Reginald condescendingly.

'No, I run it! I run it! Me, Chief Executive, Charlotte work for me,' Reginald answers, ungrammatically. Bryant now looks horrified he's agreed to this gig, correctly sussing out Eligium as a clown show. He looks over in my direction and I give him a flirty smile to perk him up. It works. Bryant walks over.

'Keep the Beaver chap away from me. Deal?' he asks.

'Of course, Geoffrey,' I say in response.

That was classic Reginald behaviour. He reacts around frontline politicians the way a teenaged girl does in the middle of a pop star convention. He's never figured out that this is literally the worst possible approach. I suppose he's never had to learn – he is living, walking proof of the Westminster axiom that middle-aged white men can only fail upwards. He is 5'5, fat but not grossly so, 56 years of age – although he looks at least ten years older than that – smokes fags and drinks any and all alcoholic concoctions at great volume, as if he's on a slow-burn suicide mission. His grouchy, perma-hungover demeanour would be half-forgivable if he was brilliant at public policy, or at least reasonably clever, but no, Reginald is an unbelievable dullard. He, like so many middle-aged white men in Westminster, is lucky to be surrounded by extremely bright junior employees who are constantly covering for his and in fact, most of his senior team's mediocrity. Not that he ever notices; he treats everyone who works at Eligium like crap, with the exception of me, only because I scare him.

Having been ditched by the worst member of Her Majesty's Government, Reginald searches around for what to do next. As ever, he alights on precisely the wrong thing. Eyeing up a tear in Violet's tights, one unfortunately very high up on the leg, he walks up to her and says:

'I bet I know what that hole there is for!'

The look she gives in response terrifies him and he immediately retreats. For a moment I think Violet might physically hurt him, such is the hatred in her eyes, so thank God Reginald possesses some instinct for self-preservation. In the age of political correctness and #MeToo, the Chief Executive of Eligium is a walking lawsuit waiting to happen.

The hour arrives and I open the doors, allowing nine poor souls to drag themselves into the room. They are the usual bunch of in-house public affairs people, think tank junior researchers and weird old men of indeterminate occupation that come to these sorts of things. The crowd is thinner than I had anticipated. I might have to flirt even harder with Geoffrey Bryant if I ever want him to speak at an Eligium event again.

'Ladies and gentlemen, thank you for coming this morning. I would like to welcome the Secretary of State for Emergencies and Contingencies, Geoffrey Bryant, to talk to us about firewalls,' I say to a very quiet room. Yes, that was not the world's greatest introduction, but I can hardly be arsed here. Bryant steps up to the podium and gets right to the point.

'Thank you, Charlotte. I have been the Secretary of State for Emergency Planning for almost nine months now,' he says, having made two major errors in the first proper sentence of his speech: besides getting the name of his department wrong, he was appointed almost a year and a half ago. 'And in that time, I have thought of many ways to try and combat the problems we face with coastal erosion. And I will say something very controversial straight off the bat here: I do not believe that setting walls on fire is going to combat the problem effectively.'

5

Jesus wept. Surely one of the Special Advisers could have reviewed this speech, one Bryant clearly wrote himself before he got here? I look over at his entourage – they are chatting to Freddie, who must have arrived just as we kicked off proceedings. Freddie is good-looking in an ageing boy band member way; he has amazing teeth, so white they feel like they could burn your eyes out if you gazed at them for too long. He is the only one of the Three Stooges, i.e. the three male Associate Directors at Eligium, that I actually like. Freddie is in his mid-thirties but could pass for anywhere between twenty-six and forty depending on how he decides to dress on a particular day. He is very posh, great fun, and cannot complete any practical task. Freddie knows far less about public policy than your average person on the street, which is an unfortunate trait in someone who creates public policy as his sole profession. Having come from extreme wealth and the connections that come with that, Freddie knows everyone and everything (gossip-wise at least) that happens in Westminster, which is why Reginald keeps him on despite his constant screw-ups and general laziness.

Freddie gives me a wave as I look over at him carrying on with the Special Advisers from the Department for Emergencies and Contingencies. None of them are listening to their minister's speech at all, which somehow manages to go downhill from where it began.

'Setting walls on fire? What a palaver! I say let's do without the fire and think about ways of moving concrete to the coasts, creating sea walls not made of flames, which would no doubt be snuffed out by the splashiness of the waves anyhow.'

I know Eligium is very possibly the crappiest think tank in Westminster, but there is always the off-chance a member of the press decides to turn up for a laugh and then you have an amazing story for any of the tabloids here. I scan the room for journos; looks like Bryant is going to get away with this one.

Jeremy is the next of the Three Stooges to arrive. He wanders in softly, trying not to attract any attention, taking a seat in the back row. Jeremy is the smartest of the Associate Directors by far but is unbelievably lazy, even when compared to Freddie. His work always gets finished off by one of Charlie's Angels, who will try to extract from the word salad she has been given, something resembling a think tank report decent enough for even an organisation as shit as Eligium to publish. Jeremy is of medium height and build, with a mane of unkempt black hair that has a lot of grey streaked throughout. He seems like he might have been good-looking when he was a young man but it's hard to tell for certain. Jeremy's general demeanour is that of a mildly pissed-off sloth or a grizzly bear seconds after having been awoken prematurely from hibernation. I've never liked him.

Bryant's speech finally shudders to a close around the thirteen-minute mark. I take over the podium to ask if anyone has any questions for the minister. No one raises their hand.

'Well then, hot drinks are available at the back of the room for anyone who would like one. Let's please give the Secretary of State a warm round of applause,' I announce to try and close proceedings. Freddie claps and cheers loudly – he is the only person who makes a sound.

Just as the punters are filing out, each of them still shaken by what they have just borne witness to, David, the last of the three Associate Directors, walks in. He looks confused. This is nothing new.

'Did I miss it?' he asks me desperately.

'Yes, David. It was doors at nine.'

'Oh, Charlotte, I'm so sorry. I thought it was half nine. Silly bugger.'

David is sweet and kind; he is also mind-bogglingly stupid, which makes him hard to like at times, although his pleasant disposition makes him difficult to hate. He is one of those poor creatures blessed with neither looks nor brains. Nor is the man svelte, to put it bluntly. Luckily for him, he had a rich daddy who sent him to the best schools, something which set him up to work in the think tank world despite his almost dysfunctional level of idiocy. Yet David is so lovely, even I don't hold this last fact against him. He does work hard and can churn out reasonable stuff when prodded and well-supported – meaning, when one of the junior researchers does most of the actual writing for him.

David at least gets stuck in to clearing the room out, and between Charlie's Angels, David, Tom, Chad Cooper and myself, we've wrapped it all up within fifteen minutes.

We all trek back to the Eligium office, about a ten-minute walk away from the venue. Mini-groups form and I end up between Freddie and Jeremy.

'That was even worse from Geoffrey than anticipated. What a complete bellend,' Freddie says.

'Bet you couldn't do his job any better,' Jeremy scowls.

'Actually, while there are few jobs I think Freddie would be qualified for in this world, he probably could run that department better than Bryant by dint of the fact that anyone with a pulse could,' I say.

'David would be worse,' Freddie says.

'You're right there,' Jeremy says.

'Yeah, probably,' I concede.

When we get to the office, it is right as the Monday morning meeting is about to commence. These can often be torturous affairs, particularly when Chad Cooper is present. He really winds Reginald up, which makes it even stranger that the Chief Executive never takes any steps to keep him out of a staff meeting that he has no right to attend.

Once we are all seated round the large table in the boardroom, Reginald begins.

'Hello all. I'd like to start the meeting with a momentous announcement. In precisely two months' time, I will be stepping down as Chief Executive of Eligium.'

Everyone is completely silent. Reginald was clearly looking for some sympathy and with none forthcoming, he looks annoyed for a moment before continuing.

'It must be said that the move is not entirely deliberate on my part. I was induced to go and thus I shall. However, there is something else I must share with you all. As a result of the same forces that have given rise to my departure from Eligium, the think tank itself will not be seeking a new Chief Executive, but rather will be shutting shop permanently in precisely two months' time.'

Pause as everyone goes into shock, having just been told in so many words that P45s will be made out for them in a few weeks.

The remainder of the meeting is mostly the three Associate Directors giving incoherent yet mercifully brief speeches about the progress they are supposedly making on various projects, all of it even more redundant following Reginald's momentous announcement than it otherwise would have been. The fact the think tank is going to close in several weeks is never reflected in any of their presentations, as if the reality of their impending unemployment hadn't yet entered their egos.

The mood in the office after the meeting is grim, with the weight of what Reginald had told everyone settling in. A lot of silent staring into the middle distance goes on for most of the hour post-meeting amongst the staff of Eligium. Near the end of this torturous period, at a point when I'm wondering whether sneaking out early for my lunch appointment wouldn't be taking the piss, Kate motions for me to come and speak to her in the ladies. I oblige.

'Is your lunch with Lawrence Milding still on?' she asks immediately once we're alone together.

'Yes, don't worry. In light of what we've been told today, I will be looking to fast-forward that situation as much as possible.'

'Do you think a job offer will be coming your way?'

She's trying hard not to sound desperate but without success. I can understand, to some extent. I have no idea how she can afford to live in London on the starvation wages Eligium are paying her, never mind how she'll get by with a sudden cessation of said pittance.

'Kate, relax. I'm on the motherfucker. It's all in hand.'

'OK, OK. Just give me an update this afternoon, please, if you would.'

She seems to feel like this last plea has crossed a line.

'If you can, of course . . . if you want to give me an update, you know, that would be great. Thanks, Charlotte.'

She cuts her losses and runs out of the toilets, leaving me alone to stare at myself in the mirror. What are you going to do, Heard? Kate is correct, of course: this lunch with Milding has moved from being important to crucial.

Chapter Two

When I first started working in the think tank world, I was incredibly naïve about it all. I thought I would be walking into this semi-mystical realm in which brilliant minds sit round and think about how to change the world for the better all day long. Instead, I quickly learned that the whole thing is a horrible grind for basic survival. Think tanks either get their work sponsored or have a sugar daddy or group of sugar daddies to keep them afloat. Either way, the think tank has to bend to the will of a third party. With sponsored work, the think tank has to please the corporate entity that paid for it, meaning everything inevitably gets compromised; if you have a sugar daddy, you have to keep them constantly happy, often churning out reports that are drivel in order to keep their bank transfers coming. If you ever find yourself wondering why we can never generate great policies to fix the problems society faces, look no further.

As I leave the Eligium office building to head to my lunch with Lawrence Milding, I spy a copy of last night's *Evening Standard*. The front-page headline reads 'Minister reveals "luck" that no one yet hit by falling debris in crumbling Palace of Westminster'. Another chapter in the long-running tale of the venerated building, in which our laws are made, falling to pieces. Political pundits like to puff this up into a metaphor about our disintegrating politics, which gets annoying somewhere around the fifty-second time you read a piece along these lines. A bit like the overuse of 'BREAKING: the government' on Twitter whenever Number 10 does something stupid (which is almost every day) or when a non-entity like Lawrence Milding gets caught up in some tawdry scandal and this is meant to signify the end of the British way of life as we know it.

Lawrence is a Tory MP in some safe-seat shire; more pertinently, he is the Parliamentary Under-Secretary for something so tedious even a Westminster know-it-all like me can't remember which department it's in, never mind what his job title is. I met Lawrence when he was a board member of Eligium a few years back, before his illustrious time in government had begun. I have been invited to lunch today to discuss a tentative job offer he has for me, at a new organisation in which he is somehow involved. If this sounds vague, apologies, but Milding has been ultra-cryptic in the build-up to this lunch. Yet he has let a few morsels drop:

'Something bold.'

'A think tank that could change the way politics is done in this country.'

'Very much like you to be involved at the most senior level possible.'

The lunch is to be held at Le Pot-de-Vin, which I think is the nicest restaurant in Westminster and I'm not alone. Any weekday between Monday and Thursday – on Fridays, MPs are mostly back in their constituencies – the place is crammed full of MPs and peers, all of them being wined and dined by donors, corporate lobbyists, or anyone who will pay for them to eat a lovely French meal in one of London's costliest eating establishments. Which means that even if the food weren't magnificent – which it is – dining at Le Pot-du-Vin inevitably makes you feel like a somebody. Someone is paying for your pricey lunch, meaning your time is inherently valuable.

I arrive three minutes early to find Milding standing by the coat check already, looking gormless as usual.

'Ah, Charlotte, my lovely,' he says and goes in for a just slightly more amorous kiss on the cheek than I feel is strictly necessary.

'Hello, Lawrence.'

'We should have a seat. The donors said they would be a little late to arrive and we should just get cracking without them.'

We are shown to our table by the maître d'. On the way there, I drift past a former Home Secretary turned backbencher seeing out the string while waiting for a peerage, as well as an ex-leader of the official Opposition, a former trade unionist firebrand turned wine-sodden Labour Lord, now seeing out *his* days being dined in posh restaurants such as Le Pot-du-Vin by corporate interests. Thankfully, the time Milding and I have to endure as a duo is brief as two obviously wealthy older men approach our table.

'Ken! So good to see you,' Milding says as he stands and vigorously shakes hands with one of them. Ken is tall and very thin, with a face that looks a bit like it has just started to melt off of his skull. I take an instant dislike to him. He seems to read my mind as he gazes at me with a sinister look in his eyes.

'Lovely to see you, as always,' Ken says to Lawrence.

'Jerry, how are you?' Milding says, turning to the other man and this time giving him a man hug. 'Sorry: Charlotte, this is Lord Bromley of Burton,' says Milding as he points to 'Ken', 'and this is Lord Smythe of Downing Heath-upon-Scratch Taven.'

Lawrence points in my direction.

'And this is, of course, the one and only Charlotte Heard.' He sits back down having introduced us all. Ken Bromley's eyes are all over me again; part lust, part deep-seated misogyny. Milding continues his role as compere.

'Now, I've told you both a lot about Charlotte and how brilliant she is, and also about how where she is working at the moment she goes very much unappreciated, which you, Jerry, will no doubt be aware of having been involved in said organisation at one point in the recent past yourself.'

13

I find it interesting to note that Smythe had something to do with Eligium before my time there began.

'And Charlotte, I haven't told you that much about the project we are all cooking up because, well, I thought it best these chaps tell you in their own words. Jerry?'

'Thank you, Lawrence. What we want to do is establish a new think tank, one that will be cross-party and deal with all relevant areas of public policy, but in particular the establishment of more fee-paying schools across the United Kingdom. And we were wondering if you would come and work for us to help build that new brand. Particularly given your links with all of the national political parties.'

Given Lord Smythe has proceeded to the money shot with almost alarming promptness, I decide to cut right to the chase.

'In exactly what capacity would you want me to work for you?' I ask him. Smythe goes a little red, which I can't interpret.

'Well, one of the reasons we were so keen to meet and break bread, as it were, was to flesh that out a little.'

'Jerry and I have some fundamental disagreements on this point,' says Ken, continuing to give me a strange combination of evil eye and bedroom eyes the whole time.

'Yes, you see, I feel confident, from what Lawrence has been telling me and of course, from your CV and all the projects you've been involved in during your time with your current employer, that you would make a very competent CEO of our new venture,' the Lord of Downing-upon-Scratch Taven says. 'As it happens, Ken has just a few more doubts than I do on this point.'

Lord Bromley shifts further forward in his seat, his eyes never leaving me for a moment.

'I have severe doubts that you are the right person to lead our organisation,' he says to me. 'You have never worked at the top level before and I think that is what we shall require of the person we employ.'

Jerry can't hold back after Bromley has gone full-frontal.

'Ken, now, that's very harsh. Like I've said to you already, it's good PR to have a woman as the CEO. And look at her! Just look! She's very, you know, presentable.'

Milding steps in to try and stop the flow of the conversation from getting any more awkward.

'Now, guys, guys, let's try and keep the discussion professional and bear in mind that Charlotte is sat right there and can hear everything that you're saying.'

'Was there some talk of the poor girl being deaf?' asks Ken with a wry smile.

The remainder of the meal follows in much the same manner. Bromley voices his concerns about my experience and suitability for this role as CEO in some think tank that doesn't even exist yet; Jerry pushes me as the right candidate based on the fact that I'm so 'presentable'; poor Milding interjects once in a while in an attempt to keep everything from getting too unbearably Tory; meanwhile, none of them ask me if doing this job they've loosely outlined is even something I would be interested in pursuing. It just so happens that I do want the role. Badly, in fact, due at least partially to having learned about my impending unemployment this morning.

The next step on my road to becoming a member of parliament is to be the Chief Executive of a think tank. Opportunities to do such a job aren't all that plentiful, particularly for a gal like me who didn't go to Oxbridge. So, whatever the shortcomings of this new venture, I need to take the job, particularly as my plan to run Eligium is no longer in play.

Lord Bromley of Burton spends the entire meal at Le-Pot-Du-Vin staring in my direction with the same mixture of desire and hatred. And I do mean the whole lunch; even when in conversation with one of his fellow Tories, Ken never turns away from me, not for a moment.

As the bill arrives and my moment to influence events is about to pass, I figure out what needs to be done.

15

'Listen, Lord Bromley. Ken. I realise you have your doubts about my ability to lead this new organisation you, Lawrence, and Jerry are putting together. I would like to spend some more time convincing you, so I was wondering,' and then I lean in toward Ken as close as I can get without having to climb onto the table, 'if you would like to come to my flat this evening so we talk about it *in depth*?'

I make the offer as seductive sounding as possible while allowing myself some wriggle room if it goes horribly wrong and he turns out to in fact be a gay man who just likes staring at women intensely. Thankfully, it's a bullseye: for the first time since we met, Ken smiles. And not just any old grin but rather a big, all-face type of smile, like the one a child gives on Christmas Day when handed their first present.

'Well, Charlotte. That is a lovely offer and one that I will happily accept. Whereabouts do you live?'

'I'm in Islington, if that's all right.'

'I am certainly willing to travel to such an insalubrious part of town to facilitate our rendezvous.'

As Jerry is paying the bill, I write my address down on a napkin and hand it to Bromley. I then say my goodbyes, telling the Tories that I've got work to attend to. While leaving, I blow Ken a kiss, which gets another happy reaction out of him. He thinks tonight is going to be his lucky night. The poor bastard.

I head back to the Eligium office on a massive high. A new CEO role is within my sights and tonight I will solidify it. My buzz is severely dampened as I re-enter HQ, however. Chad Cooper is still there, arguing with Jeremy about having clearly crossed some professional red line. It looks as if they might have been shouting at one another for a while.

'This is just not the best of days to be pulling this shit, all right? I would assume even you would be capable of understanding that,' Jeremy says with real vitriol.

'Look, you're not the only one who is losing something here. I mean, this place going down means we're all out of a job.'

'You don't bloody work here, Chad!'

I look round for Reginald who has, of course, decided to abscond, probably to the nearest pub to drown his misfortunes. As ever, I'm left to try and restore order in the playgroup.

'Right, Jeremy, calm down,' I say, stepping between the two of them. 'While it is true that Chad doesn't work for Eligium, it is the only place that gives meaning to his sad, pathetic existence. We should be sympathetic to that issue.'

I then turn to Cooper.

'And Chad: while what I've just said stands, perhaps your weird brand of fantasist's horseshit could go into remission for just this day of all days, while the *actual* staff here absorb this massive change to their vocational expectations.'

Job done, I walk away and enter the boardroom, intending to have a few hours on my lonesome in there to think about what my plan is for the evening ahead with Lord Bromley of Burton. Unfortunately, Cooper walks in right behind me, as usual not reading the social cues given to him correctly.

'Hi, Charlotte. Thanks for defusing that situation out there. Jeremy can be a real hothead, can't he? Anyways, look, given the fact that you might be leaving for a new job soon enough, or so I've heard . . .'

I panic a little as I wonder how the hell Cooper could know about the Milding situation – until I remember I told Freddie about it, which I had done in a rare, unguarded moment last week over a drink. I might as well have announced it to the whole office, thinking about it, given Freddie's incapacity for keeping anything to himself.

'I felt there was something I have long needed to get off of my chest. Okey-dokey, here goes . . .'

Cooper's American accent comes out stronger than usual; this is something big he's got to say. Oh God, I realise what it is, or at least the gist of it, just as he starts to spill it.

'I have long been an admirer of yours, Charlotte. In all this time working together—'

'We've never worked together, Chad.'

'—that platonic admiration has transformed into a more amorous feeling. I was wondering then, if you would, well, if you could, you know . . .'

Freddie picks a great moment to walk into the boardroom.

'Freddie! Just the man I wanted to see. Chad, would you excuse us for a moment?' I ask.

'Certainly,' Cooper says. 'Allow me to pick up this conversation later?'

He leaves without waiting for a reply.

'You wanted to see me, darling?' Freddie asks.

'Not really – I just wanted to use the opportunity to get rid of Cooper.'

'Very wise. I am keen to know what happened at your lunch today. Have you a safe harbour in which to escape from the insanity of this place?'

'It's complicated. But I'll get there. Do you know Lord Smythe and or Lord Bromley of Burton?'

Freddie smiles arrogantly at me, his perfectly straight, perfectly white teeth now on full view.

'I know Jerry well. Ken not so much.'

'*Ken* is being difficult. Smythe wants to give me the CEO job but Bromley is in the way. What advice can you give me on Bromley?'

'He's known as a real evil bastard, even by the standard of Conservative peers. My father plays squash at the same club as Ken, I believe. I could get him to put in a word on your behalf?'

'Thanks, but I have my own plan.'

'Of course you do, Charlotte. As always.'

There is then a moment of unquestionable sexual tension with

Freddie, as he continues staring in my direction longer than appropriate. I'm about to say something about it when he abruptly turns and leaves the boardroom.

The second after Freddie departs, David, the thickest Associate Director, enters the board room.

'Jesus fucking wept, what *do* I have to do to get some privacy around here?' I shout at David in genuine exasperation.

'I'm so sorry, Charlotte. It's just that with Reginald not around I had no idea what to do about this and, you know, you're the real boss around here anyhow, aren't you?'

I remain stone-faced, something which causes David to panic further. He continues.

'There's just this one piece of work I'm in the midst of and it's kind of politically sensitive, if you know what I mean. I didn't bring it up at this morning's staff meeting, or at any previous staff meeting for that matter due to its, you know, sensitivity.'

'I have no idea what you're talking about, David. Can you just conduct this conversation in plain English?'

'Well, it's just that, as I say, the project is highly politically sensitive and . . .'

'We all got the sack this morning, David. You are worrying about something needlessly.'

'Well, you say that. Except this is all highly politically sensitive and . . .'

'You know what, I don't need this.'

I get up, brush past David, and walk out of the boardroom. As I check my handbag to make sure I have everything I might need for the evening ahead, I notice that Jeremy is staring at me from behind his desk.

'Don't tell me you're looking to chat with me about some project you're working on that requires some sudden dick-holding too?' I ask him.

'Why would you think I'd be working on anything?' Jeremy

19

answers with a smirk. I bolt down the five flights of stairs to the building's exit, desperate to be out of there. I make the short walk over to St James's Park and decide I'm going to stay there for the foreseeable future. It's a clear, mid-September day, sun shining with only a few odds clouds in the sky. I walk toward a group of benches – only to find Reginald there, sat in a mac, trying and failing to look inconspicuous, drinking from a brown paper bag. Where does one even get a brown paper bag from in this day and age?

'Howdy, sailor,' I say as I saunter up close to him. Reginald panics but quickly realises he's cornered and eases himself into it.

'Want a slug?' he asks, holding up the bag toward me.

'No thanks. Mind if I have a seat though?'

'Be my guest.'

I sit down beside my boss on the bench.

'Why are the trustees closing down Eligium?' I ask him. 'I mean, the last accounts I saw looked pretty healthy, not that I'm an accountant or anything.'

Reginald shakes his head.

'It's not about funding. It's a political thing within the board. I tried to talk them round but it was no use. They are adamant about closing the operation down.'

'What are you going to do now?'

Reginald exhales in a thoughtful way. At least, thoughtful by his standards.

'I have no idea. No one is going to give me a job, not with my age and the seniority I'd need. I've spent the last five years presiding over a think tank that is a Westminster bubble joke.'

He pauses, taking a gigantic slug out of his bottle in a bag and then swallowing with difficulty, a couple of tears now streaming down both cheeks.

'I'm finished, Charlotte.'

I have never previously seen Reginald like this. Even when I've witnessed his state of being after more than a few too many drinks, at staff parties and things like that, he has always maintained a steady professional veneer. He's also never been half this plaintive with me.

'I should head back to the office,' I say by way of responding. I have no plan to do so, but Reginald is starting to bore me. Also, he kind of smells a bit. I start to wonder if he slept rough last night.

'I suppose you should. Lead them in my stead, good woman.'

I get up and start walking back in the direction of the office.

'I'll do my best, Reg,' I shout back at him.

In all the years I have known him, I have never called my boss 'Reg'. I have no doubt that he disapproves deeply of me having used this opportunity when he is down and out to do so. I don't look back to find out either way.

I cruise right past the office building and head straight for the tube station. I have too much preparation to be getting on with in regard to this evening's fun with Ken Bromley to waste any more time dealing with the middle-aged saddos of Eligium today.

Chapter Three

I pass Rupert Shingle in the street. He's clearly come from what they call in Westminster a BFL (Big Fucking Lunch) and is appropriately plastered as a result. He runs over and bear-hugs me before even bothering to offer a verbal greeting.

'Charlotte, my dearest. How are things at that terrible shit-show of a think tank you still bizarrely work for?'

'Everyone got the sack this morning.'

'I know.'

This is Rupert's most annoying trait: pretending he doesn't know what's going on before then revealing he knows everything. As perhaps the premier Westminster lobbyist – which he once described as 'the dark arts' to a hidden BBC camera – he is tuned in to an amazing amount of what happens inside the bubble, to a shockingly micro level. The ignorance routine is done in order to get your unguarded reaction and thus glean even more information to add to his already impressive store.

'And I'm guessing you already know everything about my new possibility?'

'Jerry Smythe is a good guy. Watch out for Ken though, he's evil.'

'Thanks, I've figured that one out already.'

'Look into where the money is coming from. I've heard some things.'

'What things?'

'Just look into it. For your own sake. Have to run.'

The tube ride on the Victoria line to Highbury and Islington seems to take ages; I realise on the way just how anxious I am to get everything prepared for the evening ahead. It has been a while since I've had anyone over to the place with anything in mind. As I leave the tube station, I note the Cock Tavern is full. Arsenal must be playing tonight. God, I hate football. The world's most boring sport.

I cut through Highbury Fields to get home. It is crammed with mothers and nannies accompanying their small children, all of them seeking to enjoy the tail end of summer before autumn arrives. The leaves have just started to fall. I take a moment to admire the scene. I'm lucky I bought my flat when I did; a combination of one of those rare dips in the London housing market and smart use of the money I'd made during the period when Kate, Aashi, Violet and I were doing 'non-think tank work' means I have a property that would now be way out of my price range.

The second I'm in the door, I set off to work. It takes me about an hour to get everything ready. My basic preparation for Lord Bromley of Burton's arrival complete, I allow myself a rest and a glass of wine. Just before I do so, I check the time: his lordship will be with me in just over an hour. Time to text the girls.

'BATEMAN RISING. IMMEDIATE AREA TO HQ, ONE HOUR HENCE.'

That done, there's nothing to do but wait.

I use this interregnum to think back over the day's events. Even though I don't particularly care any more, given after tonight I will have fixed the Ken Bromley problem and be moving into my new job shortly thereafter, I should look into the Eligium board situation, even if just for my own intellectual edification. It is strange to think that that particular group of old, fusty, indecisive men who haven't done anything for the organisation in decades just decided out of the blue that the think tank needs to close as soon as possible. Something must have spurred them to act.

23

Perhaps I'm overthinking it all. When I consider the personnel involved once again, I come to the conclusion that's almost certain. The Eligium trustees probably just got freaked out by some element of charity law none of them had bothered looking into over the past decade and then got some bum advice on how to fix it, i.e. burn the whole thing down.

I decide I want a shower, still not satisfied by this answer. After I've washed, I take a moment to meditate before getting dressed.

My mind is still filled with questions about why Eligium is folding when my front buzzer rings. Fun time is here. I make sure my top is low-cut enough to entice without being so over the top as to look desperate. This condition satisfied, I swing the door open.

'Well, hello there,' Bromley says with a huge smile. I have to contain a grin at getting the set-up so spot on. I remind myself that I can't seem too eager, not yet.

'Lord Bromley. Please, do come in.'

Ken enters my flat and has a look round.

'For someone on such a modest income and who lives in a terrible hellhole like Islington, your flat is none too shabby, Miss Heard.'

'Thank you. Would you like some champagne?'

'I'd prefer red wine, if you please.'

I curse myself for this oversight; he was drinking red at lunch and I should have taken that into consideration.

'I'm afraid I don't have any red. I have white, champers, some lager; I can make you a gin and tonic.'

Bromley wrinkles up his nose.

'Is it real champagne?'

'Yes, of course.'

'Which brand?'

'Taittinger.'

Bromley wrinkles up his nose again.

'Les Folie de Marquetterie at least?'

'It's the Brut Reserve, I'm afraid. Girl on a modest income in a hellhole and all of that.'

'Oh well, I'm not here for the quality of the drinks, I suppose. Pour me a glass of the sludge and I'll force my way through it somehow.'

I retreat to the kitchen, out of Bromley's sight for now. I can hear him inspecting the place, undoubtedly looking for chinks in the armour in order to bruise my ego in the banter that is about to begin. I pop the champagne and take out the two glasses I had already prepared, making sure to know which is mine and which is Bromley's at each and every step. A couple of years ago I came close to screwing this up and it still haunts me. I take the correct glass back out to Ken and hand it to him with a tiny curtsy.

'Salut,' he says and downs the whole glass in one go. 'I must admit, that was less bad than I had expected. Pour me another one, would you?'

'Coming right up.'

I breathe out heavily as I re-enter the kitchen. Job done, I can now relax into the final act. I pour Bromley another glass of champagne, this time sans poison, and walk back out into the sitting room where I hand it to him as he sits down on one of my sofas. I take a seat opposite him.

'Playing hard to get, are we?' he asks.

'Only for the time being,' I answer with a giggle.

'Touché for inviting me here tonight so that we can, well, negotiate.'

'I will try and keep things simple.'

Ken laughs in a way that is unsettling.

'Unfortunately, my dear, I never keep things simple. If you are anticipating that you and I will shuffle off into your bachelorette bedroom, crawl under the covers, and then within seconds of having penetrated you I will have, shall we say, exhausted your obligation to me and thus will blindly wave you into that job you so crave, I'm afraid you are in for a rude awakening.'

25

His eyes become even more creepy as he delivers what is meant to be the killer blow, the lines that are supposed to break my spirit completely.

'Nothing that vanilla will befall you this evening, I'm afraid. What I have in mind is a little bit more outré, but I'm certain a worldly girl such as yourself will easily adjust to my needs.'

He starts to laugh again; yet his fun is cut short by a sudden pain in his chest that hits him like a giant punching his sternum. At least, that was how one victim, several years ago, described the feeling to me. Bromley stops short and clutches at his shirt. He wonders for a moment what is happening – and then he looks at the glass of champagne and then back toward me with a wonder of which I hadn't previously thought him capable.

'What is it?'

'A complex compound of my own invention. All of it untraceable, meaning it will look like a heart attack on the autopsy.'

'How long do I have?'

'You've got about another five minutes. If you're lucky.'

Bromley looks at the glass again with even more wonder in his eyes.

'Had I known you were capable of this, I would have just let you have the job on principle.'

'You live and you learn. Well, I'll live anyhow.'

We both laugh at my little quip. And then Ken gets serious.

'Given the short time I have left, I'm afraid I'll have to use it to extract my revenge. You do understand.'

'Go for it, Ken. Do your worst.'

Then it starts. I have to say, Ken Bromley moves pretty fast for an old pervert. I'm required to dive out of the way in an awful hurry as he lunges at me with a taser gun he produces from God knows where like a magic trick. I guess that was at least part of what was in store for me tonight if I was a different sort of a gal.

After I quickly move down and to my right as Bromley lunges,

26

I then emerge to get myself into a position to be able to retaliate. I kick him hard in the stomach. I figure this will pretty much do it, but in addition to being quick, Ken is also tough. He jumps to his feet with an agility that would be impressive for a twenty-year-old, never mind a man in his seventies. Bromley immediately lunges at me again. Thankfully, I am well prepared for a fight after the afternoon's intensive preparations. I retrieve my nunchucks from the cubbyhole where I'd put them for just such a moment. After whipping them around my head a few times to loosen both them and me up a little, I whack Ken a couple of times round the head; he just laughs, an evil, horrible one this time round, and I wonder for a moment if perhaps he's a robot. The blood starts to trickle down the side of his head, definitely disproving that theory, but he still manages to lunge at me with that taser again, only missing by a couple of millimetres.

I realise I have to take this to the next level if I want to survive the next four minutes. I lure Bromley toward the staircase that goes up to my bedroom. I can hear him the whole way up the stairs. I run around to the far side of my bed so that at least he has to cross it to get to me. Jesus, here I am, in my bedroom with Ken Bromley. The thought is both hilarious and repulsive at the same time; I can laugh and/or wretch about it in peace in about a hundred and seventy seconds time.

'How long have I got now, do you figure?' he asks me, his voice distorted, a symptom of the poison kicking in which I'm well aware of, yet still can't shake off how demonic and powerful it makes Bromley sound.

'About three minutes.'

'When I get a hold of you, that three minutes is going to seem like an eternity.'

He then pulls an enormous, Crocodile Dundee-style knife out of the back of his trousers. I have no idea how he managed to stash that away, but there we are, he's holding it now. In fact, he's brandishing it like a mini sword.

'I have just enough time to plunge this into your midsection before I die, which will leave you powerless to move as you slowly bleed to death over the course of several hours,' Bromley says to me, the quality of his voice getting even scarier. I look round for means of escape and realise there is only one at my disposal. If I leap over the balcony railing near the foot of my bed, it's only three or four feet down to the highest bookshelf. I have no idea if it will hold my weight following such a jump – and if it doesn't, I could be in real trouble – but as I say, it is the only realistic option.

Bromley lunges; I run toward the banister. Ken thinks I'm foolishly going to attempt to go round the end of the bed and rolls off and gets himself in a position to run me through when the time comes. I am not able to see his face as I vault over the balcony and land safely on top of the bookshelf, which creaks a lot as I land, yet retrains its structural integrity.

I only have a brief window to hide while Ken gets his thoughts together and won't be able to see me as he is forced to descend the stairs again. I can hear him shout in confusion at what has just happened, his voice like something from a horror film now. I hide in one of the kitchen cupboards as he runs down the stairs. He bolts round the sitting room, opening and closing doors, crouching down to see if I'm under any pieces of furniture. This complete, he heads into the kitchen. He starts opening each cupboard, one by one. I calculate that he'll find me in the next fifteen seconds, which isn't enough time for the poison to incapacitate him. Shit, Ken Bromley is going to kill me. I have underestimated the prey and I'm about to pay for it with my life.

Bromley swings open the door to the cupboard I'm in. Face to face with him now, I make the only move I can: I kick him as hard as possible in the groin. Thankfully, I manage to connect and Ken falls back and to his right, allowing me to squeeze out of the cupboard. I go to run up the stairs to the bedroom again, sure that Bromley is seconds away from death, when I feel his hand clasp my

28

ankle, tight enough to stop me in my tracks. I look back to see him pick up the massive knife with his free hand.

'If I can't kill you, at least I can make it so you'll walk with a limp for the rest of your days,' Ken says, his voice now an inhuman, barely decipherable growl.

He winds his knife-wielding arm back to stab my calf – just as his heart gives out. He drops the weapon as he dies. I wait for a few seconds before approaching his body. I listen to his chest and then his mouth. Yep, dead as a proverbial doornail. Whew. That was the closest I've ever come to not making it out alive from a kill.

I take the gin out of the booze cupboard in my kitchen, grab a large glass and then pour myself a generous measure. I slug it down straight.

Once I'm ready, I text the girls:

'PRESENT READY TO BE BOXED.'

Five seconds later, the door buzzes. I open it to let Kate, Aashi, and Violet in. Without me saying a thing, within moments of arrival Charlie's Angels have Bromley's corpse wrapped up in bagging. A few seconds after that job is complete, the body is inside a cardboard box they brought with them. It's like watching a video of something being built on fast forward.

'Where?' Kate asks me.

'Under Lambeth Bridge, north shore. Don't unbox him until you're right in the middle.'

The three girls all nod simultaneously and they're off. Once I'm alone again, I take another large slug of gin before I ring Jerry.

'Hello?' he answers.

'Lord Smythe?'

'Yes?'

'It's Charlotte Heard.'

'Oh splendid. How did your meeting with Ken go?'

'That's the thing: Lord Bromley still hasn't arrived at my flat. I don't have his number or I would have tried to ring him myself.'

'Hmm, that is odd. Ken is normally extremely punctual. I shall try and ring him and then call you back.'

Less than a minute later, Smythe calls again.

'Any luck?' I ask.

'Afraid not, no. Just through to his messaging service. I'll keep trying him. In the meantime, don't worry too much. I'm sure it's nothing sinister.'

'You're probably right. It's just that I was hoping to impress him tonight and get this job nailed down.'

'I'm sure you will, when he arrives. And if he doesn't show up, I will simply tell Ken that he had his chance and now I'm going to go ahead and appoint you CEO, whether he likes it or not.'

'Thank you, Lord Smythe! That is ever so kind.'

'Well, Charlotte, you deserve a break, I think. In fact, this phone conversation with you now has made my mind up for me. I will be back to you tomorrow morning at the latest. When I speak to Ken, I'll tell him that my mind is now made up. You are to be the Chief Executive of the new organisation.'

'Wonderful, thank you. Have a good evening.'

'You too, Charlotte. All the best.'

Chapter Four

The first time I killed someone, I was eighteen years old.

I had spent my adolescence preparing to try and get into Oxford. This was difficult given the peripatetic nature of my father's lifestyle, one that saw me bounce from a shitty state school in the Cardiff suburbs to a shitty state school in Birmingham; nevertheless, I managed to save some money from a part-time job at a clothes shop to pay for an Oxbridge interview tutor. The interview, I had read over and over again, was everything. I had the grades to get there but not the cultural experience that would have enabled me to breeze through such a showdown without some help.

The day of the interview itself, I was as nervous as I have ever been. My whole future lay on this one half an hour slot. I'd prepared as best I could but had no way of knowing if it was enough until it would be too late.

I remember my nerves getting worse as I walked into the office of the man who was to interview me for Brasenose. Dr Salisbury he was called. He looked very posh, although to be fair, at the time I thought almost everyone who was even vaguely middle-class looked posh.

'You appear to have the jitters, Miss Heard.'

That was the first thing Salisbury said to me, which didn't help settle my nerves. It went downhill from there. I've blocked most of it out. What I do remember is pretty grim.

I asked Salisbury at the end of the interview if there would be a follow-up; he told me in a tone of voice that didn't give me a great deal of hope that the college would be in touch if they wanted to see me for a second interview.

I didn't hear from Brasenose again. I applied to several other Oxford colleges and was swiftly rejected from all of them. I figured Salisbury had put the word out that I was an idiot.

I doorstepped him one morning as he was leaving his house. It was clear he had no idea who I was at first; when it dawned on him, he was clearly mortified. I think more out of shock than anything else, he invited me into his house to talk.

'Are you married, Dr Salisbury?' was my opening question.

'That is a very personal question, Miss Heard. But since you asked: no, I am single. I live here all alone, which is how I like it. Now, you wanted to see me – the floor is yours.'

I started talking about my upbringing, discussing my father at first. I moved onto how I had not only attended bad schools through-out my life, but a lot of different ones in different places, something which had compounded the poor quality of my education. I told him how in the midst of this, I developed as an autodidact, reading the complete works of Orwell before I was fourteen; how I had taught myself Latin as well as French and a little Russian. Salisbury sat stone-faced throughout my little speech.

'Are you finished, Miss Heard?'

'I suppose so, yes.'

'You are clearly someone with a lot of energy. And I do wish you all the best with your life. However, I remain of the opinion that you are simply not Oxford material. I believe you should learn to scale down your expectations. You said you wanted to become a Member of Parliament; frankly, I don't see that as anything more than a pipe dream you would be best off discarding here and now so that it does not lead to years of unhappiness for you. It is up to you what you wish to do with yourself, but if I were giving out career advice, I would point you in the direction of say, the retail sector.'

'You think I should work in a shop?'

'I think if you worked hard over a number of years, I have no doubt that you have the aptitude to be a manager of a shop. One day, at least.'

I was deeply shaken by what Salisbury had just said to me. At that moment, he became the personification of all of the forces that had held me back in life; everything that stood in the way of what I wanted to achieve. I stood up, tears in my eyes, and shouted at him:

'You sit there all high and mighty with your doctorate from Oxford—'

'I received my doctorate from Harvard as it happens.'

'—and you think you can look down your nose at someone like me who never had the advantages in life that you've had! You presume to know everything about me having spent less than an hour in my company!'

Salisbury got angry at this point. He stood up and began pointing a finger at me as he spoke.

'*You* sought me out, Miss Heard! *You* wanted my time in order to know what *I* thought! I haven't chased you down to whatever council estate you spend your time in, have I? If you didn't want the truth, you could have minded your own business and stayed blissfully unaware!'

'You think you're so sure that I don't belong here at Oxford! Why?'

'Because you evidently do not belong at Oxford, Miss Heard! Now, I've said enough – could you please leave my house immediately!'

Tensions were high; like I say, I was upset and Salisbury had worked himself up as well. Somehow, just walking away wasn't something I felt I could do. It would have seemed like I was accepting Salisbury's decree on my ambitions. Instead, I grabbed a metal bookmark that looked like a bit like a dagger which was sat amongst a pile of books near my feet. I wielded it like a weapon at Salisbury. He laughed as I did this.

'You're going to stab me with a bookmark, are you? And what will that achieve? Nothing but sending you to prison, which is where rubbish like you inevitably ends up eventually!'

The next thing I knew, I had stabbed Salisbury through the heart with the bookmark. It was beginner's luck: he died almost instantly.

I dragged the Oxford don's body up the stairs of his house to the top floor. He wasn't very heavy, which probably explains why he was so easy to stab to death. I put him in what I assumed to be his bed. I wrenched the bookmark out of his chest, cleaned it off in the bathroom sink, and then departed the house with it in my handbag.

How I got away with it was again down to beginner's luck. No one saw me confront him the morning of the murder, nor saw me enter or leave the house. It took over a week for the police to even discover the body, as he was supposed to be on a holiday alone in Cornwall starting the day after I had killed him. They never solved the case and figured in the end some burglar must have broken in, found poor Salisbury there, and killed him to avoid detection.

I'm on edge the entire morning following the evening spent dealing with Bromley, waiting for Smythe to call and give me the official thumbs up on the job. Until that happens, I don't feel like there can be any counting of poultry. Reginald fails to show up at the Eligium office once again, which I suppose shouldn't surprise me; thankfully, no one bothers me all morning. David approaches my desk a few times, no doubt to bring up the subject of his 'politically sensitive' project once more, but all it takes to repel him is the look on my face.

Finally – finally! – I get the call around half one..

'Hello, Charlotte,' Jerry Smythe says down the line. 'I must tell you, what a day! I have some terrible, terrible news to relate: the reason that Ken didn't come to your flat last night is that it seems the poor fellow had a heart attack underneath Lambeth Bridge last night and died!'

34

'Dear God! What was he doing under a bridge?'

'I'd rather not wonder about that too deeply! Ken was a good soul but had some rather, shall we say, interesting hobbies. Oh well, poor man. Anyhow, all this means is that I think we move forward with the plan, if you're still up for it.'

'Very much so. I imagine you will need another partner, one with pockets deep enough to stand in for Lord Bromley's wallet, as it were, if that's not too crude a way to put it?'

'No, no, bluntness is absolutely called for here. Who do you have in mind?'

I take a deep breath. This is the one last potential weak spot – the final bridge to cross. Smythe and the particular peer I have in mind are old mates; yet Tory peers fall out with each other all the time and I could alight on the wrong person at the wrong time.

'I was thinking of Lord Snidely.'

'Michael? Oh, yes, he'd be perfect! Fabulous! What made you think of him?'

Snidely had, rather out of the blue, got in touch with me a couple of weeks ago and asked if I would care to have a drink with him sometime soon. Sure, I said. When? How about tonight, he asked me. When money calls and all that, so I soon found myself sat across from Michael Snidely, Lord Snidely of Grottington, each of us with a glass of white wine in front of us, upstairs at the Red Lion.

It was a strange rendezvous. Snidely said, point blank, that he was 'looking to donate to something' in the near future and was open-minded about what that might be, so long as I was involved in running it. 'A project, any project that comes up,' was how he put it. This was just before Milding had approached me with what became the Smythe-Bromley thing and I had no thought of leaving Eligium any time soon at the time, so I said I hadn't anything in the pipeline but it was a kind offer and that I would keep it in mind. He said that I should contact him about 'anything that comes up. Anything at all.' I thought it was weird, particularly given the fact that Snidely is a trustee of Eligium. Then again, rich Tories are weird, and spending a lot of time psychoanalysing them is pointless, as I had learned long ago. I just put it out of my mind. Until yesterday, that is, when I suddenly needed a replacement donor for when poor Ken Bromley met with an unfortunate accident. Snidely and his strange but generous offer seemed terribly convenient all of a sudden.

'Great. Shall I organise a lunch meeting with Lord Snidely and the two of us in the near future so that we can discuss the whole thing further?' I ask Smythe.

'I can get in touch with Michael myself. We'll sort out a date between us and then one of us will let you know next steps. Working with Michael will be a real hoot. Well done.'

Bullseye. I step out of the board room, where I had ducked in to take the call, and ask Charlie's Angels to join me inside.

'First of all, as ever, thank you for your help last night. I received a call just now that informed me indirectly that your operation was a complete success.'

'Thank you, Charlotte,' says Kate, speaking as usual for the group in these sorts of situations.

'I know the three of you have been wondering what I have in mind for all of our futures now that this particular think tank will soon be no more. I wanted to wait until it was a done deal, but now I feel confident enough to tell you that I have just got a job offer to be the Chief Executive of a new think tank and I will, of course, be bringing you all over to work there with me.'

This is a little premature given I haven't yet discussed terms with Smythe and Snidely, but I don't want to keep the girls on the hook any longer. They all erupt with joy. Kate even begins to weep a little.

'Further, you will be getting promotions. I want you all to be my Associate Directors at the new firm.'

More joy from the girls.

'What's it going to be called?' Aashi asks.

'I don't know. Haven't decided yet. Let's face it, the donors are probably going to get to choose the name, so there's no point in even thinking about it.'

There follows more weeping and hugs all round. After a few minutes of this, it starts to get on my nerves and I send Charlie's Angels out. I wait for about a minute after they leave, taking a moment to savour my impending glory as I look out the window at the Houses of Parliament before I walk to the boardroom door and open it a hair. My intention is to make a break for the stairwell and exit the building without having to speak to any other member of the Eligium staff. I think I might enjoy the free day; perhaps have a stroll round the National Picture Gallery. Haven't done that in years. Art does nothing at all for me but I like the way looking at it makes me feel about myself. Peering out from the crack in the door to the boardroom, I gaze to the right and then up and to the left . . . only to see Freddie's white-as-an-Osmond's gob directly in front of me.

'Jesus, Freddie,' I say, taken aback by his proximity.

'Apologies, Charlotte. Before you sneak away for the day, I have proposed the Associate Directors all go for a team drink to discuss recent events. We'd like to have you along, if that suits.'

'It's not even two in the afternoon yet.'

'Your point being?'

'Fine, I'll get my handbag.'

We head to the Two Chairmen, for lack of anything more imaginative to do. It's close by and that seems to be the order of the day; any further effort placed into this strange ménage a quatre would be too much. Freddie gets the first round in, as always. The pub isn't busy given the time of day, and Eligium's resident posh boy gets served straight off.

'Right everyone, here's the drinks. A big three cheers to no longer working at the dump down the road, right?'

'Easy for you to say, mate,' Jeremy scowls before taking a huge swig of his pint of ale. 'Not all of us have our father's bank account to keep us going.'

Freddie appears taken aback at this comment.

'Don't be gloomy, old chum,' Freddie says. 'Perhaps you can apply for a job at Charlotte's new think tank.'

Freddie cannot contain a smile which he unsuccessfully hides behind his glass of gin and tonic as he spills the beans, thereby setting up an awkward and otherwise unnecessary conversation here and now.

'You have a new think tank, Charlotte?' David asks in his usual, artless way.

'Not yet, no. But it is looking good.'

'She's not going to hire the likes of us,' Jeremy says in that bitter old sea dog voice of his.

'No, I'm not,' I say, wanting to kill this before any even partial expectations can be formed.

'Is that true, Charlotte?' David asks with such unguarded stupidity, I can't control myself. I burst out laughing, spitting some of my wine onto David. This sets Freddie off as well.

'You don't have to be so nasty about it, you know,' Jeremy says with a real twinge of hurt in his voice as Freddie and I chuckle. It seems out of character for the annoyed sloth. 'To those of us for whom the closing of the think tank could represent vocational oblivion, this isn't a laugh.'

'Give me a break,' I say to Jeremy, not feeling in the mood for any of his self-pity. 'White male privilege got you to where you are already: a not very talented, not very imaginative, lazy bloke who nonetheless has a job most PPE students coming out of Oxford or Cambridge would wet their pants for. You had a good ride and now it's over. Retire to some decrepit coastal town and put your feet up. I'd say you earned it, but you haven't.'

There is a moment of tension as Jeremy looks angry; this ends when he bursts out laughing. The tension broken, Freddie and I laugh along with him. David joins in as well, although it's clear from his facial expression he has no idea what's going on.

'As ever, a rapier wit. I shall miss thee, Charlotte Heard,' Jeremy says, raising his pint. We all clink glasses in the middle, David the last to join in. There is a vague feeling of camaraderie that disperses rapidly.

'Can you tell us more about this new think tank you might be starting then, Charlotte?' David asks, again not understanding that the conversation we just got through was a social minefield. Thankfully, after a brief silence caused by me ignoring the question, David and Jeremy break off and talk to each other about golf. I turn to chat with Freddie.

'What are you going to do now that you're unemployed?' I ask him.

'One of Daddy's mates has a place in Rhodes. And not one of his weird, creepy gay mates who might be trying to bum me but one of the good ones, you know.'

After Rhodes, Freddie's plan is to head to South America.

'Not sure where, but I've never been there and think it's well overdue. Might just go to Buenos Aires and see where the adventure takes me from there.'

After one more drink, gracefully purchased for the group by David, I leave the pub intent on going home and doing little else with the remainder of my day. I think I fancy a night in, impose an early bedtime upon myself. Then, I get the call.

'Hello, Charlotte? Jerry Smythe here. Listen, I've spoken to Michael and yes, I think this is a goer. We'd both like to meet you as soon as possible – tomorrow if you can manage it – to finalise your terms and conditions. Can you do tomorrow?'

We work out the details, agreeing to meet at Le Shard café in Mayfair the following morning at 11a.m. As my head spins at just how epoch defining this moment is – I've made Chief Executive! – I decide I no longer want to go home. I text the girls:

'HIGH OCTANE EVENT. MEET AT CAT'S MEOW IN 20.'

Kate texts back almost immediately:

'WE'RE ON.'

As I walk toward the place I've just arranged to meet Charlie's Angels for an evening of adventure, my sense of victory is massive. I can't resist – I jump up and punch the air, letting out a squeal of delight as I pass by Westminster Abbey. I then walk across Parliament Square, staring up at the Houses of Parliament. I have just moved one step closer to being in the Commons.

Nothing can go wrong from here. Nothing.

Chapter Five

My alarm goes off at 8 a.m. Wednesday morning like a hammer to the forehead. My plan had been to sleep late, not bother going into Eligium at all, and simply get dressed and turn up at the 11 a.m. rendezvous with Smythe and Snidely in Mayfair. In my drunkenness, however, I forgot to change my alarm.

My throat feels like sandpaper. My headache is so bad I wonder for a moment if having a brain tumour could possibly feel worse. My stomach is churning like a washing machine and I'm so thirsty I feel like a could drink an entire lake, if only my poor stomach would allow me to ingest that much liquid.

Charlie's Angels and I, as you can no doubt already guess from my state this morning, had a hell of time last night. After having one drink at the meeting spot, we moved on to a cheesy bar on Haymarket that had been Aashi's suggestion. At least there was some ridiculous happy hour on at the time, for girls only, in the establishment's clear effort to make it less of a dude-fest. Something along the lines of a 'look like you probably have a vulva, get two drinks for one' thing common to such establishments. We loaded up on cheap booze at the cheese den before we moved onto to somewhere hipper in Soho, where the drinks were pricier but the boys were grown-ups and I could at least half relate to the music they were blaring at head-crushing volume. Getting close to the point of no return alcohol-wise already – I decided to go for it, from the start – Kate and I found a relatively quiet corner and started talking about our impending moment of triumph.

'We did it, boss,' she said.

'That we did. Congratulations to us.'

We clinked glasses – then her face became all serious.

'What?' I asked.

'I've been thinking about my future.'

'OK.'

'I don't know if I want to do it for ever.'

'Do what for ever?'

She rolled her eyes at what she interpreted as my intentional naivety.

'The things we do, Charlotte.'

'It shouldn't be necessary for much longer.'

'That's what we told each other three years ago.'

'But look where we are now! So close to having a funded think tank all to ourselves. I'm inches away from being in a position to run for Parliament now!'

'And I'm happy for you. But I don't know what I want any more. I just . . . I was thinking last night about everything we've done over the past few years. And the moral weight of it was pretty overwhelming.'

'Don't think about it then.'

'That's easy for you, Charlotte.'

'Not easy. Just necessary. Are you telling me you're out?'

'No, of course not. Just giving you the heads up that in the next couple of years I may want to retire to the countryside with some banker who will keep me.'

'It won't be as nice as you think it will.'

'At least it won't be murder.'

We traded smiles and silently agreed that we needed to find the other two and get on with our evening.

The Angels and I ended up next in some place near the river that was closer in spirit to the Haymarket cheese den but without the inexpensive drinks. The higher price tag at least convinced me to slow down a little, which was a good thing in retrospect. After a couple in this new place, I told the girls I'd had my fill and wanted to go home. They all being notably younger than me meant they were having none of this, and thus Charlie's Angels coaxed me onward. I relented for some reason, saying that I would go to one more place so long as it was closer to Islington. We ended up in Vauxhall – which is actually farther away from home, but there you go. We got in the queue for a club called FIST ME; when we arrived at the front and face to face with the bouncer, he laughed at us and said he wasn't going to let us in.

'You're all dressed too club,' he said after I had asked him why several times.

'Listen, mate, if the idea is you won't let us in because we're women and you think we're going to be flinging ourselves at all the gay blokes in there, I am having none of this sexism!' Aashi yelled at him.

He laughed, shrugged and drew up the velvet cord.

'Remember: I tried to keep you out of it,' he said as we walked past, and even in my extreme drunkenness I could tell by his face that perhaps we had just bitten off more than even we could collectively chew. Sure enough, not only were we the only women in the club, we were the only people wearing any clothing. I found myself in a room filled with men who were all naked save for Doc Martens boots. A surprising number of them seemed to have surgically implanted horns in their skulls. To make the scene all the more vivid, every single one of them seemed absurdly well hung, so it was like being in a room full of nothing but massive penises and artificial antlers. Several of the blokes were copulating on the dancefloor. Through sheer bloody-mindedness, we all stuck around for one drink before dispersing.

'You aren't thinking of leaving me too, are you?' I asked Aashi while a man in front of us swung his dick around like a vertical heli-copter propeller. This question of mine came out of the blue, and with her having no idea what Kate and I had discussed in Soho, it would have landed on her with no context.

'What are you talking about? I would never leave you! Especially not in a place with a bunch of naked dudes with horns growing out of their heads and with the music like the eighties but with a particu-lar something to it that I—'

I don't often talk to Aashi one on one and that moment in FIST ME was a good example of why. Since we don't chat alone much, whenever we do she feels she has to keep talking and talking and talking out of fear the conversation will end. I eventually shut her up by walking away and talking to Violet instead, who was hypno-tised by all the genitalia. Poor girl doesn't get a lot, at least from what I've been able to gather.

'You OK?' I asked her.

'I'm great,' she said. 'Like, really great.'

She was still staring at cocks and evidently enjoying it. I recall deciding that perhaps I would pick the conversation up with her at a later date, when there weren't naked men everywhere you looked.

I don't remember getting home.

Just as I'm feeling like I might survive the hangover with a bit of coffee and a pastry, there comes an insistent buzzing at my door. I wrack my brain for any recent Amazon purchase and cannot recall one. I do up my robe a little more tightly, check my face in the mir-ror for vomit, and then walk to the door and open it. Jesus fuck: it's the fuzz.

'Charlotte Heard?' comes the voice of the male cop standing in front of me, beside a small but fierce-looking black woman in a smart outfit.

'Yes?' I say.

'I'm Chief Inspector Watkins and I'm here with DCI Murray. Are we OK to come in and ask you a few questions?'

'Of course.'

They enter. The white man copper, who is the size of a tree, walks in first and the short but kick-ass DCI Murray follows in behind. Their faces tell me this is no routine call. Whatever it is they want to chat about, it's heavy business.

I curse myself – why did I choose Lambeth Bridge to dump Bromley's body? That was me showing off. CCTV must have caught something; they've probably talked to one of Charlie's Angels while she was still drunk from last night and the beans have been spilled. I try and contain my panic, which the severity of my hang-over greatly impedes.

'Ms Heard, how well do you know Lord Duncan of Beaver-brook? Crossbench peer, just to jog your memory?' DCI Murray asks me the moment we are all parked in my sitting room together. This question throws me completely.

'Um, I don't know him at all.'

I'm telling the truth. I wrack my brain for a Lord Duncan and come up blank. Meanwhile, the two coppers turn to look at one another and each of them smirks. DCI Murray opens a file she has been holding and produces from it a picture: it is of me standing next to a man dressed in a suit, both of us holding glasses of champagne and appearing to be deep in discussion with one another while at a drinks reception.

'I take it that's Lord Duncan?' I ask them. They both nod.

'Look, my life is going to Westminster receptions. I don't know the bloke, we clearly just chatted once at a party and . . .'

DCI Murray gets out another picture from her file. This one is of Lord Duncan and I having lunch or dinner together at a restaurant that looks like it is probably Le Piège Doré.

'OK, so I might have had a meal with the guy. Like I say, I don't know him. What is this about?'

'Where were you last night?' DCI Murray asks me. Given I have no idea who Lord Duncan is, truth is my best ally here.

'I went out with three of my work colleagues drinking. We started in the West End and then finished off in a club in Vauxhall.'

'Which club in Vauxhall was this?' she asks. I pause, feeling embarrassed to have to share this information with any human being.

'It was called FIST ME.'

'Excuse me?' Watkins asks.

'FIST ME. Gay club. Naked guys all screwing each other. It was a poor move and we all headed home after one drink there.'

DCI Murray removes another picture from her file.

'Is this you, Ms Heard?'

It is a grainy picture of what does look a lot like me in front of Vauxhall bus station.

'It could be, I suppose.'

'This was taken at 1:04 this morning near Vauxhall bus station, which you've just confirmed was the last location on your evening out.'

'Like I say, looks a bit like me but who knows. The end of the night was a little fuzzy.'

DCI Murray produces another photo.

'This is what appears to be you, walking up behind Lord Duncan.'

She gets out a stack of pictures and then hands me the next one on the pile.

'And this is what appears to be you attacking Lord Duncan with what turned out to be, upon forensic enquiry, a surgical scalpel.'

I go through all the photos, each one of them a few seconds later than the last, all of them together telling the story of this poor Lord Duncan chap being savaged by someone who admittedly looks a lot like me, reducing the man in several quick strokes to a corpse.

'I take it Lord Duncan didn't make it,' I say. DCI Murray smiles in spite of herself.

'This isn't me,' I continue.

'Are you sure?' DCI Murray asks.

'Positive.'

'Even though you say the end of the night was "a bit fuzzy" and you confirm you were in the Vauxhall area around the time the incident took place?'

'Look, it wasn't me, all right?'

Although, I'm now starting to doubt the veracity of that claim myself. Could I have done this? If it was a random person I had drunkenly attacked, the fact that it turned out be a peer of the realm, never mind a peer that I had dined with and yet couldn't recall, seems to be a massive coincidence.

'Ms Heard, although we cannot say anything more at this time, we would ask that you not travel beyond the M25 until further notice. You may be called in for further questioning.' Watkins tells me.

They then get up to leave. Watkins leaves without a further word. Once he's gone, DCI Murray shuts the door and addresses me alone.

'Charlotte, I've been watching you for a long time now. Just so we're clear what's happening, I know what you've been up to.'

I struggle to stay cool, maintaining eye contact with her.

'You've never slipped up, even once, before. But now, I'm very close to proving it was you who murdered Lord Duncan.'

'I didn't murder him.'

It feels strange to be saying this to a policewoman and for it to be the truth.

'I don't have enough to push it to trial yet, or even have you arrested, but I'm close. I'm very close.'

She opens the door.

'See you soon.'

She departs, closing the door behind her.

I begin cursing, stomping around my flat. I'm furious with myself for having got pissed with Charlie's Angels last night; I let my hair down, thinking everything would be all right. Now I find myself under suspicion of murder – and the cruel irony is, it isn't one I'm even remotely involved with.

I force my hungover brain to recall the pictures depicting Lord Duncan and me together. I try and remember having ever met him. The photo at the restaurant is the one that gets me; OK, fine, I might have been talking to some boring crossbench peer at some Westminster reception and forgotten all about that, but if I've dined with someone, particularly a man, never mind a bloke who has been ennobled, I remember that kind of stuff. Yet I cannot recall having ever met Lord Duncan, no matter how hard I try.

I get a sudden brainwave. When I got home last night, I went to my home computer and created a Word document containing draft names for the Milding-Smythe-Snidely think tank, the question from the girls about what it would be called clearly gumming up my head. I run over and switch the PC on. Once it has booted up, I look through recently created documents and find the one I've entitled 'fdksjafdsa', which upon inspection is definitely what I created to capture the brilliance of my possible names for the new think tank I will soon be running (sample suggestions: The Big Pee and Smack You Foundation). Bloody fantastic: it was created last night at 12:53 a.m. I was home in Islington and typing out embarrassingly terrible names for a think tank eleven minutes before Lord Duncan was murdered on the streets of Vauxhall. Although I could never use this as evidence to a third party – I could have rigged the time on my computer – it at least lets me know that I definitely didn't kill the poor chap.

Someone must be setting me up. The scary thing I can't be sure of is whether this person trying to frame me for the murder of Lord Duncan has a straightforward political motive for doing so – as in, it's something to do with the new Lord Smythe think tank – or it is someone who is aware of my nefarious nocturnal activities involving the three Eligium junior researchers and homicide. Then it occurs to me that it could be some combination of both. Yet if the person trying to frame me for the Duncan murder knows about the other people I've killed, why bother to go to the trouble of murdering a whole separate peer and then try and hang it on me? Why not just turn me in to the cops for Bromley? Or better yet, why not try and, you know, extract something from me after having revealed their knowledge of my aforementioned nefarious activities, given this is the way these things are supposed to work?

Christ, maybe it is just a twisted coincidence after all. I laugh out loud – after all of the bodies I've buried in this town, literally, I am going to go down for the murder of some bloke I can't even recall ever meeting and whom I definitely did not kill.

I walk into the kitchen and get down the bottle of gin. I pour what looks to be about two measures for myself and then down it in one go. I almost puke but through sheer concentration manage to just keep it down. I think about having another one but figure it's too digestively risky.

I disconnect my phone from its charger and call Kate.

'Are you in the office?' I ask her.

'Yes.'

'Are Aashi and Violet there too?'

'We're all here.'

'Great. I'm coming in. Code Magenta.'

'Fuck me solid.'

That's the first time I've ever heard Kate swear in all the time I've known her; despite the grave situation, I afford myself a smile for having managed to get that out of her.

I have a quick shower, throw on some clothes, and then dash out of my building. Luckily, a black cab is passing by the road outside and I flag it down.

'Take me close to St James's Park tube station?'

He nods, I get in, and we're off. This is a terrible extravagance, but I do need to speak to Charlie's Angels as soon as possible. I start to figure that perhaps I can claim the cab ride on my last Eligium expenses.

'Shame about that geezer from the Lords, eh?' the cab driver barks back at me.

'What?'

'Haven't you seen it? Fucking bloke, excuse my language, was torn to pieces like a wild bleeding animal.'

I spot a copy of *The Sun* on the front seat. Its headline reads: 'Butchery in Vauxhall.'

'Apparently, they figure it was some brunette woman who approached him in the street and just started ripping him apart with some sort of medical instrument. Fucking mental!' the cabbie continues.

'Could I have a quick look at that paper?' I ask.

The taxi driver hands one of the corners to me and with some effort that might be comical to an outside viewer, I manage to pry the newspaper through the little hole between the driver's area and the back. I flip through it until I get to pages four and five, which is a two-page spread on the murder. It features several CCTV captures documenting the progression of the killing, from the mysterious woman who does look a great deal like myself creeping up behind Lord Duncan, to her pouncing on him, to her leaving him behind in a pool of his own blood. It's all a low-res version of what DCI Murray had shown me back at my flat.

'You bear more than a passing resemblance to the attacker, if you don't mind me saying so, miss!'

He laughs.

'Wouldn't have any sort of medical instruments on you at present, would you now?' he continues in a light-hearted way.

'You might find out if you don't shut your fucking mouth and just drive the cab,' I say, deadpan. He turns to face forward and doesn't utter another peep for the rest of the journey.

When he drops me off, I give the cabbie a healthy tip and ask for a receipt for the lot; I've decided Eligium are indeed going to pay for this trip. I stop at the newsagent and buy a copy of every major tabloid before rushing up the stairs to the office. When I get there, I see Kate and Aashi – but no Violet. I silently ask the two present where Violet is; they simultaneously point to the board room. As I open the door to the board room, I hear the unmistakable sound of Chad Cooper's voice.

'Thing is, Violet, if you and I can pull this thing together before Eligium shuts, you will have something to show for yourself CV-wise out of all of this.'

'Chad!' I shout, and Cooper jumps and falls out his chair as if he were a character in a comedy routine.

'What have I said about corralling the junior staff?' I ask him as he stumbles to his feet.

'Sorry, Charlotte. Won't happen again, promise.'

He recoils as he shuffles past me, as if expecting me to assault him as he goes out of the room. Not that such a thing isn't tempting. I stick my head out of the doorway once Cooper's ass is clear of it.

'Kate, Aashi.'

The other Charlie's Angels join Violet and me in the board room. Once they are all sat round the table, I lay out the whole scenario for them, at least as much as I know, including the fact that the CCTV stuff is all over the tabloids.

'Someone's trying to frame you for this?' Aashi asks me.

'I have gone back and forth on that all morning,' I answer. 'The cops have pictures of me with Duncan even though I can't remember ever meeting him. Then someone who looks like me ends up killing him – in Vauxhall, where I just happen to have been last night. I don't think this can be anything other than someone attempting to set me up for murder.'

'Just so we are clearing all other possibilities from our minds,' Kate says gingerly. 'Is it possible that, in your drunkenness, you did carry this one out?'

'As you say, we were all in Vauxhall around the same time it happened, and I do remember not being able to find you for about

51

twenty minutes. Are you absolutely sure you didn't do it?' Violet asks me.

'I'm 100 per cent positive I didn't do it. I know for certain I was at home when Duncan was killed. And the reason you couldn't find me, Violet, was because you were entranced by male genitalia at the time.'

I have a sudden panic attack. I look at my watch: 9:55. Shit, the meeting with Smythe and Snidely is about an hour away and I didn't even consider that when I got dressed. I don't have any makeup on – I don't even have any makeup *with me*. I tell the girls they weren't mentioned at all by the police, so no worries on that front; they tell me if I need them to act as an alibi for last night, as much good as that might do given we were all pissed to the gills and at a club called FIST ME, to put them forward. I thank them and then dash off. I buy some makeup at the John Lewis on Victoria Street and do my face in the loos there. Classy. I decide the dress I yanked on isn't going to cut it, so I buy another one and wear it out of the shop. I now feel a bit more prepared for the meeting ahead.

I'm the first to arrive at the café, which soothes my nerves a little. Until I find myself face to face with James, an ex-boyfriend.

'Heard! Looking good these days. Here for a hot date with a rich bloke who'll take away your worries?'

James and I dated about a year and a half ago. I broke it off; the breakup did not go well. He acted nonchalant at first. Then, a couple of days later, he showed up unannounced at my flat, which given my lifestyle, it was lucky I didn't have my hands full at the time. He asked to come in and I felt temporarily weak and allowed it. He started crying and then when I went to get him a drink, he grabbed the little guitar I got as a leaving present from the trustees of the think tank I left Eligium for that used to sit in the corner of my sitting room. After clearing his vocal chords for about twenty seconds, James began to sing me a notably terrible version of 'Purple Rain'. When he finally finished, I told him that if he didn't get out within

52

the next ten seconds I was going to rip the little guitar out of his hands and then break it over his head. He didn't listen and yes, that is why the little guitar *used* to sit in the corner of my sitting room. James screamed the place down and said he was going to try and get me done for attempted murder as he kept wiping his hand over his skull, seemingly hoping for there to be blood present.

'Got a job offer and we're discussing terms over coffee,' I say to James.

'Moving up in the world, good stuff. Jesus, did you see that malarkey about poor old Duncan getting butchered in Vauxhall?'

'Yeah, brutal stuff.'

'By a woman as well, how strange. You remember John from when I introduced you, right?'

'John?'

'John Duncan. I introduced you at that party down the road from here. When we were still together, remember?'

'I've never met John Duncan,' I say, knowing that photographic evidence exists that tells me this is a lie, even if I still can't recall ever meeting the bloke.

'I distinctly recall introducing you two, so that's not true is it now?'

James's tone is becoming increasingly weird and aggressive.

'What does it matter when the guy is dead?' I ask. I realise this is a foolishly insensitive comment to have uttered, particularly while I'm under police investigation for having supposedly murdered the man in question, but it just slipped out. Something about James' behaviour is having an unbalancing effect on me.

'That's awfully kind-hearted of you, Charlotte. Reminds me of the compassion you showed to me when you decided to chuck me overboard and then a few weeks later break a miniature guitar over my head. Have a nice meeting.'

The nasty turn that conversation made for no discernible reason, coupled with James' insistence about having introduced Duncan and me, has my head spinning a little. I now suspect James of being involved in framing me. Revenge for dumping him, perhaps? I'm off again, in my own little paranoid world: who is the woman in the CCTV footage who killed Lord Duncan? Why does she look like me? I need to calm my brain down ahead of this meeting and fast.

'Charlotte! How are you?'

I look up to see Jerry Smythe headed my way. Right behind him is Michael Snidely, looking even more emaciated than usual, like he'd just crossed the Sahara and then got himself cleaned up and into a posh suit.

'Hello, Jerry. Hello, Michael,' I say.

'Let's have some tea and discuss this exciting new venture!' Smythe yelps in a slightly unhinged way.

'Let's,' I reply, trying to match his excited tone and not quite making it.

We have a seat at a table that is unfortunately within direct eye-line of where James is sat. My ex-boyfriend of 'Purple Rain' fame sees me take a seat and then begins staring in my direction in a Ken Bromley-like fashion. He continues doing this throughout the whole of my meeting with Smythe and Snidely, making the whole thing even more difficult for me to get through on an even keel.

'We are keen on you starting immediately. How soon can you get out of your contract at Eligium?' Smythe asks me.

'As Michael will already know, Eligium is closing down. And Reginald has stopped coming into work and the whole place has crashed to a halt. So, the answer to your question is, I can start tomorrow if you like.'

Smythe and Snidely both look pleasantly surprised at this news. I have the urge to ask Michael about why Eligium is shutting down but it feels inappropriate to the meeting.

'That is amazing,' Smythe says. 'Truly amazing. Now then, down to practicalities. I can confirm that your title will be Chief Executive, as I believe Lawrence mentioned that you wanted. You will have managerial control of the organisation, reporting to the board. There are some pieces of bad news, however.'

Shit, here we go.

'I can't recall if we discussed yearly budget or not,' Smythe says. We hadn't. 'But I'm afraid it's going to be a little thin at the beginning.'

'Define thin?' I ask.

'About a million pounds annually, give or take a few grand,' Snidely says in a rare intervention. I struggle to look disappointed at the reveal of this massive figure.

'Right. Well, we'll have to make do, somehow,' I say.

'That's the spirit, Charlotte!' Smythe shouts. 'Great to hear it. There is one other piece of bad news, though, and I can only hope you'll take this on the chin in the can-do spirit as well. It's about your remuneration package. It's, well, like the budget, a little smaller than we had initially hoped. But in light of the smaller budget than we had anticipated, we just felt there was no real choice. Charlotte, I'm afraid that for the first year—'

'Only the first year!' Snidely interjects in a panicked voice, waving his arms hysterically as he does so.

'Yes, just the first year,' Smythe continues. 'We can only afford to pay you a hundred and twenty thousand.'

It requires the acting job of a lifetime to remain poker-faced. I had figured, coming into this meeting, that they were going to offer me 50 or 60k and I was going to have to haggle them up to 65k, 70 if I was lucky. Earning £120,000 a year is a bona fide lifestyle changer for me.

'A hundred and twenty? Jeez,' I say, feigning disappointment.

'It's only the first year! We can raise it after that!' Snidely shrieks.

'OK. I'll settle for one twenty. But first year only and we talk in the new year about a raise,' I say.

'Absolutely, Charlotte, absolutely,' Smythe says. 'And thank you for being such a good sport on this front, we very much appreciate it.'

'What can I say? I just want this whole project to work.'

Smythe witters on about the work of the think tank as he sees it, with the odd nonsensical interjection now and again from Snidely. I tune out completely and think about what my new salary will bring with it. I can buy a house. On my own. I can buy a car – a nice car at that. I'll buy designer clothing without having to save up for it. Holidays will become a whole different experience.

While I'm thinking all of this, I find my eyes drifting back over towards James. He's still staring at me, as if I'd dumped him two minutes ago as opposed to almost a year and half back. His weird behaviour gives me an idea. I get out my phone and, rather cheekily, I start texting Aashi then and there:

'JAMES, MY EX, IS ACTING STRANGE. CODE PUCE.'

I'm asking Aashi to follow James until further notice.

'ROGER THAT,' she texts back almost instantly. I put the phone down and tune back into Smythe.

'I think one of our first projects should be on how we get young people to vote Conservative again.'

I make the appropriate noises about needing to crack on with my day and that helps us wrap things up. I ask them to email over a contract. Snidely gets a physical contract out of his inside pocket and hands it to me then and there.

'Look it over carefully. We'd like you to start, as you mentioned, as soon as possible. Perhaps next Monday if you're happy with the contract as it stands,' Snidely says.

I say my goodbyes and depart. I am in such a hurry to get out of there, mostly because of James, but also because it is my modus operandi whenever I'm forced to hang around with older Tory men that when there is no additional booze, food, or anything else of intrinsic value to be had from the situation, I skedaddle as soon as is comfortably possible. You never know when the wandering hands might make an appearance. It's always best to get out while you're ahead.

I'm now at a loose end, wondering what I should do next. That's when my phone rings. I look at the display to find it's Reginald calling. Perhaps he's decided to start coming into work again and is wondering where the hell I am in the middle of the day.

'Hello, Reginald.'

What confronts me down the line is, to say the least, unexpected. Reginald is crying.

'Hello,' he says in a broken voice.

'Jesus, what's up with you?'

'We need to talk. Can you leave work and come meet me at a pub in Mayfair called the Roaring Lion? It's on Charlemagne Street. If you can get here as soon as you can, please.'

'Sure, I'll leave now. What's up? Can you give me at least a hint while I head over to you?'

'I'll tell you everything when you get here. Why Eligium is being wound up is part of it. I just need to talk through some things and you're the only person I trust right now.'

Since when does Reginald trust me? But hey, whatever.

'I'll be there as soon as I can. Hang tight.'

I'm now in the surreal position of being a less than a five-minute walk away from the pub I've just agreed to meet Reginald in, wondering if I should kill time to make it look like I came from the Eligium office or to just sod the pretence and get there as soon as I can. I decide I can't be bothered with the charade that would inform the former course of action and head straight for the Roaring Lion.

I get lost on the way there, taking a wrong turn down Hill Street and then wandering around Berkeley Square for longer than should have been necessary, trying to get my bearings. By the time I arrive at the Roaring Lion, I've almost unintentionally killed enough time to make the idea that I've come from Westminster look realistic.

When I walk in, the pub is totally deserted, which gives me the chills. No one behind the bar even.

'Hello?'

Nothing. I look round, wondering what to do and then decide to

57

call Reginald. Just as I'm getting out my phone, however, I hear someone crash out of a door which sounds like it is near the back of the pub. I look up to see what's happening and catch a woman in a black jacket similar to the one I was wearing yesterday, her brunette hair bearing a distinct resemblance to my own flung across her face, obscuring it, flash past and out the far door. I run to the window to see her jogging down the street at a reasonable pace. From behind, she looks exactly like the woman caught on CCTV killing Lord Duncan last night. That is to say, she really does look a lot like me, at least from a distance. I run to the same door she left from and down the road after her. I see a black Citroen pull up, the back door flings open, and the woman with the black jacket and black hair jumps in. She looks back momentarily and I catch a glimpse of her face. She looks so much like me, she could be my long-lost identical twin sister. She shuts the door and the car whisks off, leaving me in the dust, breathing heavily. I get out my phone again and call Reginald. No answer.

I walk back into the Roaring Lion, which is still totally deserted. I hear someone moaning in what sounds like brutal pain coming from within the establishment. I move toward the sound and it takes me to the door of the gents. I open it, where I come face to face with Reginald, who is lying on the floor having been stabbed multiple times in the chest and abdomen. Seeing me, he tries to say something but all that comes out is blood. He points to the far wall of the bathroom. My eyes look to where he's pointing; there, scrawled upon the wall in what I assume to be Reginald's blood but I suppose could be anyone's are the words:

'CHARLOTTE HEARD DID I . . .'

The 'I' of the message just trails off, as if Reginald wrote it as he was dying. I turn to Reginald to speak to him; unfortunately, he's already passed away. My next immediate instinct is to wipe the blood message off the wall. I stop myself before making that rookie mistake – it would only cause me to get blood on my clothes and put my prints all over the wall, worsening my defence – and decide that it would be best if I just got the hell out of there as quickly as possible, particularly as I can hear a load of wailing sirens heading my way.

I heave it to Green Park tube and hop on the Victoria Line headed south. I have no specific destination in mind, other than wanting to get out of central London. I then remember that Violet lives in Brixton and considering the advantages of her location more and more, I decide to get off at the end of the line.

I remember the first time I ever exited Brixton tube station. I was fourteen years old. I was with a school friend named Marlene. We'd run away from our homes to come to London and then specifically Brixton for some seemingly outré purpose, the exact nature of which I cannot now recall. As we came out of the tube station entrance and walked to the left, I almost immediately came face to face with an elderly black gentleman who was wearing nothing but a pair of underpants – and a living snake, which was perfectly coiled around the top of the man's head and spitting its tongue out at passers-by. Marlene was so freaked out by the snake that we had to abandon whatever it was we'd come to Brixton to do and retreat to the West End immediately.

Coming out of the tube station now, all I see is middle-class hipsters on the phone to their agents or their web designers. I suppose eighteen years is a long time. I go into the nearest pub, order a white wine and once that's in hand, I get out my phone to call Violet.

'Good news?' she asks, wondering about her job prospects.

'Yes, but I've also been dumped into a fresh pile of shit. I need to stay with you for a while. Is that OK?'

'You want to sleep at my flat? Of course! Of course!'

'Shhh. I don't want anyone else in the office to know.'

'Even Kate and Aashi?'

'I'll let them know myself so that you can obey the following rule: don't tell anyone about the fact that I'll be staying with you.

59

Anyone at all. Not members of your family, not Kate and Aashi, no one. Understand?'

'Got it. What time do you want to come over? Do you like horror movies? We can watch loads of horror movies!'

'Remember to keep your voice down, please.'

'I'm the only one in the office right now anyway, so relax.'

'It's that bad?'

'I'm only sticking around because I can stream pirate-related porn on Tom's awesome big screen.'

'OK, another ground rule while we're roomies: I don't want to know more about your personal life than is absolutely necessary.'

'Gotcha. No porn talk.'

'If it's all the same to you. Be at your place for five on the nose so I can get in.'

I hang up on Violet and start considering how to kill several hours in Brixton.

Chapter Six

I go shopping, sparing no expense in buying several outfits that are fabulous and don't look like something my murderous twin would wear. I get them from New Look and a few of the Brixton indie shops. I turn up at Violet's flat feeling like a million quid.

'Right, just a word of warning, the flat is a little untidy,' she says just before opening the door. This gives me the jitters. With good reason as it turns out; entering Violet's flat for the first time kills my clothes shopping spree buzz completely, sending me sharply back to Earth.

The place is a total dump. A depot for used takeaway containers, scattered all over the floor, covering it almost completely, the land-scape only broken up by the odd rotten piece of furniture it seems like Violet must have picked out of someone's bin. Then there is the lone tower of used takeaway containers that stands in the middle of her sitting room, hundreds of them stacked one upon each other, a sort of aluminium miniature of one of the World Trade Center buildings. The smell of the flat is revolting: stale Chinese food meets stale Indian food meets the cheap perfume Violet has clearly taken to using in a lame attempt to cover up the foul odours.

This barely scratches the surface of the flat's awfulness, however. Each time you investigate more of the dwelling, some new level of decrepitude reveals itself. The fridge is a no-go area, containing nothing but mouldy horrors. Yet it's the little surprises that await you in places you assume are safe. Within my first few minutes in the flat, I go to grab what looks like an untouched packet of biscuits from one of the kitchen cupboards, only to find my arm covered in a brownish pink goop that smells like a combination of old socks and a used tampon. I am so embarrassingly keen for the biscuits that I carry on trying to get them – only to find once I'd opened them, done after I'd thoroughly washed all of the smelly gunk off of my forearm, that they had morphed into an alien creature, having been soldered together via biological processes months and perhaps years in the making, the whole thing now having the look and texture of a slightly damp cardboard box.

I picked Violet's flat as my hideout for several key reasons. The first plus it has going for it is that she is the only genuinely single one of the three girls. Kate has a boyfriend who comes and goes when he likes – don't ask me why she puts up with it – and whom I would certainly not trust with my freedom. She says she wants to run off with some banker; the upside of that plan would be leaving her current bloke in the dust. Aashi is technically single but sleeps with so many random people of both genders each and every night that she'd probably bring home DCI Murray within a week just by dint of churn. There are other advantages to Violet's flat: her listed legal address is her parents' place in Hampstead and her mother and father are not even aware of the flat's existence, Violet having told them she was living with Kate (it was the only way they'd let her live in London without them, bless). Her name isn't on the lease, she having taken it over from a friend and the paperwork never altered because the landlord insists on cash payments and may not even understand that Violet is not the person to whom he is now renting the flat. Therefore, Violet is all but untraceable to this address, at least without some heavy digging.

If you're wondering how the hell a young woman on what I have already described to you as starvation wages affords a flat to herself in Brixton, Violet is the one Charlie's Angel who comes from a wealthy background. She tells her parents she needs a few extra grand a month to get by in London than she in fact would need if she was sharing a flat with another person and they shell it out, no questions asked.

Her socio-economic status is part of what makes Violet so strange and despite the large advantages I've just laid out to staying at her flat, after two nights and an entire day here by myself I'm wishing I'd taken a chance with one of the other two girls' abodes. Kate and Aashi had spells within organised criminality for almost entirely financial reasons; Violet was drawn to it purely for kicks.

The only child of a hedge fund manager and a successful writer, Violet has told me that she was mostly raised by cable TV, where she soon found out where the horror films played. She enjoys the spectacle of violence more than any woman I have ever met.

This is part of what has made the prior two evenings so awful to bear; we have to spend them watching extreme horror movies. The first night, we watched this German thing called *Necromantik*. It's about a guy who works for a company that cleans up body parts from the roadside following traffic accidents; he takes the bodies home and has sex with them while keeping the various limbs in formaldehyde. While it was on, I would look over at Violet whenever there was a particularly gruesome bit that I didn't want to watch (which was every two minutes or so) only to find her sat there with an expression on her face that if you didn't know what she was looking at you would assume to be the very definition of innocent joy, wearing as she did the uncomplicated smile of a small child. All as she watched a man shoot blood from his erect penis after having stabbed himself in the abdomen.

When the film was mercifully at an end I asked Violet what she liked about it.

'It's a viewpoint into a lifestyle that I hope to one day have myself.'

This was baffling to me.

'You want to take dead bodies home and have sex with them?'

'That would be lovely. Some day. Some day.'

I told her I was going to settle in for the night at that point. I often wonder whether or not I'm a psychopath; spending time with Violet makes me realise how far I am from the real deal.

Then there is, of course, the horrors of the flat itself. As I sat down to watch television this afternoon, I was hit with a putrid smell that I had not previously discovered. It was horrible even by the standards of the rest of the flat, emanating from the corner of the room. Without a huge amount of investigation, I discovered the source: a dead mouse that was half-rotted away. Bear in mind that this is in the home of a woman who knows every technical way to dispose of a human body in order to put it beyond police inspection, and yet it turns out she can't even get rid of rodent corpses in the corner of her own sitting room in anything approaching a timely fashion. I then recalled her views on necrophilia; it occurred to me that perhaps she keeps tiny rotting animals lying around the place intentionally. I decided to think about something else instead.

Violet did manage to cut my hair well, so I should I give her some credit for that. I now have a bob that I've been thinking about getting for ages. Not exactly changing my identity, but I'm less conspicuously that woman who killed the peer in front of Vauxhall bus station now.

Today I'm doing what I did yesterday: watching daytime TV and reading and then re-reading the newspaper Violet fetched me in the morning. Every so often I turn on my phone to check and see if I have any messages. I have none, not even from Smythe and/or Snidely – which come to think of it, worries me a little. They were in such a hurry for me to confirm my walk out on Eligium in order to start on the new venture next week, i.e. immediately after the weekend that starts tomorrow. Have they heard about my being a wanted criminal? Strangely, there has been nothing on the news or in the papers about Reginald's murder whatsoever.

In the evening, it is film night at Violet's again and with it, another round of terrible horror films. In the middle of the second one – yes, a double feature this time out – I tell her I'm too tired to continue watching. I realise as I lie in her guest room, trying not to think about another terrible smell that has emerged from somewhere, that I need to get out of Violet's flat as soon as possible.

I wake up on Saturday morning, day three of the Violet excursion, with my urge to act undiminished. The cops are going to figure out where Violet lives eventually and when they do, there goes my freedom, of which I am making nothing at present. Unfortunately, my options are limited; anyone I reach out to other than Charlie's Angels puts me at risk of being shipped. I turn my phone on with the idea of going through my contacts list for inspiration only to find a text from Tom pop up:

'HEARD YOU'RE AT VIOLET'S. CAN I COME VISIT?'

Over the next three seconds, I vacillate between telling him yes and texting him no. There are pros and cons on either side. Ultimately though, Tom knows where I am – which irks me, as that means either Violet told Tom or she told one of the girls who then passed it onto Tom – so he could have sold me out to the police already anyhow if he had wanted to.

'OK,' I text him back.

It only takes him about twenty minutes to get to Violet's front door, which means he was either already on his way here or else got extraordinarily lucky with his travel route. Standing there in front of me, having not been around a man in several days, I get the urge to grab his shirt, haul him inside, and then jump all over him, which I suppress.

'I like the new hair,' is the first thing Tom says.

'Thanks. Tea?'

'Do you have any coffee?'

'Violet doesn't drink it, so no, I'm afraid.'

'Tea is fine.'

He stays standing, looking round Violet's sitting room with a bemused expression, clearly taking delight in the horrible state of the place.

'Been eating a lot of takeaways, I see,' he says, kicking the Sears Tower of trays, almost causing it fall over before he skilfully rescues it.

'How is the mood in the office?' I ask while not caring about the answer and yet feeling like this is what the social situation calls for.

'Bleak. Kate and Violet still come in most days, for at least some of the working day, but no one else bothers.'

'Other than you, of course.'

'Someone has to answer the phone.'

'Wait a second: even Chad Cooper has stopped showing up?'

'Well, to be fair, not quite. But he has become spottier in his appearances. Still calls me every day when he won't be in to let me know, of course.'

I hand Tom his cup of tea.

'Milk, no sugar, right?'

'I usually take sugar, but that's OK.'

'Not that I wish to seem discourteous but why have you come see me, Tom?'

'I spoke to Kate about everything. Among the Eligium staff only she, the other girls and I know about Reginald being murdered. She said you were under investigation for the whole thing but that you had been set up by someone. Not that I would hold that crime against you, when I think about it – joking, of course. Sorry, that was in bad taste. No, she said you had been framed for murder, were staying at Violet's flat and then asked if I could do anything to help.'

'Thanks. But I don't see how you can help me.'

'There is one practical matter to note: I have come as a messenger on behalf on someone you know.'

'Who?'

'Aashi. She wants to come and see you. Says she has some ideas about your current predicament.'

66

'Why the hell did she send you to ask me this? Has the poor girl not heard of text or email?'

'She's worried that you might be angry at her if she asked directly.'

'She could have asked to come via Violet then!'

'Don't shoot the messenger. Should I tell her to come or not?'

'Sure, let her come. All I'm doing round here is suffering anyhow.'

'What, here in paradise?'

'Violet makes me watch terrible horror movies all night. And I try and talk to her but all she's interested in are these horrific films and pirate porn.'

'Is she the one using my computer to watch pirate porn? I was bloody wondering. She could at least erase them from my history after she's finished.'

Tom looks at his teacup in a way that signals that his mission having been accomplished, he'd like to get out of the awful flat pronto.

'You need to go, don't you?' I ask him, even though I wish he'd stay.

'I probably should, yeah. Listen, I was wondering . . .'

'Yes?'

'Once you've put all this trouble behind you, maybe you and I could have a drink together.'

My word – Tom just asked me out on a date. I find myself saying, before I've stopped and thought about it:

'I would love that.'

He smiles, puts down his tea and departs, leaving me alone in the flat from hell once more. I consider what I've just done and conclude its fine. We don't work together any longer, so if it doesn't work out between Tom and I, it's no big deal. I find myself unreasonably cheered up by the prospect of a date with Tom, which I internally chastise myself for. What do I think, Tom and I are going to fall in love and get married? Have kids? I don't think I'd like to raise a kid inside of Holloway prison, which seems to be where I'm headed someday soon.

I'm alone all day today as Violet is back in some Tory shire, talking to Mummy and Daddy about how flats in London cost five thousand pounds a month these days. I scan her shelves for something remotely entertaining to watch. Violet has no subscriptions of any kind to online media service providers, relying solely on DVDs to provide her with entertainment. To be fair, I can imagine a lot of the crap she watches wouldn't be featured on Netflix. I've done this exercise who knows how many times since I began staying with Violet a few days ago, always hoping, as I am now, to stumble upon some previously hidden gem within her little DVD collection. Such a thing is unforthcoming yet again.

Instead, I try and sleep, but to no avail. I decide I need to text both Jerry Smythe and Michael Snidely to find out where I stand with the new think tank project we had all pencilled in for me to start on Monday, the day after tomorrow. Two hours after texting each of them, I've still got nothing back from either.

I'm feeling bleak about the world when Violet's buzzer rings. I answer the door to find Aashi standing there, looking terrified.

'Why are you shivering?' I ask her.

'I'm still worried you'll be angry at me for knowing you're staying at Violet's.'

'Who told you I was staying here?'

'Violet.'

'Why would I be angry with you instead of her then?'

Pause.

'I don't know.'

'Just come in,' I say to her.

I make her some mint tea by request and we sit on Violet's vile sofa, both of us completely silent for about two minutes. I have made the decision that since she requested this little get together, Aashi should be the one to break the ice. Yet I can now sense that we could sit here for the next hour or maybe even longer unless I make an intervention.

'Tom said you had some ideas about how I might escape my current predicament,' I have to say to get things rolling. It has the effect of uncorking Aashi; now that I have given her the permission she was searching for, she's off and running.

'I have been thinking non-stop about this over the last few days, since I found out that Reginald was dead and you'd been set up again to look like the murderer, that this must have something to do with a past kill that we were all involved in. You know, some guy you killed, like, years ago and now, like, his family or his friends or even, you know, his ghost has arisen and is determined to make you fall for this, 'cause you know, like, as in, this is a big-time revenge type of thing. I have some ideas about who it could be, starting with the ghosts of people we buried . . .'

Aashi continues talking for the next ten minutes in this vein. She runs through a list of people I killed and she helped to dispose of, going through each of them as a possible reason for my current dilemma in a massive amount of detail, talked through at an insane speed that somehow manages to gather pace as she proceeds. She also says a lot more about ghosts being involved than anyone would think strictly necessary. I sit and listen to it all, partly because I hope she might accidentally stumble on to a good idea, but mostly because I'm so lonely I'm just happy hearing another human being talking to me, even Aashi.

After several minutes of her rambling, I decide to stop her, having suddenly remembered the Code Puce I had texted her a few days back.

'Aashi. Thank you for coming by and downloading all of this. I have one question that has occurred to me: why aren't you still tailing James like I asked you to?'

'Don't worry – he's working today. I followed him to his office this morning. He's got a meeting there at three p.m., so plenty of time left before he's on the loose again. Although, I suppose I should get there early just to make sure I don't lose him.'

'Anything interesting to say about his movements over the last few days?'

'Not really. He goes to his flat at night. Wakes up, goes to work. Eats lunch at the same place every day. All pretty boring stuff.'

'Keep on him for another few days, if you would.'

'Will do. Apparently I'm not missing anything at the Eligium office anyhow. Of course, you know the whole thing about the Russians and why Eligium is shutting down already, you know, it all sounds so dodgy, and I still haven't figured it all out, you know, like why would Russians want anything to do with some old boring think tank and then I get to thinking—'.

'Hold on, stop there. What's this about Russians and Eligium?'

'You know, the way the think tank has to shut down because Russians were using the organisation's bank account to launder money.'

'Who told you that?'

'Freddie did.'

Note to speak to Freddie as soon as humanly possible.

'Start tracking James again, but in the meantime could you also ask Freddie to come see me here? As soon as possible, today if he can manage it.'

'OK. All I know about the Russian thing is that apparently they used Eligium because it was really well-established and I think that's what you need when you do this sort of a thing. Also, being old, there would have been a lot of ghosts hanging around . . .'

'Thanks, Aashi, off you go.'

She departs. The mention of the Russian thing is interesting but probably a red herring. The idea of Eligium being used as a rouble-rinsing factory strikes me as absurd.

Poor Aashi. Her life story is a pretty brutal one; it's amazing that she's such a delicate flower, at least on the surface. She's handy with a dagger, which she learned on the streets of Karachi as a kid. She was abandoned by her parents when she was a baby because they wanted a boy. Aashi lived at a Christian orphanage until she was nine; she was made homeless when a suicide bomber destroyed it. She was taken into a crime syndicate who wanted to turn her into a prostitute but set her to much more challenging work after they saw the full gamut of her skills at play. When she was thirteen, she was smuggled into the UK to work for the same gang in Yorkshire. After a few years up there, she escaped and claimed asylum in London. As a refugee, she was put into hiding in a flat where she was not to have any contact with anyone she had previously known for her own safety. Deciding she was going to make the best of the situation she had found herself in, she travelled back up north one day and killed the whole of the gang, obviously unbeknownst to the authorities. All ten of them, single-handed, with the same knife. She returned to London the very same day.

Shortly after the dectuple murder, Aashi entered into a sham marriage with a hippie named Ben who, it seems, really loved her. At least that is the only logical explanation for a lot of his behaviour that I've ever been able to come up with. This is how she acquired British citizenship. I think she and Ben are officially still married to this day although I'm not certain.

Aashi met Kate when boredom saw her drift back into organised crime on more personally alluring terms. Their rough upbringings give them a bond with each other that neither of them have with Violet, although I don't get the sense that Violet minds this, or indeed, has even noticed.

Kate was born in Hull, the daughter of a woman who was a junkie and a man with a serious drinking problem. She emerged from her mother's womb addicted to methadone. Child services were quick on the draw and little Kate soon found herself in what sounds like a particularly horrible orphanage. She managed to be taken in by a foster family – who it turned out were drug dealers.

Kate was assimilated into the family business; she once told me that she learned how to get rid of a fully grown man's corpse in under half an hour while making no part of the DNA traceable to police before her tenth birthday.

In her early teens Kate's foster father was arrested and she was taken away by Child Services once again, this time into a nice, middle-class home. She proceeded from there to private secondary education. It was tough at the all-girls school she attended, as she was still adjusting to the mores of the upper-middle classes. As you can already imagine, her training in the criminal underworld came in handy a few times.

Just as she graduated from secondary school and looked to move onto university, her foster parents died in a traffic accident. They had left nothing to her in their will, and she was, once again, penniless and all on her own.

After she failed to get into Oxford, she ended up going to University College London. It didn't take her long to decide that she was going to pay her way through her university years using her skills once more, this time working for a large crime syndicate, disposing of bodies.

The strangest thing about Kate is that despite her difficult upbringing, she's remarkably normal. You also would have no idea she hadn't lived her entire life within the purview of the upper-middle classes either, unless you really got to know her.

I spend Saturday evening alone in Violet's flat. I have terrible nightmares all night long, waking me up every couple of hours or so. I have a lot of dreams about my father; they focus on the period when he started drinking a lot, the Birmingham era, that point when he decided he had given up on life. In the nightmares, my father had found out about all of my crimes and was shouting about taking me to the cops unless I did something for him that seemed vague and difficult to understand, in that way that things can often seem vague and difficult to logically comprehend and yet seem so very real in an emotional sense within a bad dream.

The following day, mid-morning, Freddie shows up at Violet's flat with Kate in tow.

'Took your sweet time then,' I say to him.

'Sorry, darling. I did come as soon as I could. Do you have any alcohol? I could use a nip after the evening I've just experienced.'

'Afraid not. What's all this about Russians using Eligium as a money-laundering source?'

'Could you actually let me into the flat and give me a cup of tea first? I promise to tell you all I know, darling.'

Kate and Freddie negotiate where best to place themselves within Violet's disgusting sitting room while I boil the kettle. Once we're all sat with warm beverages in hand, I start staring at Freddie with intent.

'All right, here's what I can tell you,' he says. 'The reason that Eligium is being closed down is because either the charity commission, the cops, or possibly both have got wind of the fact that the think tank has been taking money from some Russians who may or not be part of a criminal syndicate.'

'Why would anyone use a charity to launder money? How do they get their money out the other end if there's no profit to hide it in?'

'Bogus suppliers, darling. You just create paper companies, get them bank accounts and away you go. Unless the Charity Commission dig into it with real intent, you're sorted.'

'Who at Eligium was involved?'

'Difficult to say. Reginald must have been, given his position,' Freddie says.

'What about Lord Duncan?'

Freddie shakes his head, looking very confused at my question.

'Not sure what to say on that one,' he says. Freddie seems like he's now hiding something from me. I consider that perhaps I'm just being paranoid, having been cooped up in this ghastly flat for the last four days.

'How long have you known about all of this?' I ask Freddie.

'I always know everything that's happening, darling, you know that.'

'Why didn't you tell me about all this?'

'Come now! You were much happier living in ignorant bliss, were you not?'

'Which has led me to being framed for murder!'

'I can see how that has been inconvenient, yes. But have no fear: I come armed with a solution.'

'OK, what is it?'

'A connection of mine wants to speak to you about everything that you're caught up in. Knows far more than I do about it all, as hard as that is to believe.'

'What connection?'

'They prefer that their identity remains secret until you are face to face.'

'What is this cloak and dagger bullshit, Freddie?'

'They are waiting in a café in the West End right this moment, anxious to speak to you as soon as is convenient.'

'Forget it. No way.'

'Suit yourself, darling. But ask yourself what your next move is if not this. How long are you planning to stay in this decrepit flat with Violet, being forced to watch her terrible horror movies every night?'

'You know about the terrible movies?'

'First-hand, I'm afraid.'

I want to know more and yet, really, I don't. Freddie getting off with Violet does make a certain amount of sense when I think about it.

'All right then. Lead the way,' I say.

As we all get up, I'm suddenly reminded again of Kate's presence. She had still not said a single thing since arrival and had been so ethereal that I had forgot she was even there.

'Before you go, could I have a quick word with you alone?' Kate asks me.

'I'll see you outside, Charlotte,' Freddie says, and then departs.

'What's up?' I ask.

'I want to apologise for what I said to you at the bar the other night. You know, about not wanting to do it all anymore.'

'Did you mean it?'

She pauses for a moment to think.

'I'm not sure. But I want you to know that I have your back. You don't need to worry about me not being all in here. I won't let you down.'

Kate looks on the verge of tears. I think she's scared of me being angry at her and frightened at the prospect of losing my friendship. Not only did I meet Kate first of all the Charlie's Angels, she is the one with whom I have always had the closest relationship. Kate is also the only one of the girls who deeply cares about having a career in Westminster, with Aashi just pleased to have a real job as it allows her a veneer of respectability missing from most of her previous life, and Violet simply happy to be part of a team of kick-ass women who kill people every so often.

'I've forgotten all about it, don't worry,' I say. 'Except to mention that if you do meet a banker who turns out to be Mr Wonderful, I won't hold that against you.'

We hug, the first time I can remember doing that in ages.

'You shouldn't keep Freddie waiting,' Kate says.

'Sod the bastard, he can wait. Although, I actually really do need to get the hell of this flat.'

I take one last look around Violet's abode.

'Remind me never to come to Violet's flat for any reason ever again,' I say to Kate as I shut the door behind me.

Chapter Seven

Exiting Violet's flat, I find London a little overwhelming for the first ten minutes. The brightness hits me first and hardest; I end up blinking for ages to try and adjust my eyes. Then the busyness of the streets, filled with Sunday shoppers and hipsters, finds me feeling a touch agoraphobic. What helps me through this unfortunate period is how fresh the wind smells, which is worrying given I am inhaling the worst air quality in all of Europe. Anything smells good after Violet's flat.

Freddie and I walk silently past the skateboarders who do their thing in that park with all the bumps near the Brixton Academy. At least, I think the Brixton Academy is nearby; not being in any way a 'rock' sort of a person, I secretly don't know where the hell the Brixton Academy is located. There is a bottleneck at the tube station entrance which has me feeling a strange combination of agoraphobic and claustrophobic that is all kinds of awful.

We hop on the Victoria line and change to get off at Charing Cross. Throughout the entire journey, Freddie is completely silent, which is very out of character.

'Where exactly are we going?' I ask Freddie as we emerge into Trafalgar Square. It too is rammed with tourists; what strikes me as a massive number for mid to late September. I think to ask Freddie if there is something on in central London today but then think better of it given how reticent he's being.

'Not far. Justin's.'

I giggle. 'Seems a little common for the likes of you.'

'Suits my contact. Not everyone who is helpful in my world is posh, you know.'

By the lions underneath the column, I see a woman taking a picture of what appears to be a heterosexual couple, both of them holding each other tight with Whitehall as the backdrop. Once the picture is finished, they meet in the middle, with the woman who took the picture grabbing the gal who posed with her boyfriend and kissing her on the mouth, a full-on snog. Then the bloke joins in by embracing the two of them in a way that suggests they'll all be sleeping together later. As Freddie and I move out of sight and earshot of this trio, I can hear them speaking a language that is eastern European, but definitely not Polish or Russian.

My next dilemma is the pigeons. Don't laugh at me too hard here – I'm suddenly a little freaked out by them. So much so, I come to a complete halt on the pathway as a coterie of birds blocks my path.

'What are you doing?' Freddie asks, not unreasonably. I try and think of something face-saving but can't come up with anything. I am forced to tell the truth.

'I'm frightened of the pigeons.'

Freddie bursts out laughing.

'Charlotte Heard, did you have a traumatic incident befall you whilst you stayed at Violet's? That's the only way I can begin to let you off the hook for this appalling behaviour.'

'I don't know what's going on. Maybe all of those horror films traumatised me somehow. OK, here goes,' I say before shutting my eyes and walking forward. I can hear the stupid birds flapping their wings furiously as they move out of my way and the only thing holding me back from screeching through it all is my desire to avoid Freddie not only laughing at me again but him chalking it up as one to mention whenever he wants to make me feel embarrassed for the remainder of my time knowing him. If this happened, I'd have to kill Freddie and I'd rather not.

'OK, let's keep moving,' I say, determined to get over myself.

It is at this moment I notice something even more alarming than my sudden ornithophobia. About twenty feet away, trying to hide behind one of the fountains but not doing so effectively, is James. He's clearly been following me; this means he must have known I was in Violet's flat and either waited for me outside or had someone tailing me. I now feel certain that he has something to do with the Lord Duncan murder and set-up; his sudden reappearance in my life and subsequent stalking of me can't be a coincidence.

I have the urge to shout at him, demonstrate to him that I know what he's up to. But then think it best to check in with Aashi first. I call her.

'Have you lost sight of James?' I ask her after she picks up.

'No, I'm on him. I'm behind the fourth plinth.'

I turn to my right to see Aashi's delicate right hand popping out behind the statue.

'You said he was at work this weekend.'

'He didn't go into today, for whatever reason. Came to Brixton and waited outside for you instead. Should I keep following him?'

'Yes, please,' I say to her.

'On it.'

Freddie and I manage to get out of Trafalgar Square without further bird-related incident and walk down Pall Mall. We turn down a side street to get to Justin's, a low-end café frequented by political journalists. We grab a table; I order a gin and tonic and Freddie gets himself a Diet Coke.

'I'm afraid that I have a busy day ahead, darling,' he says in response to my staring at him in menace for not joining me in an alcoholic beverage.

'Right, we're here: tell me who this contact of yours is and how they're going to help me,' I say to Freddie.

'Be patient. All will be revealed soon enough.'

My heart jumps into my throat as into view hovers DCI Murray. I look to Freddie who smiles and shrugs.

'Thanks for selling me out, Fred,' I say with real anger in my voice. I cannot believe what he's just done to me, shipping me to the Met.

'Sorry, darling. I can see that you two have a lot to talk about, so I'll be on my way now. Toodle-oo.'

Freddie gets up and departs the café. DCI Murray takes his place at the table.

'First of all, I'll explain why you aren't under arrest,' she says as an opener. 'As I'm sure that will be your first question.'

'You would think that, wouldn't you? In fact, I was wondering why I hadn't stabbed Freddie in the eye with a pencil when I had the opportunity.'

'He's been a big help with my investigation, Freddie. As I'm sure you're aware, he's the nephew of Lord Duncan, which is how I first came to speak with him.'

I had no idea that Duncan was Freddie's uncle. I'm even more annoyed with Freddie given he hadn't bothered to mention this fact to me, even when Duncan had been explicitly mentioned by me in the conversation between us at Violet's.

'I know you didn't kill Lord Duncan. Or Reginald Meavers either,' DCI Murray continues while I'm still pondering Freddie's motivation for not telling me the person I'd been accused of killing was his relative.

'How do you know that then?'

'The DNA evidence at the Duncan scene was almost non-existent, but the killer got sloppy with the Meavers pub murder. The blood on the wall was clearly not Meavers' and we found traces of DNA in several different places in that toilet that belong to someone we've been tracking for some time now, a Russian individual under ongoing investigation.'

Hearing about the Russian connection from DCI Murray makes my stomach hurt a little. Coming from the DCI investigating the case, I can no longer dismiss the connection via Freddie between Eligium taking money from a Russian source and the attempt to frame me for murder.

I start piecing together a possible scenario: Smythe was getting money from the Russians to launder through this new think tank he picked me to run via Lawrence Milding; when the Russians got wind of this, they wanted me out of the way. But it's here I get stuck: the elaborate and bizarre method of trying to eliminate me from the picture makes no sense. Had I been arrested and then questioned, I might well have told them everything I know about Smythe and the new think tank venture, which would be a bad thing from their perspective. Why not just kill me instead? And how does Eligium link in? Also, if Smythe was getting money from the Russians ,why did he need Ken Bromley or Michael Snidely at all? And then there is James, the ex-boyfriend. It's impossible to fit him into this Russian-flavoured picture. He's the son of a retired hedge fund manager and would have no need and isn't the type to dabble with rich foreigners, particularly dodgy ones.

'The Russians, eh?' is what I say to DCI Murray to keep the conversation moving.

'Yes. As I told you when we met at your flat, I have been investigating a series of crimes in which the common denominator seems to be you for several months now. I have also, coincidentally, or so it seemed at the time, been investigating several Tory peers as well as a current Parliamentary Under-Secretary in the FCO for their Russian connections. When I found out that the investigations criss-crossed, with two of the peers involved in the investigation interviewing you for a position in what was likely a new money laundering operation, I had a twenty-four hour tail put on you.'

I get that heart in the mouth feeling again until DCI Murray's next words put me at ease.

'Due to limited Met resources, I wasn't able to get someone on you until the following evening, at which point one of the Tory peers under investigation had already died in what was officially deemed natural causes but because of the timing and circumstances, I deemed suspicious. You seemed to be on your way to a club in Soho on the night of Lord Duncan's murder. The tail stayed on you the rest of the evening, through your little escapade at the FIST ME club, following you back home. Beyond the DNA evidence, that let me know you couldn't have possibly killed Lord Duncan yourself.'

'If you knew I hadn't killed Duncan, what about the heavy visit to my flat the next day?'

'I hadn't had the debrief from the tail at that point. And who knows, I might have wanted to use the opportunity to put the shivers up you anyhow, given you're somehow in the centre of all of this.'

'Why didn't I read about Reginald's murder in any of the papers?'

'We put a press ban on it due to the suspected Russian involvement. It's been classified as a matter of national security.'

'So now you want me tell you what I know so you can find this Russian operative?'

'I have her in custody already. And yes, the lab results confirm she was Meavers' killer and she confessed to the Duncan murder under questioning. You might find her mugshot interesting.'

DCI Murray pulls a photograph out of her handbag. It is of a woman who looks so much like me, we are almost each other's doppelganger. I knew she looked a lot like me from having seen her as she sped away from Reginald's murder scene but seeing the likeness in a photograph is something else.

'Jesus,' I say.

'I don't suppose you are aware of having a long-lost twin?'

'No, I'm afraid not.'

'Svetlana Deseroyova is her name. Came to this country by means of a visa I still don't understand. I'm now thinking perhaps instead of you being the person I should have been investigating all these months as a murderer, it was this woman the Russians placed to draw suspicion in your direction. So, in answer to your question, yes – I need to know everything you know about the Russian connection to Lord Smythe, Lord Bromley, Lord Snidely, Eligium, everything, so that I can figure out why one of them or some combination of them would have tried to frame you for all this. As I say, I still don't understand why you seem to be in the centre of everything.'

'I had no idea the Russians were involved in any of this until the weekend just gone.'

DCI Murray looks at me sceptically.

'Come on, Charlotte. You are a bright woman. You must have known the Russians were putting money into the old think tank at the very least.'

My confused face reveals the truth.

'You really didn't, did you?' DCI Murray says. 'Wow. OK. I'm assuming Lord Smythe is still interested in you heading up this new project he's launching?'

'He hasn't been in touch since I met with him Wednesday morning to talk about the details. Given I was supposed to be starting on the job sometime around now, it seems to have gone to pot.'

'I propose that you call Jerry Smythe tomorrow and report back to me everything he tells you. Try and dig a little.'

'I think I'd rather get on with my life and leave all this to the professionals, if it's all the same to you, starting with finding a new job.'

'Surely you have an interest in seeing the person or people who tried to frame you for a double homicide at least, perhaps many more murders, brought to justice?'

Brought to justice of a sort, yes, but not of the kind DCI Murray has in mind.

'Like I say, I would rather put this all behind me.'

'I will be coming across information that will help keep you alive, particularly if the Russians are the ones killing everyone here.

It's likely you'll be on the hit list at some point if what I now think is happening is the case.'

I give myself a moment to take stock. Not only am I off the hook for the murders of Lord Duncan and Reginald, killings I had nothing to do with, DCI Murray now thinks all of the murders I did commit over the past couple of years were done by this Russian bird she's taken into custody. Given the extreme, instantaneous turn around in my fortunes, as well as the fact that DCI Murray may well be a good source of information over the coming weeks, I decide I should play nice with her, at least for the time being.

'All right then. I'll see what I can find out. After I call Jerry Smythe, I'll give you a bell.'

We shake hands and DCI Murray departs. I think for a moment about bringing up the fact that my ex-boyfriend is following me everywhere and that I think he must be involved in all this somehow; I decide on a whim to keep the information to myself for now.

It's time to get to work. No one is going to try and frame me for murder and think I'm just going to let it slide. Given I'm no longer a suspect and can go about my business unhindered, I will be able to extract my revenge from whichever poor twats have brought this upon themselves, be they Russian, English, or otherwise. If James is involved, he is going to pay for it with his life. They all are: I won't rest until I've killed every last bastard involved in this scheme to frame me for the Lord Duncan and Reginald murders. I don't care if they are the hardest Russian gangsters known to mankind, no one messes with Charlotte Heard like this and gets away with it.

I head towards Islington on the tube. After several nights away, I am looking forward to being in my own flat again. I can't stop my brain trying to piece together Freddie, Smythe, Bromley, Milding, Snidely, these mysterious Russians that seem to be the money behind everything, and my strange ex-boyfriend. I get nowhere. Nothing adds up. There are too many pieces of the puzzle missing for me to see what the overall design looks like.

I enter my flat and turn the lights on. It takes me a moment to notice someone is there in the kitchen already. When it hits me, I jump back as I let out a little shriek. It's James, my stalker, standing there in a suit that looks rain-sodden even though it's been sunny in London all day long.

'What the hell was that, Heard? Losing your tough exterior?'

'Did you break in?'

'You never asked for your key back. Rookie error.'

'Why are you here, James?'

'Since we ran into one another the other day, I have been thinking a lot about you. A lot about our time together as well. Like the hair, by the way. Always thought you should wear it a little shorter.'

He starts to circle around the furniture, slowly but with an intensity that tells me he has something specific in mind here. I begin to get nervous.

'Thought a lot about how you broke up with me as well,' he continues. 'I've come here tonight to offer you a choice.'

James then takes a small gun out of his inside jacket pocket and aims it straight at me.

'Listen, I don't know what's going on here with you and Smythe and the money-laundering, but I think we should just sit down and have a nice, quiet chat about it all,' I say. James looks completely baffled.

'What the hell are you talking about?'

'It's OK, James. Let's just talk this through.'

'You're trying to confuse me and it won't work. The choice here is that you either agree to be my girlfriend once more, or . . . or . . .'

I begin to laugh, not being able to help myself.

'Hold on: you following me for days on end, breaking into my flat and pointing a gun at me; this is just about you wanting to date again?' I ask. He looks taken aback by my reaction. I'm trying to stop giggling but can't get there. Somehow, this weakens his resolve to the point of no return. The gun starts to droop in his hand.

'Watch it, James – you're about to shoot my floor,' I say, still trying to stop chuckling.

'Just tell me this at least: why did you dump me? Huh? What wasn't good enough about me?' he shrieks. I decide I have to pull myself together and talk him down before someone gets hurt here, namely me if the gun goes off by accident.

'Nothing in particular. It just didn't click between us. It happens, mate. You're a good-looking guy. Lots of women will want to go out with you.'

'The women who do seem to want to go out with me are all stupid nobodies. You're the only one I have ever been with who is a real woman. You're the only woman with real emotional depth I've ever been with.'

'Stop looking in the Westminster village for love,' I tell him, still trying my best to sound supportive so that I can get him and his gun out my life as quickly as possible. 'Check out internet dating. Don't even put anything about politics in your profile.'

'I just want to be with you!'

I find my patience with James and his vulnerability at an end.

'Look, James, I feel for you here, but I'm tired and I've had a hell of a week, so can you put the gun away and shove off?'

I should have tried to be nicer about it, I realise in retrospect. But the whole angsty adolescent, 'why does no one love me?' routine just started to get on my nerves in a way I could no longer disguise. Unfortunately, this tactic is ill-judged. Without another word, James takes the gun and places it in his mouth.

'For fuck's sake, James, no!' I shout. He then pulls the trigger, blowing his brains all over my kitchen floor.

I take a moment to consider next steps. This is clearly not my fault, and the forensics will demonstrate that it's a suicide. However, it will open up my whole flat to a pretty thorough examination and I decide I can't risk it, particularly as I've just got off the hook for all my past misadventures. I take my phone out and call Aashi.

'How the hell did you lose track of James?' I ask her harshly.

'He just slipped away from me. Must have known I was tracking him and made a move that threw me somehow. How did you know?'

'Because he is lying dead on my floor, having blown his head off with a pistol in front of me.'

'Oh shit, Charlotte. I'm so sorry.'

'You can make it up with me by taking out my dirty laundry and having it washed since I don't have the time. Use the other girls if you wish, just get it done.'

'On it.'

'Text me when it's done.'

I leave the flat, which is a little risky until the morgue service arrives, but I decide it's something I need to do for my own sanity. Witnessing an ex-lover shoot himself in the face in front of me and then having to make the decision about what to do about it all has left me flustered. I walk to one of my locals, the type of place I never frequent because I always go out drinking either in Westminster or the West End. Upon entering I ask the barman, who I instantly identify as trouble, for a small glass of white wine.

'You live round here?' he asks me as he places my order on the bar.

'Maybe. Maybe not.'

He's an Aussie, of course, as all those who work behind a pub in Islington inevitably are, but he has a particularly fresh off the boat feel about him.

'Crazy what's going on in British politics at the moment, right?' he asks me, having not taken my snarky response to his questioning my post code as a sign to leave it there. I decide I'll have to engage a little if I want any peace.

'What in particular do you find crazy about our politics at this exact moment?'

'That whole bridge to Norway thing. Jesus, why the hell did you guys have a referendum on that when there was no way to deliver it, eh?'

Dear God, the bridge to Norway: the world's most boring topic. About a year and a half ago, the then prime minister had a huge split within his party about the building of a bridge between Inverallochy, Scotland, and the town of Haugesund in Norway reach a long brewing point of no return. Just for reference, the length of such a bridge would be 311 miles, notwithstanding any need to deviate here and there for any natural impediments. It all started as a joke one charismatic Tory MP wrote about in his *Daily Telegraph* column ten years back. The gist of it went: if we built a bridge to Norway we'd be able to bypass the French and supposedly add about eighty kazillion pounds a year to our GDP along the way. Only, a lot of Tory voters seemed to respond positively to whole thing, which meant that Tory MPs started to pay lip service to the bridge to Norway while still thinking it was bonkers. Over time, having spoken about the bridge to Norway so much, having to defend it as a concept many times at constituency meetings and on television, they all started to genuinely believe in the concept. Given the ridiculousness of it all, this belief, in order to be maintained, had to harden into a dogmatic faith of a quasi-religious nature. Right-wing think tanks began writing reports supporting the concept of a bridge to Norway, using arguments that any reader of the *Daily Mail* or the *Daily Express* would quickly become accustomed to hearing a lot: it will pump billions into the UK economy; will only take a few weeks to build; it will be cheap, or even if it isn't, we will somehow get the Norwegians to pay for most of it.

The divide in his party between those who advocated for a bridge to Norway and those who still talked about it in a more realistic way had become out of control. The prime minister felt the only way to get out of his dilemma and re-unite his party was to let the people decide via a referendum. Surely the British public, so noted for their conservative common sense, will reject the silly idea of building a bridge to Norway. Then we'll be done with it, the idea rejected for ever.

Except that the British people voted fifty-three percent in favour of building the fucking bridge to Norway.

This has resulted in a year of a new Conservative prime minister endlessly saying that the result of the referendum must be respected, while simultaneously knowing that building a bridge to Norway is almost impossible, and even if it wasn't, would be a massive waste of resource with no financial justification. British politics has become absorbed with this problem of the bridge to Norway, with those who argue quite rightly that building the bridge is stupid deviating from logical argument and instead becoming obsessed with conspiracy theories about why anyone would countenance such a massive white elephant in the first place, with the pro-bridge people getting more and more deliriously bonkers as the downsides of their precious venture become ever more apparent.

'I don't want to talk about the bridge to Norway, thanks,' I tell the Aussie barman.

'I know, right! But it is a stupid idea! Like, the currents alone are such a problem. The Norwegian sea is all wrong for building the—'

'What part of "I don't want to discuss the shitty bridge to Norway" do you not understand?' I snap at him, cutting him off. He finally gets the message and leaves me alone.

As I sit by myself, sipping my wine, waiting for Charlie's Angels to clean my ex-boyfriend's brains off of my kitchen's linoleum and dispose of his body, I think again about the Russians framing me for murder using an operative that on one hand was made up to look so much like me it seems like something from science fiction, yet so sloppy in execution that the Met caught her within a matter of days. And this has all seemingly been done because I'm loosely involved in some half-arsed venture of Jerry Smythe's and/or work at Eligium. It's so nonsensical, I try and force my mind in the direction of something, anything else, and all I can come up with – thanks to the Aussie bartender – is that stupid bridge to Norway again.

How could anyone think building a three-hundred-mile-long

bridge to Norway is a good idea? That's the point: no one does think it's a good idea. Like everything else in the Twitter age of politics, stupid ideas just take on lives of their own. You wouldn't think your average middle-aged English woman, one whose understanding of international relations doesn't even extend to knowing that the reason you have to take a ferry to get to France is because Britain is an island, would be the type of person to show up in Parliament Square brandishing a placard bearing the legend 'Norway is the only way!'. Yet amazingly, you'd be incorrect on a semi-mass scale.

My phone buzzes – a text from Kate.

'EX-COMMUNICATION HANDLED. HOME BASE CLEAR FOR RE-ENTRY.'

Charlie's Angels have saved me again, bless them.

Chapter Eight

I set my alarm for nine a.m., Monday morning. I bolt upright when it goes off, ready to spring into action, revenge heavy on my mind. I can't wait to find out who tried to frame me and then proceed to wipe them off the face of the Earth. Step one: call Jerry Smythe.

'Oh, Charlotte! Just the person I wanted to speak to! How are you?'

'Good, thanks. Just wondering where we are with the new think tank?'

'Yes, on that front: Michael and I have had further discussions now and I have some bad news to report, I'm afraid. Are you free to come to the Lords this afternoon, say, around two? I'd rather I told you about it all in person.'

'Two p.m., let's see.'

I pretend to look at my diary in order to buy time. I want to silently fish around for information on the rest of Smythe's day.

'Or any time really,' he says, falling into my trap. 'I'll be in the House in around an hour, an hour and a half, and I'm planning to be there all day until about five o'clock.'

'Two p.m. is perfect. Peers' entrance?'

'I shall have your name put on the list. See you then.'

What Jerry doesn't know is that now that I know he'll be in the Lords all day, I intend to pay him a visit a lot sooner than two in the afternoon.

I call DCI Murray to ensure I'm keeping up my end of that deal.

'I'm seeing Smythe today at two in the afternoon.'

'Great. Did you get anything from the phone call with him?'

'Only that he's clearly flustered. He wasn't giving away anything on the phone, telling me he wants to say everything he has to say to me in person. I'll make sure I squeeze him for information.'

'Fantastic. Give me a call straight afterwards.'

I hang up. Oh yes, Jerry Smythe is about to be squeezed for information all right, particularly now that there's no job for me left in everything. I have been used by Jerry in some little game of his – and he is about to find out he crossed the wrong person.

Lord Gin is one of my most valued Westminster contacts. He's a hereditary peer and comes from extraordinary wealth. He has a drinking problem but given his heritage – his forefathers invented gin – I can't blame him too much for that. He is the first person I call when I need a no strings attached entrance onto the parliamentary estate; perfect for the immediate situation, as someone who will let me into the House of Lords and then be happy to allow me to roam the corridors by my lonesome.

'Here to see Lord Gin,' I say to the policeman at the peer's entrance. I get a chill when he looks at me a funny way, having to reassure myself that I'm no longer on the run from the law thanks to DCI Murray's excellent detective work. The cop grabs an iPad from the little booth they have there and scans it for the meeting of Gin's name with mine.

'Yep, go on through.'

Ginny never lets a girl down. I used to think the reason he always bent over backwards for me was because he thought we'll get off with one another someday. If that's the case, he's happy to be playing the long game, as he's been doing me ridiculous favours, many of them of a dubious legal nature, for almost ten years now.

'Charlotte, my lovely, so wonderful to see you.'

'Likewise, Ginny. How are you?'

'A little kettled, I'm afraid. Got into the red wine early in the day with Lord Brewster and still feeling it. I take it you just want in the building and don't have need of my actual company?'

'That was the idea.'

'Wonderful. I'm going to have a nice lie down in that case.'

He goes to walk away to the right but then stops and turns back to add one last point.

'Used to be that you could have a little snooze in the chamber. Now they have cameras on the whole time and if you had a kip in there you might end up on the cover of *The Sun* on a particularly slow day. Means you have to nod off in the bogs instead. I tell you, being a Lord is just not what it used to be.'

Ginny leaves on that note and I get to work. I walk along the corridor with my head held high, looking like I know where I'm off to, all the while hoping to God one of the clerks doesn't notice I'm alone with a visitor's pass and I have to call Ginny again (and get the poor sot into trouble to boot). I pop my head into the tearoom and do a quick scan: Smythe isn't there. As I turn round to start looking elsewhere for the roubles-soaked shit of a Tory peer, something falls in front of me, less than ten feet away. It is a piece of stone, a rather large piece of stone at that, which I can tell from the trickle of rubble that continues in its wake came from the ceiling. Almost immediately, a team of four small, immaculately dressed men, all of them around 5'0, 5'1 perhaps, emerge holding brooms and dustpans. They remove the offending piece of fallen stone within seconds. I look round; no one else seems to have noticed that Parliament is falling apart around them, and that it's down to postcode lottery whether you end your days here or not, a victim of falling debris, just outside of the Lords' tearoom.

Having survived that little travail, luck smacks me in the face again a few seconds later: there he is, Lord Smythe of Devonish cream on Smack Tavern or whatever; Jerry, the man of the hour, saying goodbye to a group of Tory peers before nipping off to the loo by himself. I walk as quickly as I can toward the gents' without drawing attention to myself, take a quick scan of the horizon to make sure no one is looking in my direction, then duck into the men's toilets myself.

Smythe is the only one present. He is whistling to himself 'The Grand Old Duke of York' as he micturates into a urinal. I walk up behind him and withdraw from my coat pocket my trusty jack knife. The sound of it clicking open causes him to freeze. If you're wondering how I got it onto the estate, past security, it's a combination of two things: one, the security at the peers' entrance is pathetic. I suppose being mates with a Lord is one of the few things to still buy you that level of trust in our society. Two, it's made entirely of ivory as opposed to metal and gets through any metal detector I've ever encountered without a squeak. I had it carved for me by an old Kiwi hippie a few years back.

'Put your dick back in your trousers, your Lordship,' I tell him. I hear his zip go up a second later.

'I take it you've figured out that the job offer is no longer available then,' he says. By way of an answer, I stick the knife into his back, through his jacket and shirt, but only so that the very, very tip of the knife pierces his skin. He wails like a toddler anyhow.

'Next time you make that sound, this knife is severing your renal artery. Got it?'

'Understood.'

I take him into one of the stalls and lock it behind me with my free hand.

'Tell me everything you know about why Eligium is going under, what it has to do with you, what it has to do with dodgy Russian money, and how that all connects with why you hired me to run the new think tank. And finally, why either the new think tank isn't happening now or you don't want me in the picture any longer. Keep it brief and to the point.'

'Lawrence Milding came up with an idea for all of us to make a lot of money. The arrangement was simple: Ken Bromley could get money from various Russian contacts looking to launder, while Lawrence and I had a way of spreading it amongst a network of trusted suppliers which meant we could skim off the top for ourselves.'

'Sounds both dodgy and stupid.'

'Scoff all you like but it worked a charm, at least for a little while. We got in touch with Michael Snidely about the venture and he offered up Eligium as the vehicle, which worked well, for a time at least.'

'Which is strange given Michael Snidely was my suggestion to you in the first place.'

'After Michael had summoned you already to place himself prematurely in your mind for just such a situation, you see.'

'Did you set me up to murder Bromley?'

'Of course, you silly girl! That was the main reason why you were offered the job at the think tank in the first place. Coupled with the fact that you seemed to have the type of character that would be guided more by personal gain than moral compass once the real reason for the think tank's existence was inevitably revealed to you.'

'How did you know about my, for lack of a better word, talents in this regard?'

'I had heard it rumoured. Then your Eligium colleague Frederick D'Hondt was the one who confirmed that your reputation in this regard was merited.'

I pause for a moment to take in this information about Freddie not only knowing about my extracurricular activities but spreading it around Westminster – and what that might mean for me.

'Why did you want rid of Bromley?'

'Ken got greedy. Wanted a much bigger cut, saying he was the contact to the money so he should get more. He also threatened to take the whole thing to the authorities if we didn't comply with his demands, saying he could get off the hook himself. By that time Michael had got to know the key Russian contact, won him over as well, and so Ken had become a costly and dangerous burden to us.'

'What about Eligium shutting up shop?' I ask.

'Ken must have suspected we were trying to get rid of him and made good on his promise. He almost certainly went rogue and told all of the Eligium board members about what we'd been up to. They, predictably, flew into a tizzy and wanted to all quit. They decided that the only logical solution was to shut the whole operation down as quickly as possible.'

'Are you pushing ahead with the new think tank without me now?'

'That whole arrangement has gone belly up over the past weekend. The Russians are not best pleased with the way things have turned out and are pulling their funds altogether.'

'What about the death of Lord Duncan? How the hell does that fit in with all of this?'

'What? Nothing to do with me whatsoever. John was never involved with any of it as far as I'm aware and I was at the centre of the whole thing. You really didn't kill him yourself?'

'No, I didn't. What about Reginald?' I ask. 'Surely the Russians had something to do with that?'

'I have been wondering that myself. His murder has been a massive inconvenience as it means the Met are sniffing around the corpse of Eligium in a way that could create unnecessary problems for both them and us. It was Reginald's unfortunate passing in fact that led directly to the Russians ending our otherwise fruitful arrangement, so I remain confused as to why they would have killed him.'

'Who is the main Russian contact?'

'I don't know. Michael keeps the contact to himself.'

'Bullshit! Snidely couldn't keep anything to himself. Tell me, Jerry.'

'I can't tell you that!'

'Tell me or I'll kill you,' I say, inching the knife a millimetre further into Smythe's back.

'All right, fine. His name is Vladimir Kostchenko.'

'Where can I find him?'

'I don't know but a word to the wise: don't underestimate

Kostchenko, whatever you do. He's a real miserable bastard who would shoot his own son in the back if he thought there was a few quid to be made out of it.'

'Thanks for that, Jerry. Afraid I'll have to leave it there.'

'No hard feelings, I hope. Sorry it didn't work out with the new think tank but you know, easy come, easy go, eh?'

Conscious that I am still on the parliamentary estate and holding a lethal weapon at the vital organs of a peer of the realm, I withdraw the knife, place it back in my pocket, and skedaddle. I walk as quickly as possible back toward the peers' entrance, exit the estate, and then head up Victoria Street. As I pass the building that houses the Department for Business, Energy, and Industrial Strategy, I run into Rupert Shingle, again looking like he's just come from a gigantic piss-up.

'Charlotte Heard, we must stop meeting like this.'

'Always there when I need you. What do you know about Vladimir Kostchenko?'

Rupert's eyes go big. Then his hand creeps up to his mouth and then he starts slowly backing away from me, all this done in pantomime, Rupert clearly finding my question hilarious.

'Don't be a drama queen!' I say.

'You've got yourself in deep! I would take the time now to move to one of the smaller Indonesian islands, whilst you still have that option.'

'How do I find the guy?'

'You sure you want to know?'

I nod. Rupert takes a pen and a small piece of paper out of his jacket pocket and uses the wall of DBEIS to write something down. He hands me the paper.

'That's his address. I would go armed if I were you.'

Shingle blows me a kiss and then retreats. I look at the piece of paper, which reads:

'12 ARCHERY LANE, W2 5ZZ'

I consider my situation and appropriate next steps. Having to extract my revenge from Russian gangsters as opposed to Westminster apparatchiks does up the ante by some margin, regardless of what I have previously said about not caring who did it. I consider whether to pursue this or to cut my losses and leave it all behind. I decide that I don't care if ninjas tried to frame me for murder, I'm not letting them get away with it.

I remove my phone from my pocket and call David, the Eligium Associate Director who is sweet but useless. It should be said that calling David is an extremely rare move on my part and a desperate one at that. Yet I am short of allies here, particularly as I've learned Freddie can't even be marginally trusted and, who knows, may even be directly involved in this whole mess himself. Also, David is the only person I know in London who owns a car.

David answers after one ring, as if he spends every waking hour staring at his phone, desperately hoping I'll call at some point.

'Charlotte! How are you? So glad to hear from you!'

This opening salvo from him makes me feel unclean; David sounds like he's literally jizzing himself as he says it.

'I need your help. Are you at the Eligium office?'

'I'm at home but rest assured working on an Eligium project. Shame about Reginald, isn't it?'

Word seems to have got as far as David on that front now at least.

'I've been crying my eyes out over it. Can you be in Westminster within the hour?'

'Of course. What's going on?'

'I'll tell you when you arrive. Bring your car.'

'My car? But where will I park in town?'

'Do you want to help me or don't you? I'm sure Freddie could get hold of a car for me within the hour, so perhaps I should just call him instead.'

'No! I'm coming, I'm coming!' The unfortunate turn of phrase here makes me gag a little. 'Where do you want me to pick you up?'

'Right in front of the office. We're going up to Marble Arch.'

David takes less than half an hour to get to the Eligium offices, driving up at a ridiculous velocity that suggests he has broken speed limits all the way here in a desperate attempt not to fail me in my one-off hour of needing him.

'I got here as fast as I could.'

'That much is obvious. Like I said on the phone, head for Marble Arch. I'll explain on the way.'

I hop into the passenger's seat and close the car door.

'You changed your hair. Looks nice,' David says as we pull away from the Eligium offices. I then hear someone in the back seat and whip myself around, ready to strike. It turns out to be Jeremy.

'What the hell is he doing here?' I ask David.

'He was at my flat when you called me. I had no real choice in the matter; he was insistent about tagging along. Look at it this way: wherever we're going, this is going to be a real Eligium staff day out!'

'Why didn't you tell me Jeremy was coming along on the phone?'

David goes a deep shade of red.

'I was scared you might not let me come and pick you up if I mentioned it.'

I give David and Jeremy a PG, slightly altered version of why we're heading up to Kostchenko's place as we make our way there. The story is that I think the Russian is the one behind Eligium folding and I want to stake out his place to see what I can find out and from there try and prevent the think tank from going under.

'There is a possibility you can save our jobs here, Charlotte?' David asks in such a cloying manner it makes me a little sad. Jeremy is much more cynical and asks a lot more questions.

'What does this Russkie have to do with Eligium folding exactly?' he asks.

'Like I said, money was being passed to Eligium as a charity to avoid tax on monies begotten from money-laundering operations.

98

Seems that they were on the verge of being found out and decided to close the whole thing down.'

'Discovered by whom?'

'I don't know. The cops maybe, the charity commission possibly, the latter of which would have led on to the police.'

'Where did you get this information from?'

'I have my sources, all right?'

'And how will finding out what this dodgy Russian bloke is up to save Eligium and by extension our jobs?'

'Look, I have another project to go on to,' I lie, 'so I can just turn around and walk away. I thought it would be better if I used my information to do everything I could to help save Eligium and your jobs, but I suppose if that help isn't going to be appreciated, you can just let me off at Marble Arch and I'll take the tube home.'

'No!' David wails. 'Please stay and help us keep our jobs, Charlotte! Please!'

We are soon parked in front of number 12 Archery Crescent, which is a large Georgian place in the style of every other house in the area. It probably costs the annual GDP of a small African nation if you wanted to buy it. For the first hour that I am parked in front of Kostchenko's house in a terrible car with two people I usually avoid like the plague when I'm not being paid to be in their presence, I find myself questioning if I'm doing the right thing. Not only in terms of pursuing Russian gangsters for bloody revenge but with regard to my wider future. Losing the think tank CEO position disappoints me more than I have so far been willing to concede. Perhaps instead of trying to get another think tank job, I should do something else with my life. It could be that my long-term aim of becoming an MP is just out of my reach and I should consider other options. As soon as this last thought emerges, I see Dr Salisbury in front of me, telling me I should give up on my 'pipe dream'. I then realise I need to see all of this out to the bitter end.

We end up sitting in that terrible car for hours, until the early evening arrives. At the appropriate time, I call DCI Murray and give her a false account of the two p.m. meeting with Smythe that never took place. Jerry was a stone, I tell her, giving me nothing.

Around half five-ish, I am about to tell David that this whole stake-out plan was a bad idea and could he please just drive me home, when someone emerges from the front door of Number 12. I take a pair of mini-binoculars from my handbag – like the ivory jack-knife, this accompanies me everywhere I go – to get a better look. The first person out is hard to see clearly because of the bad light available on an overcast day; after a few seconds, I'm sure it's Kostchenko. No one who isn't Russian looks that Russian. Then, the lightning bolt strikes – next out the door at Number 12 is none other than the Honourable Lawrence Milding. Looks like Snidely and co may have been squeezed out of the Russian picture while Lawrence has managed to keep his toe in.

As he steps out into the street, Milding places his arm across the back of the Russian like the two of them are old pals. Just when I think I can't be any more gobsmacked, a third figure emerges from Number 12; this time, it's Chad Cooper.

'Is that Chad?' David asks, confused.

Cooper walks up behind Milding and Kostchenko and puts his arms around both. Milding looks annoyed at this move; the Russian jerks his shoulder in a manner that flicks Cooper's advance away. It's clear neither of them are happy with Cooper's presence there – he must be doing a one-off for them. But for what reason?

The three of them begin to walk down the road together. I know this is a golden opportunity I can't let go to waste.

'I'll be back in a second,' I say to David, before noticing he's fallen asleep. I turn toward Jeremy to address him, only to find him unconscious as well. I jump out of the car, creep up and past Milding, Cooper, and Kostchenko with the intention of setting myself up so that I can meet them all walking the other way, as if I just happened to be wandering around north of Hyde Park and accidentally bumped into Lawrence, Chad, and their Russian mate.

They turn the corner, which temporarily disrupts my plan, but I get there in the end.

'Lawrence!' I shriek in an attempt at feigning genuine surprise as I approach the unlikely trio.

'Charlotte!' Milding says with real terror in his trembling voice. He tries not to panic, mostly succeeding. Meanwhile, Cooper fails utterly in this same task, looking round from side to side and then simply running away from us in the direction he had just come as fast as his legs will carry him, all without saying a word to me or indeed, either of his two companions before taking off.

'Who is your friend here?' I ask Milding, deciding to just ignore Cooper's runner for the time being.

'This is, uh, this is . . .'

'Vladimir Kostchenko,' the Russian steps in with to save Milding from his quandary. He shakes my hand and glares at me in a pervy way that lets me know I'm probably his type Although to be fair, Kostchenko's type is probably 'any white female between the ages of sixteen and forty who doesn't look knackered'.

'It's a pleasure to meet you, Vladimir. Lawrence, now that we've run into each other in this completely random way, we might as well confirm our appointment together for tomorrow afternoon.'

'Excuse me?'

I then over-enunciate in order to press home the point I'm trying to communicate to Milding.

'You recall, don't you? The appointment we made to talk things over tomorrow at eleven a.m. in the House of Commons. You know, to discuss the very, very important matter to us both that has emerged rather suddenly?'

He finally gets it.

'Oh yes, of course, of course. Eleven o'clock. I will pick you up from Portcullis House reception myself.'

'Always the personal touch with Lawrence.'

I giggle at this and Kostchenko strangely joins in.

'Vladimir, it was wonderful to have met you,' I say.

'Miss Heard, it was truly *my* pleasure to have met *you*.'

He kisses my hand and then shudders a little, as if he just came in his pants. I then quickly saunter off, walking back toward the car. Opening the passenger door to David's shit box automobile doesn't awaken my snoozing Eligium colleagues, so I resort to slamming the door extremely hard to rouse them, which works.

'Right, right, staking out here, staking out,' David says, getting himself together.

'I got what I needed. Let's head home,' I say, as I hear Jeremy slowly sitting up in the back seat.

'What about Chad? What was that all about?' David says, getting panicky now.

'I've done all I can,' I say.

'Oh no, Charlotte, does that mean you can't save our jobs?' David asks, setting a new low in whiny behaviour, even for him.

'I have to level with you here: it's looking mighty grim, David. Mighty grim indeed.'

'Oh, Blarney!' he says and covers his face with his hands. He then completely recovers from this quasi-meltdown in an instant, starts the car, and we're on our way.

David kindly drops me off in Islington first, even though that makes little logical sense, to the obvious annoyance of Jeremy who lives in the opposite direction.

Chapter Nine

The first few minutes of the meeting with Milding are embarrassing for us both. He sits there, across the table from me at the Sports and Social Club, looking as if he were my husband whom I had caught in bed with the nanny and this was our big talk to discover whether or not the marriage could continue in light of this new information.

'I am so, so sorry, Charlotte.'

'Stop laying on the penitent man shtick with a trowel, it's fucking me right off.'

'OK, I'll stop. I just want to say that I was always acting in what I thought was your best interests.'

'For future reference, trying to ensnare me in an organisation that is being funded by dodgy Russian money and then pulling the rug out from under me without any explanation is not what could be defined as in my interests, just in case this comes up again in future.'

'I thought the whole thing would be straightforward. Bromley's, you know, ahem, shoved aside, Snidely gets the money in from the Russians, we use the new organisation run by you as the replacement vehicle, everyone's a winner. Except Ken Bromley, I suppose, now that I think about it all again. Oh, God, Charlotte, I'm so sorry.'

'Stop apologising, Lawrence!'

'OK, sorry.'

He holds his hands up by way of letting me know he's sorry he keeps saying sorry.

'How did you manage to make contact with Kostchenko? And how have you kept the contact when Snidely has been squeezed out of the picture?'

'Vladimir is extremely unhappy with the ways recent events have unfolded. Nevertheless, we have a friendship, he and I, that has matured beyond strictly business affairs.'

'You and the Russian are fucking each other?'

'No!' he shouts, drawing attention from nearby tables. He then lowers his voice. 'No, no, that's not what I was inferring. Just that Vladimir still has interests in this country and wants to know how he and I might work together to our mutual advantage.'

'You figured out a way to the Russian and then convinced him to keep funding whatever you're up to at the expense of your so-called partners in crime. Does that pretty much sum things up?'

Lawrence shrugs by way of confirmation. Jesus, what a scumbag Milding turned out to be. A corrupt, backstabbing sack of shit. As I stand up to leave, Milding grabs my hand, hard.

'Before you go, I must know something,' he says.

'What?'

He pauses in a ridiculously over-dramatic way.

'Are you going to kill me because of the think tank job falling through?' he asks in complete earnest. This is too much: I burst into laughter.

'Stop being such a fucking idiot, Lawrence, of course I'm not going to kill you.'

He instantly relaxes by a factor of about fifty. This annoys me; I decide to wind him up a little as a result.

'But I'd watch what you do in the near future or that could come back onto the menu in a hurry,' I say. I pause as I watch his tension level start to rise again.

'Just kidding!' I say, laughing. He laughs as well, although cautiously this time. Then I make my face all serious again.

'I'm not kidding, you know,' I say. He looks terrified again. This is fun.

'I do have one final question for you,' I continue. 'Why the hell was Chad Cooper at Kostchenko's place last night?'

Lawrence chuckles a little, his mood instantly lightening.

'Oh yes, that. Vladimir is getting increasingly nervous about the Eligium being wound up situation in terms of legal complications. He wanted to speak to an employee about it all and so I invited Chad to come and try and allay his fears.'

'But Cooper doesn't work for Eligium.'

'What? He told me that he's worked there for over a year.'

'I can imagine that he told you that, but no, he doesn't work there.'

'He used to work there?'

'Chad Cooper has never worked for the think tank. Ever.'

I leave Lawrence confused, departing the tearoom. I exit the estate, leaving through the Carriage Gates. What greets me there on the pavement in front of parliament is somewhat unnerving: a string quartet, playing Pachelbel's 'Canon', while down on one knee in front of them, holding in his hands a dozen red roses, is none other than Vladimir Kostchenko himself.

'My dearest, Charlotte. Though we have met but once, I felt that meeting to be fateful, for you are the most beautiful woman I have ever laid eyes upon. Please, will you accompany me to dinner tonight? Any restaurant in London of your choice.'

This is a lucky result; I now get to explore the Russian connection in all of this first-hand. I agree to meet Kostchenko at Le Pot-Du-Vin at seven p.m. that evening. He asks if he can have a car sent to ferry me to my overpriced meal and I decline, insisting on meeting him there. That arranged, I walk up to the junction of Parliament Square and Great George Street closest to the river. As I stand by the traffic lights, waiting for them to turn in my favour, a female voice beside me says:

'Nice move last night, arranging to "bump into" Kostchenko and Lawrence Milding on the street. Notable detective skills on display there.'

It's DCI Murray.

'Have you been following me step by step since we last spoke, despite you telling me I'm no longer a suspect?'

'You may no longer be a suspect, but you're still smack in the middle of this whole mess whether you like it or not.'

'Has following me around revealed to you anything helpful to the investigation?'

'Nothing I didn't know already.'

'Do you mind if I ask you something personal, Detective Chief Inspector?'

'Go on.'

'You seem young to be such a high-ranking officer,' I say, mostly as a diversionary tactic. I want to end this conversation.

'I'm twenty-nine, so yes, you're right.'

'How did you pull that off then?'

'I work too hard to give questions like that much thought. Are you happy to keep trading information?'

'Of course. Are you going to keep following me?'

'It's been enlightening so far, so I would consider that probable. Was Lawrence Milding of any help in there?'

She can't have me followed on to the estate – not legal – which is why she has no idea I pinned Jerry Smythe to the wall of a toilet using an ivory jack knife yesterday.

'He knows nothing of any use. I'll tell you what: I will find out all I can from the Russian tonight and then call you afterwards. Can I call you, even if it's late?'

'You can call me anytime, Charlotte.'

She turns down the little side street in front of the Red Lion as we approach, parting ways with me.

I head back to my flat where I have a brief nap before getting ready for my date with the Russian. I have a sex dream about Tom which turns at one point into a whole different thing involving Freddie and I on a tour of America as a duelling banjo duo. It leaves me feeling icky during the duration of my shower, both my obvious obsession with Tom and the thought of touring the United States with Freddie as part of a novelty act. I perk up once I'm dry and think carefully about the dress I'm going to wear. The Russians never want you to seem like you're throwing yourself at them, at least until they have a few vodkas in them, so I need something with enough restraint to satisfy his Orthodox guilt pangs while simultaneously sending the signal that I'm up for grabs, so to speak. I pick a long black number that will only put on display the kind of cleavage that would have made the average man drool in 1908, so perfect for the evening ahead.

I arrive at the restaurant early to find that Kostchenko is already seated. Let it be said, he's certainly keen, this one. When he lays eyes on me, it is like he's seeing the Archangel Gabriel for the first time following death by motor accident.

'Charlotte, my beautiful one. Please, have a seat.'

I do as I am asked and what follows immediately after is an awkward silence. It becomes clear that if I want to get what I'm after from this evening, I'm going to have to be the one to break the ice.

'How do you know Lawrence Milding?' I ask.

'Lawrence is one of the best people in your parliament. I have only met him recently but already he has helped me so many times. You know, so many of your Members of Parliament, they have these scruples. They do not feel comfortable taking money to do things, to ask questions in Parliament for instance. Lawrence is so open-minded, it is refreshing.'

I have never heard corruption described so eloquently.

'Yes, Lawrence. Always one to count on in that respect. What is he working on for you now then?'

'He is helping me wield my influence in this country. He has his ideas about how to do that and I trust Lawrence implicitly.'

He's being coy, which is irritating. I keep digging.

'What is it exactly that you are looking to achieve? Or is that top secret?' I ask, batting an eyelid as I do so.

'I do not wish to discuss business all evening. I would rather talk of romance.'

'Talking of romance' turns out to mean Kostchenko regaling me with hyper-dull tales of his youth on the 'tough streets' of Volgograd. It's an all too predictable hagiography of a man always destined for success even though his father was but a mere multi-millionaire as opposed to the billionaire he has managed to become. The Russian definition of a 'self-made man' made explicitly pukeworthy. I smile and nod through the whole thing, planning my next move.

As the pudding plates are cleared, I place my hand on his forearm and say:

'I was wondering if we could continue this conversation elsewhere?'

He laughs.

'You British women! Yes, yes, I would like that. My club is nearby.'

'I was thinking we might want to have a little more privacy than that.'

He doesn't laugh this time, but rather gets that serious look men do when they are at a strip club and the woman on stage is about to drop her knickers.

'Would you like to come back to my place?' he asks, a little nervously.

'Yes, I would. I just need to powder my nose and then let's be off.'

This makes him laugh again.

'You British women! So direct!'

As soon as I'm in the loo, I take out my phone and text Kate.

'ANGEL AMBER. 12 PARK LANE CRESCENT, RIGHT OFF HYDE PARK. FIND THE NEST. ASAP.'

The drive toward Marble Arch in the back of Kostchenko's black

Mercedes, driven by chauffeur, is perilous; now that I've made my intentions clear, the Russian has become all hands and I'm having to invent a latter-day chasteness to fend him off.

'Come on now, big boy. Let's wait until I have you all to myself, alone.'

'The driver doesn't give a shit, darling Charlotte.'

'I know, but I do. We British women move in strange ways, you know.'

'I certainly hope so!'

And then he's all hands again and I'm thinking about slapping him in the face and giving up. Yet as soon as I've seriously considered this move, we pass the Arch and I realise I only have two more minutes to hang in there.

Once we arrive at the house, Kostchenko thankfully reverts to his more austere persona, as we have to walk past the number of servants one would think necessary to run a large hotel.

'Shall we have a drink in the Bevington Suite?' he asks me.

'Sounds delightful,' I say, thinking I want to give the girls as much time as possible, so I'll see what I can do to stretch this out before Mr Hands make his return and a retreat to the bedroom becomes unavoidable.

'How did you first meet Lawrence Milding?' I ask him as he pours us a couple of glasses from a bottle of Crystal he's just removed from a mini-fridge that is a feature of the 'Bevington Suite'. It's an oak-panelled room with pictures done in the style of the seventeenth century. Or at least, that's what I think at first until I remember that I'm with a billionaire oligarch, meaning I am probably sitting underneath priceless originals from the actual period in question.

'You want to talk business at this hour?' he asks back.

'I'm just curious is all. I like to know what Lawrence gets up to when I don't have my eye on him.'

Kostchenko suddenly gets a little uppity as a thought occurs to him.

'Have you had relations with Lawrence Milding?'

This makes me laugh out loud.

'Definitely not, no,' I say through my giggles. This reaction seems to satisfy the Russian's sense of honour and he returns to himself again.

'I met Lawrence through Lord Snidely. Do you know Lord Snidely?' Kostchenko asks.

'Yes, I know Michael.'

'Michael is a man I once trusted as I now trust Lawrence.'

Vladimir's eyes go cold and then he adds: 'Until recently, I thought Michael could be trusted. Now, I do not believe this to be the case.'

'Why, what did Snidely do?'

The cloud around Kostchenko is whisked away in a flash and his blank, doting smile is back.

'I am tired of all this discussion of business. I want to speak of more romantic things. Shall we retire to the bedroom?'

I haven't received a text from Kate giving me the all clear as yet, so I need to stall Kostchenko in this ridiculous room a little longer.

'In a moment,' I say. 'First, tell me more about your childhood.'

Thankfully, this hits the target and Kostchenko is regaling me again with more stories about the rough life of the son of a multi-millionaire in post-communist Volgograd. I try and tune out as much as possible, but as his teenaged years hover into view some of the dodgy details can't be ignored completely ('I suppose this would be described as rape in your country'). In the midst of a mildly interesting anecdote involving a donkey, a mango, a pack of cards, and a flamethrower, I receive a text from Kate:

'NEST READY.'

I manage to read it without Kostchenko looking, so lost is he in his role as raconteur. I grab his chin while he is in mid-sentence, turn it toward me, and say:

'I'm ready for the bedroom now.'

'You British women!'

I follow him up a set of stairs, Kostchenko bounding like a child on his way to the entrance of his favourite theme park. At the top, he leads me down a corridor until we come to what must be the master bedroom. He turns the doorknob and enters the room. I walk inside behind him. Once I'm there he shuts the door, turns around and smiles – but then the grin fades, replaced by a coldness that is impressive in its totality. Kostchenko points to the bed.

'Lie down, with your face in the pillows,' he says in a voice that indicates that the time for playing nice is now at an end. Charlie's Angels do not require a better cue: within seconds all three of them jump out from hiding and have the Russian incapacitated. Kate with a large knife at his throat, Aashi with an even larger knife pointed at his heart, and Violet with what could only be described as a sword dangling close to his crotch. He is understandably terrified by this sudden turn of events.

'Is it the Georgians who are paying you? Is it? I will pay you more! Whatever they have offered you I will double! Triple!' he shrieks.

'I'm not working for anyone,' I tell him. 'I'm after information. Lord Duncan and Reginald Meavers were killed by the same assassin, a Russian woman. They tried to frame me for it and I want to know who they are and why they did it.'

'I have no idea who either of those people are!'

'Reginald was the CEO of the think tank you funnelled money through. Are you telling me you never met the bloke?'

'I told you! I trusted Michael Snidely on all such matters!'

It must be said, his chat downstairs on this subject *was* fairly convincing if minimal; he did seem to leave it all to Snidely, until things went pear-shaped anyhow, which isn't that peculiar as these things go. It does mean I'm going round in circles here: neither Smythe, nor Milding, nor Kostchenko seem to know anything that leads me to a plausible explanation as to why someone wanted to frame me

111

for the deaths of Lord Duncan and Reginald, or even what connects the two murders beyond having the same assassin. Neither of the homicides seem able to fit into the Eligium folding story. As Smythe rightly pointed out, Reginald's murder was counterproductive to everything Kostchenko and his shadowy international bunch were trying to do – and Lord Duncan doesn't seem to fit into the equation at all. His murder, in fact, would seem to be random, were it not for the fact that the same Russian killer did in Duncan and Reginald and tried to make it look like I did it. I decide the next person I need to have a little sit down with is Michael Snidely.

I'm about to tell Charlie's Angels to retreat and for us to leave Kostchenko in the dust – until the stupid, macho Russian decides he's not about to be bested by bunch of ladies and takes matters into his own hands. He elbows Kate in the guts, causing her to unconsciously withdraw her knife from Kostchenko's throat; he moves back and to the side in order to avoid the other weapons in his way. Mostly at least – Violet does manage to cut his thigh a little. However, Kostchenko quickly recovers from this wound in an impressive manner – perhaps he did learn a thing or two from the mean streets of Volgograd – managing even to dislodge the sword from her hand and grab it for himself. Violet, now defenceless, escapes out the room's open window, leaving Kate, Aashi and me staring down the newly armed Russian as a trio. Aashi tries to strike early, stabbing at what she no doubt figures will now be his weak side, the left, where he is nursing the wound from Violet. This doesn't work – he punches the knife from her hand and then tries to run her through with the sword. Aashi just manages to dodge getting killed, then escapes out the open window uninjured.

Kostchenko takes a moment to get his breath back as he watches Aashi flee – and to take the time to close the window before turning back to Kate and me. During the micro break, I manage to pick up Aashi's knife. Kostchenko turns toward us as the only foes left; we outnumber him, but he has a mini-sword and we now only have knives at our disposal. Also, this is his house and he has a plethora of staff. I am amazed no one has yet come to his aid.

We circle each other for what feels like an eternity, the whole time convinced several heavies are going to pop through the door and finish us off. Yet the thugs never arrive. Kostchenko makes a lunge at Kate, stabbing her shoulder but thus allowing me the opportunity to slice at his arm at the same time. He collapses to the floor and I motion for Kate to escape. When she realises I'm insistent on this, she chucks me her knife, runs over to and then opens the window, hurriedly fleeing the scene.

Kostchenko is soon up on his feet again. Now, it's just him and me. Having two knives helps me a lot as he attacks; for several minutes, I manage to fend him off without too much stress, without ever being presented with a moment to give up the defensive and strike. I realise that even with two knives in hand, Kostchenko is too much for me alone; my new plan is to manoeuvre myself close to the window and follow the girls out the same way. Unfortunately, Kostchenko then makes a silly move that causes me to have to move instantly to Plan B. He lunges with his sword at me in such a way that I have to stab him in order to protect myself from being run through. Just as his sword cuts my head slightly, right below the hairline, I get him right in the heart with the knife I got off of Aashi. Kostchenko dies instantly.

Surveying the scene, the full enormity of what I've done sets in. Just for starters, DCI Murray or at least one of her minions surely witnessed me entering this house. This not being my own space, I have no materials with which to hide the DNA evidence, and even if I did, I have no time or any remaining Charlie's Angels with which to do it. There is then the even bigger problem of having just killed a Russian gangster; I can't imagine his other partners in crime tend to be terribly forgiving about such transgressions. This would have been worth it if Kostchenko had been the one who framed me and revenge had been served; I now feel almost certain that this is not the case. Despite my doppelganger being Russian, Vlad had no clear motive for framing me and in fact, several clear reasons for at least not wanting Reginald to be murdered at all.

I lose vision in my left eye as something liquid hits it – my own blood, pouring from the wound Kostchenko inflicted on me before dying. I grab one of the Russian's embroidered handkerchiefs and wrap it around my head as a bandage.

I can hear footsteps coming up the hallway, so I exit out the open window that Charlie's Angels had taken advantage of only moments earlier, pausing briefly for just one last look at Kostchenko's dead body as I leave.

Chapter Ten

Charlie's Angels end up staying at Violet's 'secret' flat in an attempt to avoid police attention in the immediate aftermath of the unfortunate Kostchenko incident. Following my previous experience there, I can't face it. Instead, I do something that is probably ill-advised, at least from a long-term perspective: I call Tom and ask for his help. To his credit, he drops everything and comes to pick me up.

'I didn't know you had a car,' I say to him as we drive westward on the M4. After the incident involving the Russian, I got on the first bus heading westward and sat there for a while, in a daze, applying pressure to my head wound. When I looked up, after what had been about half an hour, I was in Chiswick, which is where I met Tom.

'There are lots of things you don't know about me,' Tom says with a wink.

We drive out past the M25, into Buckinghamshire. As we cross over the circular road that goes round and round London, I think about the fact that Chief Inspector Watkins' instruction not to travel beyond the motorway, given to me at my flat a week ago, was never officially rescinded and so I've very possibly just broken the law again. During the car journey, I tell Tom pretty much everything about what has been happening to me since I'd last seen him at Violet's place. After about twenty minutes in the countryside, Tom turns the car off onto a side road. Following another five minutes of driving, we pull up in front of a modest yet gorgeous country house.

'Don't tell me you own this,' I say to him as we come to a halt. 'There can't be that many things I don't know about you.'

'It's my parents' place. Don't worry, they aren't here at the moment. They spend half the year in Spain and aren't due to be back here until the start of October.'

'They spend the summers in Spain and the winters in England?' I ask, confused.

'No, no, my dad doesn't like English Septembers for some reason. No, they come back for a few weeks in October to sort things out and then go back to Spain again, where they'll be until May.'

Tom and I walk into his parents' house. He takes me on a tour of the place and then shows me to my room.

'Cosy enough?' he asks as I sit down on the bed.

'Very cosy, thanks.'

'Let's tidy up that cut on your head.'

We head to the upstairs bathroom, where Tom cleans the wound with iodine and then applies a plaster to it. Soon enough we're back downstairs in the sitting room, an unwelcome sexual tension descending upon proceedings.

'I would offer you a drink, but I don't think there's much around.'

He walks to the kitchen and has a look through several cupboards.

'There is some Drambuie and . . . some Crème de Menthe. I could try making something with those ingredients, I suppose.'

'How close is the nearest pub?'

'About two minutes' walk down the road. But I thought you were in hiding.'

'From the London Met, Westminster types who know who I am, and Russian gangsters. A one-off quiet drink in Buckinghamshire shouldn't blow my cover.'

'I don't know, you'd be surprised how many Russians have houses round here.'

We set off down the road, side by side. The country walk has me feeling more chilled out already.

'Did you grow up in that house?' I ask.

'I did.'

'When did you move out?'

'After I got out of uni, I moved to London straight away. I've been in London almost seven years now.'

'Wait, how old are you?'

'I'll be thirty next January.'

'Jesus, I thought you were twenty-six, twenty-seven at most.'

'It's all this Buckinghamshire air I grew up breathing, I guess.'

As we walk into the pub – which is lovely, I have to add here, with that atmosphere only nice English country pubs have – I consider the reveal that Tom is older than I had reckoned. He is much closer to an age where it wouldn't be unreasonable to date him after all, as well as the fact that we are no longer working together; the combination of those two things might even make it acceptable for me to try and jump all over him when we return to his parents' house. No, no, I tell myself; my life is in his hands for the moment. Best not to foul that up. There's nothing to definitively suggest he fancies me anyhow, he could just be a nice guy. OK, a really, really nice guy when you take everything into consideration, but jumping the man still contains an element of risk I can't afford just now.

I grab us a little table in the corner, conveniently hidden from the rest of the pub, while Tom gets a round in.

'Nice place, eh?' he asks.

'I can see you grew up on the wrong side of the tracks out here.'

'Where did you live when you were a kid?'

Funny – the asking for personal details way beyond anything I have ever previously shared with Tom was something I should have

117

expected and been prepared for, given he is sheltering me from the law and Russian mobsters in his parents' house, and yet it somehow catches me off guard.

'I grew up all over. My parents divorced when I was young and I bounced between my father and mother, who themselves bounced from here to there. Reading, Exeter, Norwich, a brief spell in Dublin. Cardiff, Birmingham for a bit. I didn't enjoy moving around at all. I always wanted somewhere that I truly thought of as home.'

'When I was a kid, I always wished we had moved around. You know, just to experience different places. But now I'm glad I grew up in one place.'

We talk a little bit more about our childhoods, me being lenient with real information, but much, much, much more forthcoming than I usually am in that sort of social setting. I suggest we get another round as last orders arrive. Tom says that he'll get it in, citing my need for cover. I offer him the money but he refuses.

The walk back to Tom's parents' house is lovely, with a clear, early autumn sky letting me see the stars in a way that is impossible in London. We use the time to reminisce about our days together at Eligium, hitting the usual high notes: Reginald's often sweary moments of misspeaking, Chad Cooper's quasi-employment at the think tank that he kindly offered pro bono, David's almost miraculous stupidity, the ridiculously posh nature of Freddie. We laugh together and it all feels comfortable.

When we get back to the house, I tell Tom I'm tired from the last few days and I'd like to go to bed. He checks the time and ponders that it is late now anyhow and he's going to turn in himself. We pause for a moment before parting ways. I think for a moment he's going to go in for a snog; I have no idea how I will react if he does. Thankfully, after a tense moment or two, Tom smiles and wanders off to his bedroom. I go to my room, strip off and lie myself down in the comfy bed Tom has provided for my stay. I figure the events of the last couple of days contain so much to unpack that I'll be awake for some time. However, I fall asleep within minutes.

The next day is peaceful and allows me to recharge my batteries a little. Tom still goes off in the morning – not to Eligium, for even Tom has thrown in the towel on that front, but to various job interviews. He comes home that Wednesday afternoon with several new dresses, undergarments and other clothing accessories for me. They all fit and are to my sartorial tastes.

'How did you know my size?' I ask him, stunned.

'I'm a stickler for detail. It's how I managed to keep Eligium afloat.'

'Speaking of which, do you think we'll still be paid at the end of this month?'

'Good question. I might swing by the office tomorrow while I'm in town and get the lay of the land.'

Tom returns to the house Thursday evening, after I have spent an embarrassing portion of the day binge-watching *Friends* on digital television. I hate to admit it, but the snowflakes might have had a point about the show – it is pretty socially retro. Tom gives me the Eligium update.

'No one was there at all. Weirdly though, the lights were on as well as some of the computers, you know, like as if someone had been in, making themselves at home in our absence.'

'It's probably the Russians, looking for information.'

'That's not at all discomforting then.'

'On the flipside, it could just be Chad Cooper continuing to make his presence felt.'

'Anything exciting happen to you while I was in town?' Tom asks.

'No, nothing at all.'

That's a lie; there was one notable phone conversation I took part in. DCI Murray texted me in the morning.

'LET's TALK.'

I ignored the text. Another one from her arrived about an hour later.

'I KNOW YOU KILLED KOSTCHENKO IN SELF-DEFENCE. WANT TO TALK ABOUT SOMETHING ELSE.'

Ignored her again. About half an hour after the second one, I got this text from her:

'I NEED YOUR HELP. SOME OF YOUR WORK COLLEAGUES COULD BE IN DANGER.'

The last one made me think of Tom and then convinced me to get in touch with DCI Murray. I ventured out into the village nearby and picked up a Jeronum mobile phone from the newsagents. They are the cheapest burners available on the market, come with their own SIM card with ten pounds pre-paid on them – and happen to be almost completely untraceable, unlike most burners these days. My theory is that the company intentionally created them for the drug-dealer market.

It took me about five minutes to get the piece of shit technology I was working with up and running as I returned to the house. I dialled DCI Murray's number as soon as the burner was ready to go.

'Hello?' she said, answering almost right away.

'It's Charlotte.'

'Thought it might be.'

'This is a Jeronum I'm calling on so don't bother trying to trace the call.'

'I'll take your word for it. You didn't stick to your word and call me after your date with Kostchenko. But given the way the date seemed to have gone, I'll forgive you for that.'

'Thanks. I travelled beyond the M25 as well. Wasn't clear if that request was still a live one.'

'It was a grey area, I suppose. Lawrence Milding has received a death threat.'

'The Russians are threatening Milding now?' I ask.

'They say it is in retribution for Kostchenko. The gang call themselves Soldati Smerdi.'

'Death's soldiers?'

'You speak Russian?'

'A little.'

'We have a police detail protecting him. In the meantime, I want to ask you about Freddie D'Hondt.'

'What about him?'

'I am beginning to think he might be involved in all of this in a big way,' DCI Murray says.

'What makes you think that?'

'He is the only person who connects to both Lord Duncan and Eligium. Also, he's gone missing. I can't find him anywhere. The Home Office assures me he's still in the country so we're still looking. Once I find him, I'm going to bring him in for questioning. If you hear from Freddie, will you let me know?'

'Depends. Am I under arrest for the Kostchenko thing?'

'There is a warrant out for your arrest in relation to the death of Kostchenko. There's nothing I can do about that, I'm afraid.'

'I remain in hiding then.'

'Or you can come in and we could clear this all up quickly. It seems like a self-defence plea can be put forth given what I've seen at the crime scene. You'd still have an evading arrest charge to talk through, but again, you can say you feared retribution from the Russian gang and that might get you some leniency.'

'Forgive me if I'm cynical for now.'

'Will you at least get in touch if Freddie contacts you?'

I leave a little pause for her to sweat.

'OK. If Freddie calls, I'll let you know.'

Tom is making me dinner, just as he did the last night. I enter the kitchen to see that Tom's dinner plans have progressed already to an almost alarming extent. Chopping of vegetables has taken place and a pan full of something delicious smelling simmers on the stove top.

'Curry?' I ask.

'Lamb pasanda. My speciality. There's beer and wine in the fridge, if you fancy a drink.'

I crack myself open a tall tin of Cobra and take a moment to admire Tom. Jesus, the guy can cook as well. I soon find myself asking him things about his life without either trying to kill time or because I'm trying to fish for information, but because I genuinely want to know.

'Are you an only child?' I start with.

'Yeah,' he says, as if it were an affliction. 'You?'

'I had a sister once.'

'Had?'

'She died when we were both young. An accident.'

'Jesus, I'm sorry.'

'I don't remember it and I know it's kind of strange, but I never asked my parents anything about it at all.'

'Were you close to your sister before she died?'

'I think so. Again, I can't remember.'

'How old were you when the accident happened?'

'I think I was about twelve.'

Tom pauses from stirring the lamb pasanda to look up at me intensely.

'Twelve? And you can't remember anything about it other than it was an accident of "some description"?'

'That's weird, right?'

'It's peculiar, yes.'

'This coming from the guy who's in his early thirties and still lives with his parents.'

'I'm not thirty yet. And I'm only spending the time here at present because of you.'

I feel a little guilty for the jibe, which was foolish under the circumstances.

'Fair enough,' I say. 'I'm sorry.'

He smiles.

'It's OK, Charlotte. You're going through a lot.'

Over dinner, we talk further about his parents.

'My dad was a banker before he retired. Made enough money to stop when he was fifty-five,' Tom says with a touch of insecurity peeking through. He is not on course to retire in his mid-fifties, is our Tom.

'Why did you decide to work for a think tank?' I ask.

'My mum is where my interest in politics comes from. She ran to be the Labour MP around here several times.'

'This must be the definition of a safe Tory seat.'

'It is. But she never lost her deposit, which is fair going for the area.'

'It's your mother that turned you into a soggy leftie then?'

'Pretty much. My father isn't too right-wing, for an ex-banker anyhow. What about your parents? What did they do for a living?'

'My father was a failed entrepreneur. That was one of the reasons we kept moving around. He tried to open a restaurant and that went bust; then a furniture shop and that went down; several other failed businesses followed that; what sank him was an attempt to open a large wholesale carpet store.'

'Sank him?'

'He retired to the dole, a sitting room sofa in Birmingham, and a daily bottle of Tanqueray. Drank himself to death before my A levels were finished.'

'Sorry to hear that.'

'He was a prick, so don't sweat it.'

'Your mum?'

'She was always a broken person, from as far back as I can remember.'

'Although given you can't remember back further than when you were twelve, who knows what that tells you, right?'

Tom smiles. I feel a little tingly. I suppose the thing I like about the guy is that he is at once kind and giving, yet at the same time he isn't at all drippy or overly sensitive.

'I just always remember her walking around like life beat the crap out of her,' I say.

123

'Is she still alive?'

'I don't know. Once I came to London, I broke contact with her.'

'What, all contact? With your mum?'

Having Tom question me about this portion of my past makes me feel guilty about having done this to my mother, something I had never previously felt bad about. Part of it was what I had done to Salisbury; somehow after that, I couldn't talk to my mother again. I think I was worried that I would confess the crime to her and that it was not information with which my mother could in any way be trusted. Still, it was a very shitty thing to do to one's mother, however much of a mess she is.

'She was a bad influence. After I moved south, I just decided I couldn't handle my relationship with her any longer,' I say by way of explanation.

From there our conversation regresses into more standard first-date style rubbish: favourite movies, holiday experiences, past sexual relationships. Not only do I find myself going along with it, I find myself enjoying the whole experience. We open another bottle of wine, which turns out to be unwise, for within ten minutes of doing so I find myself snogging Tom furiously.

From there, it doesn't take long before Tom and I are in bed together. We have sex three times that evening. The first time is a little awkward, as first shags inevitably always are, but the next two are amazing, as if Tom and I had been lovers for years already.

We are awoken the following morning by two loud old people, whom I quickly learn are Tom's parents. They stomp into their son's room and proceed to jump onto the bed; once there, they hug us both while we are still starkers.

'You've found a girlfriend!' Tom's mum yelps after she kisses my cheek. 'And she is a total babe to boot!'

'Oh aye, son, she's a real corker you've landed yourself there. Well done, son. Well done.'

Tom's father is shaking his son's hand as he says this.

124

'Mum, Dad – what are you doing home? I thought you weren't back until next month.'

'Oh God, it was so boring in Spain, we just couldn't handle it,' Tom's mum says. 'All anyone could talk about was that bloody bridge to Norway.'

After a few minutes of forced smiles and awkward conversation, we manage to get them to leave us alone long enough so that we can get dressed, but only on the proviso that we join them in the sitting room for coffee to explain our 'marvellous new pairing'.

'What have you told them about me? About us?' I ask Tom frantically as we speed dress.

'Nothing on either front. They had no idea of your existence until they met you when you were naked a moment ago.'

'What's all this "girlfriend" nonsense about then?'

'My mother saw you nude in bed with me and made the assumption.'

It's clear that Tom is telling the truth, so I relax a little.

'OK, fair enough. That was kind of funny, I suppose.'

'I'm glad you can already see the humorous side, Charlotte. It may take me a little longer yet.'

We head downstairs to the greeting I would have expected had Tom and I just been married. His father opens his arms up wide as I approach; he then throws them around me, wrapping me up in a bear hug that causes me to have to think about my oxygen intake for a second.

'Welcome to the family,' he says. As weird as this whole thing is, I like the way I can feel the depth of his voice reverberating across his chest.

'We don't even know her name yet!' Tom's mother shouts.

'I'm Charlotte,' I say, wriggling free of the father's embrace. 'Lovely to meet you both. Sorry, didn't catch your names.'

'I'm Barbara and this is John,' the mother says.

I think I'm through the worst of it – until the tea is poured and

Barbara decides she's known me for five minutes now, which is apparently long enough to ask of me the following:

'Charlotte, I was wondering – how do you style yourself downstairs. Your pubic hair, I'm referring to now.'

'Mum!' Tom shouts, embarrassed, covering his eyes with his hand.

'No, I'll field this one,' I say, figuring it's best to just ride the wave. 'I prefer what amounts to au naturel. Perhaps some slight tweaking at the edges, but that's as far as I'm willing to go.'

'So glad to hear it,' Barbara says. 'Good to see a young woman taking that sort of principled stand in this day and age. Also, I know Tom is partial to a nice bit of full-grown minge anyhow.'

'Mum! Stop!'

I get the sense that having to live with his mother's 'lively outbursts' has been part of Tom's life since he learned to understand English.

'I'm sorry, love,' Barbara continues, playing out this Freudian nightmare to the bitter end. 'I've just always noticed that tendency in your choice of pornography is all.'

John thankfully takes us away from the topic of genital hair styles and onto the details of how Tom and I met. I allow Tom to field this one as I don't wish to interfere on what information he wants his parents to be in on and what he wishes to leave out. It's a short history: we met at work, we had never been out with each other, we're still deciding on next steps. He leaves out the 'Charlotte is on the lam while hiding out from some Russian gangsters' bit, which I appreciate for several reasons.

'An office romance!' Barbara shouts, and I'm starting to think the woman has only one gear. 'You're being sheepish here, Tom, but I can see the love between you two, clear as day.'

I look at Tom intending to trade cynical glances; instead, I find myself in a 'moment' with him. Oh Jesus, I think I've fallen in love with the bloke. That's inconvenient for many reasons.

126

I manage to break away from my makeshift new family by declaring my need for a shower. I get a strange sensation as the soap and water flows off and away from my body; I feel a sense of loss involved in losing the remnants of Tom's pheromones from my skin. Jesus, what the hell is wrong with me here? It's like I'm changing into a different person, someone I'm not sure I like.

As I get dressed, my phone starts to vibrate. I figure it must be one of Charlie's Angels. Instead, it's a text from DCI Murray.

'WHY DID I TRUST YOU? YOUR PLAN WORKED: FREDDIE HAS FLED THE COUNTRY.'

I grab the Jeronum and call her.

'Lawrence Milding, Jerry Smythe, and Freddie D'Hondt left the country aboard a yacht this morning,' DCI Murray says.

'What? I thought you had Milding under police protection.'

'We did. He escaped after you told Freddie he was under investigation and he decided he would take Smythe and Milding and flee the country before either of them could tell us what they knew about the murders.'

'I didn't tell Freddie anything! I haven't even spoken to him since I last saw him in Justin's when you and I met there!'

'I shouldn't have trusted you with the information I did. Just so you know, you are now wanted for conspiracy to murder given Freddie is wanted for double homicide.'

She hangs up.

Trying to find the silver lining here, at least this cures me of thoughts of puppy love for the time being.

Chapter Eleven

I spend the next twenty-four hours in a panic after discovering that my rap sheet has another notch, my brief time of being off the hook for all criminal activity having come to a shuddering halt thanks to bloody Freddie. Tom doesn't have any interviews, meaning he doesn't need to go into town – 'I don't do interviews on Fridays,' he tells me – added to the fact that Barbara and John have decided to take an impromptu trip to Cambridge in order to 'leave the house to the lovebirds', which means that Tom and I have the house all to ourselves. I can scream about the fact that it looks like I've just been framed for something again without worrying about alienating any future in-laws. Together, Tom and I go over scenarios one by one and what becomes clear the more we talk is that I can't allow Tom to be exposed to any further legal danger. He's harbouring someone under investigation for conspiracy to murder; if I'm caught here, he's going down for a while himself. I come to the conclusion that what I must do is go back into London and turn myself in to DCI Murray. Tom and I will spend one more night together and then I'll go first thing the next morning.

We spend most of the rest of the day having sex, talking little on the topic of conversation staring us in the face, i.e. my impending incarceration. A few times it can't be avoided, however.

'Given you are innocent of all charges, you'll get off.'

'You say that, but whoever is doing this all is extraordinarily professional.'

'There can't be anything but circumstantial evidence to try and pin you to anything.'

We sleep a lot between sex sessions. The only odd slice of business that Friday throws at me is a text from Michael Snidely.

'Just wanted to assure you that I am still keen to push ahead with the new think tank. When could we meet to discuss?'

Interesting. Seems that Jerry skipping the country has brought the think tank job back into contention somehow. Swings and roundabouts. I suppose there's no harm in keeping options open here.

'A bit snowed under at present,' I text Snidely back. 'Be back to you soon. Look forward to speaking about it further.'

Despite sleeping for significant sections of the day, Tom and I pass out around ten that evening anyhow. I manage to snooze straight through without a strange dream hitting me or indeed experiencing anything other than deep slumber for the next nine hours. As I wake up the following morning, stretch and then open my eyes, prepared to get myself ready for the trip into London to turn myself in, it is fair to say that my day does not start as planned. That is because there is a gun pointed in my face. At first, I am resigned about this fact, figuring that this must be the cops – until it hits me a second later that this is a long way from any ordinary police procedure. My eyes focus on the man holding the weapon: he's Slavic-looking and in his mid-twenties. As it becomes clear to him that I am now awake, the man with what I've now figured out is a Glock 22 in his hand, pointed right at me, starts to shout at an unseen companion in Russian, something about having found the subject and to come quickly. Shit: Death's Soldiers have tracked me down. I suddenly feel stupid for not realising that this was almost certainly inevitable.

Tom is awoken by all the Russian flying about, at which point he then gets a gun pointed in his face. For a moment, I'm thinking that's it, these guys are going to ice us right here in Tom's bed. But then, another Russian man walks into the room, this one mercifully unarmed as well as equipped with a demonstrable ability to speak English.

'Good morning, Charlotte Heard.'

'It's me that you want, not Tom. Do whatever you need to do to me but please don't hurt him.'

This feels strange coming out of my mouth and does so without forethought. It's hard to recall another time when I would have instinctively tried to surrender my life for someone else's.

'Do not worry, we have no intention of killing your boyfriend. As long as he plays nice, you come with us without any problems and do everything we ask, I won't touch a hair upon his head.'

I get dressed quickly and then follow the Russians out to a car they have parked in front of Barbara and John's house. I want to wave to Tom as I go, but I'm afraid they'll think I'm signalling him about something and get itchy trigger fingers. I just smile at him, as best I can under the circumstances, as I leave our little love nest. Tom gives me a faint smile back.

We drive for a bit in silence, the two goons on either side of me pointing their Glocks in my direction the whole time, their eyes never leaving me for a single moment. I don't even catch either of them blinking.

I notice we're on the M40, heading further away from London. Are we going to Oxford? Birmingham? Stafford? Some isolated spot where they can execute me in peace?

'Allow me now to introduce myself,' says the Russian who spoke English back at Tom's parents' house. 'My name is Sergei Mikhailov. Your life is mine for the moment. If you do everything I say, you have every chance of making it out of this predicament alive. Is that understood?'

I nod.

'Good,' Mikhailov continues. 'You recently became acquainted

130

with an associate of mine, Vladimir Kostchenko. Unfortunately, Mr Kostchenko met with an unfortunate demise at your hands subsequent to the two of you, how do you say, getting to know one another.'

'Look, it was an accident, I didn't mean to—'

Mikhailov puts his finger to his lips and softly shushes me. I immediately stop talking.

'I will let you off for that outburst this time, Charlotte Heard. Next time, you'll receive a punch in the abdomen. After that, it's a bullet in an extremity. After that, I don't think you need me to tell you. Is this rule clear?'

I nod.

'Good. Now, as it happens, you are in some luck here. Vladimir was becoming a liability to the organisation. We had even gone as far as looking into having him eliminated. There is a viewpoint in your favour which could be expressed as you, Charlotte Heard, did us a favour by getting rid of Vladimir for nothing.'

He pauses to take a cigarette out of his pocket and then lights it with a match.

'Yet despite this fact, Vladimir was still one of us. And I cannot allow English serial killers to murder my men without recourse, now can I?'

He smokes for a while in silence. I think of asking him what he wants from me – since it is clear he wants something, otherwise he would have just killed both Tom and me back in Buckinghamshire – but then I remember the punch in the gut warning and wait for Mikhailov to speak again.

'In light of Vladimir's standing prior to his death, I am willing to make you an offer, Charlotte Heard. I want to use your skills pro bono one more time, as it were. You undertake the job I am about to describe to you without any blowback on us, within the time frame given, and then you are off the hook for killing Vladimir.'

Mikhailov hands me a picture. It takes me a moment to recognise the face but when I do, I almost shit myself, literally, right there and then in the Russians' car.

'You want me to kill the Foreign Secretary?' I ask softly.

'Yes.'

'Why?'

'Yours is not to know why, it is simply to do.'

I pause for a moment to get my head together. My thoughts are all over the place.

'Does it matter how I do it?'

'As long as he is dead and it is not traceable back to us, then no, I don't care how you do it.'

I look at the picture again. It seems a ridiculous thing to even think about attempting, particularly given I am a wanted criminal with a conspiracy to murder charge hanging over my head. Mikhailov then takes something out of his inside jacket pocket and hands it to me. It is a delegate's pass to the Conservative Party conference. It has a picture of a woman that I know isn't me but looks exactly like me with the name 'Oxana Deseroyova' on it. I instantly note the surname: Oxana shares it with Svetlana, my other doppelganger, the one arrested for killing Duncan and Reginald.

'You want me to kill him at the Tories' party conference?' I ask, taking the pass off of Mikhailov.

'That is the idea.'

'Anything I should know about Oxana?'

'She is one of us. We have been assured that she has been cleared and will face no problems in terms of access to the conference.'

'Assured by whom?'

'The top.'

I know better than to pry into what 'the top' means. Jesus, what are Number 10 doing, allowing the Russians unquestioned access to their own party conference, with the entire government in one building, knowing what they know about what that could possibly mean? It's an offshoot of the usual thing every Western government does, I suppose: the Russians wouldn't do anything *really* brazen, would they?

'You have until the conference ends on Wednesday afternoon to kill the target. If you don't succeed by then, I will kill you, your boyfriend, and both his parents, the lovely Barbara and John.'

I quickly come to the conclusion that I can't allow anything bad to happen to Tom and his parents.

'All right, fine, I'll do it. Remind me: where is the Tory conference this year?'

Please say Birmingham. Or Manchester. Just not . . .

'Blackpool.'

Fuck. I hate Blackpool. Not just for all the reasons most middle-class southern people don't like the place – although despite not having been raised in the south of England and hardly being able to call my upbringing in any way middle-class, I dislike Blackpool for all of those reasons too – but because I had a particularly horrible time there once with my parents. It is one of the only holidays I can ever remember going on with both of them. It was definitely after my sister died, but not long after, so I must have been in my very early teens. We stayed in a terrible hotel near the beach and my parents fought mercilessly with each other the whole time. The 'highlight' of the trip was all of us going to the top of Blackpool Tower together – and my father coming down in handcuffs, having grabbed my mother and dangled her over the edge, threatening to kill her in front of several bemused Lancastrians.

It's getting colder as we move north, the Indian summer we are experiencing in London no longer applying as we head into the Midlands. This part of England is as home to me as any part could claim to be; watching it scroll past, I feel nothing for it.

The two goons either side of me put their guns away somewhere near the turn off for Coventry. From there we stop only once, at a service station just outside of Stafford, for food and a piss. I'm in no way guarded while away from the car. I suppose the Russians figure

I either get a ride with them to Blackpool or run off and find my own way there; either way, I'm on the hook for exactly one dead Foreign Secretary.

The service station is filled with families on outings, probably most of them off to some overpriced theme park the kids will complain about the whole time, wanting to be home playing video games instead. There is one particularly cute three-year-old boy who is trying to get his father to buy him a Peppa Pig doll (without success), a gorgeous creature with bright blue eyes and curly blond locks. The little man makes me feel broody, which immediately causes me to think about Tom again.

The concourse has a sushi place, a Tex-Mex restaurant, and a Thai place – all of them closed. The only place to eat that is serving is the resident chippie, a place that looks like it probably hasn't shut once, even for Christmas, since it first opened in 1974. As I think about the job ahead while eating my way through an unappetising chicken and chips, I begin to relish the idea of assassinating the Foreign Secretary. If there is one member of the current cabinet I would like to take out, it would be the fat, posh, stupid man that disgraces the hallowed halls of the FCO. The Right Honourable Stephen Bishop, a man mostly infamous for three things: his ability to put his foot in his mouth during any media appearance; a stunning lack of knowledge about the wider world that would be unforgivable in any Member of Parliament, never mind a Foreign Secretary; and last but certainly not least, a misogyny combined with an unguarded racism that is something to behold. I have only met him once; it was after an event. I'd had to corner him for a chat because Eligium were doing a project about Slovenian prisons at the time. He responded to my query, something boring about jails in Ljubljana, with a short answer that communicated to me that he had confused Slovenia with Singapore ('The thing runs well enough, but then again it's a city state off the coast of Burma run by the slanties, so I hesitate to draw too many conclusions there') before looking down my top and

134

saying 'nice tits' before walking off. Most sexism tends to be innuendo-driven; I suppose I should give Bishop points for being so brazenly old school. Perhaps I'll consider that while I'm severing his femoral artery.

This final thought makes me panic. I didn't bring my usual hand-bag, the one that has my ivory jack knife in it. This already difficult job just got much trickier.

We all pile into the BMW again. I fall asleep around Warrington, only to be roused by a Russian elbow to the ribs as the car pulls up outside of the Blackpool convention centre.

'I guess this is goodbye then?' I ask once I've got my bearings.

'For now,' Mikhailov says. 'Here is a card with my number on it in case I can help you in some way that is beyond your immediate reach. Otherwise, we will meet at this spot at either three p.m. on Wednesday afternoon, or one hour after the news of the Foreign Secretary's death has hit the news, whichever arrives first. I wish you luck, Charlotte Heard.'

I get out and the BMW drives away. I suppose it is time to see what I'm made of; this will be the biggest kill I've ever tried to pull off by some ways.

The smartest thing for me to do would be to try entering the conference on this, the opening night, to see if this pass in the name of Oxana works. I chicken out. I'd rather give it a go in the morning when I'll hopefully feel more up to the stress of it all.

The immediate priority then is to find a roof over my head for the night. I go from B&B to B&B in the centre of Blackpool trying to get a room, which is of course impossible given the conference of the governing party is in town and everyone booked their rooms months ago. After the fifteenth establishment turns me down, I decide to lower my standards and attempt to get a bed at a hostel. Even then it takes me three of them before I find something.

'One night?' the bloke behind the counter asks me with a Scouse accent so thick you could win the European Cup with it.

'Yes.'

'That'll be fifty pounds, please.'

'Fifty quid! You must be joking.'

'Conference prices, luv. Take it or leave it.'

It's possibly the only place available to sleep under cover in all of Blackpool, so I have little choice. I slap two twenties and a tenner on the counter, which thankfully I already had in my trouser pockets.

'There's one toilet on the wing, down the end of the hallway. Be careful where you're walking, like. Some of our longer-term tenants are prone to accidents.'

Luckily, I don't require the loo. I simply hunt out my bed and try and fall asleep as quickly as possible, despite the fact that it's only half six in the evening. And wouldn't you know it: my next-door neighbour is a talker.

'What brings you to Blackpool, luv? Looking for some spice? I can get you some like, no problem,' is her opener.

'No thanks, I'm covered in the spice department already.'

'I get it, don't worry. Was he rough, the last one?'

'Excuse me?'

'The last bloke, I mean. Was he bad to you?'

She thinks I'm a victim of domestic abuse. It's the cut on my forehead from the Kostchenko incident added to the fact that I look like a bag of shit. I decide my best course of action is to play along.

'He was pretty bad, yeah.'

'Local lad?'

'Russian.'

'Jesus, luv! Well, best off out of that, I say. Name's Georgina.'

'Lovely to meet you, Georgina. I'm Oxana. Now, if you don't mind, I need some sleep.'

To her credit, Georgina obeys my wishes and I'm soon out like a light.

Chapter Twelve

Mid-September of every year, party political conference season begins. For three weeks, parliament is in recess while in turn, the Liberal Democrats, Labour, and the Conservatives gather together amongst themselves to discuss their own internal greatness. This used to happen in seaside towns like Margate and Scarborough until MPs decided this was all a bit insalubrious and chose instead to have these solipsistic affairs in large cities, or at best Brighton as the one nod to the old way that was still suitably upmarket. It was all part and parcel of the gentrification of party politics, as people with degrees in PPE from Oxford and Cambridge decided having to go to Morecambe every autumn when Manchester is on a much more reliable train line from London and at least has some nice restaurants on Deansgate was outmoded.

The Tories have decided this year to go old school and have it in Blackpool again. It's probably all part of their misguided attempt to bond with 'real people'; the party thinking it has to have its conference in a northern hellhole in order to reconnect with something, although no one could possibly define to what they are being reconnected.

I wake up early, a little before six, and proceed to get the hell out of the hostel as quickly as I can. I need a shower and have no idea how that's going to happen if I don't have one at the hostel, yet the idea of me being naked in there fills me with such dread that I can't face it.

Now I'm walking down Church Street, in the direction of both the seafront and the Winter Gardens where the conference is already into its first full day, regretting that I didn't take the shower opportunity while it was there. I stop in front of a shop and look at myself in the mirror to discover that I look like a street sleeper. I can't see how I'm getting into the conference looking the way I do, and even if I manage that there's no way anyone of any import will talk to me, particularly with the phony accent I'll have to adopt for the part of Oxana. Given all this, getting the Foreign Secretary alone has gone from being analogous to trying to climb Everest with a dessert spoon as my sole implement, to trying to get to the moon using only my leg-strength.

And there's no way out of my dilemma unless I leave Blackpool. Yes, that's what I'll have to do: take the train to Preston and hope I can get a room there. Buy a new dress, clean myself up and then get back here and hope I have enough time remaining to kill Bishop and save Tom and his parents' lives, not to mention my own.

I'm about to put the Preston plan into action when I hear someone shouting at me in the near distance.

'Charlotte! Is that you?'

It's David, my old Eligium chum who picked me up and helped me stakeout Kostchenko's house before he fell asleep. I see him approaching me with a huge smile on his face; directly behind him is Jeremy being his usual cantankerous self.

'Hello,' I say to them both as warmly as I can manage.

'What are you doing here? Up for conference, I take it!' David says.

'Yes, I am. What about you guys? You already have new jobs that have assigned you Tory conference?'

David looks baffled by this question.

'We're here on behalf of Eligium, of course,' he says. I can't help but laugh a tiny bit.

'Who's been in the office lately to tell you to come up here?' I ask David.

'No one, as it happens,' David says, like this is the first time that fact had occurred to him. 'But we had the trip planned for months before the whole shutting-down business came to light, so of course we couldn't just not come. Seemed not in the spirit of things. What happened to your head?'

'Small kitchen mishap, nothing serious.'

I make a mental note to lose the plaster asap. It is then that the fortuitous nature of this random meeting of the Eligium duo suddenly occurs to me.

'Do you guys have a hotel room in town?'

'It's a room in a B&B,' David says.

'Could I use it to have a shower and get changed?'

The idea of me washing my body in the same cubicle he used that very morning strikes a chord with David, who now looks like imminent orgasm may be possible.

'Of course, Charlotte,' he manages to say through his cloud of ecstasy.

'Hold on a moment, it's my room as well and I don't like this idea,' Jeremy butts in with.

'Please, Jeremy? Look at me! I need a shower!' I squeal.

'Yes! She needs a shower!' David shrieks, not willing to let this long-held fantasy of his slip out of reach on account of his grouchy quasi-workmate.

'I won't stand for it,' Jeremy says, deciding he's going to at least attempt to die on this hill. 'I'm sorry, Charlotte, but you can get your own room. We're late for an appointment as is and I'm not handing over my key to the likes of you or letting poor David here be conned out of his key.'

Desperate times call for desperate measures.

'David, here's the deal: I need a dress and I need a shower. If you come with me to get some clothes and then let me into the room to wash myself,' I pause, steeling myself for the offer I'm about to make here, 'I will let you watch me while I shower.'

139

This time round, it's possible by the face he pulls that I've just caused David to ejaculate into his pants. Jeremy sees his cause waning and rolls his eyes.

'Don't be manipulated by her, David. She's just using you to get what she wants,' Jeremy says as a last-ditch attempt to get his way.

'Charlotte, please lead and I will follow,' says David as he recovers his wits a little.

David and I walk toward Bank Hey street, leaving Jeremy in the dust without a further word. When we arrive there, I go to the nearest ATM and withdraw the maximum amount allowed using the dodgy, untraceable bank card attached to a Belarussian account I have in reserve for these situations. I soon see what is probably going to be my best bet in terms of getting a dress that will pass muster at Tory conference. As I walk into the dress shop, I am treated by the salesclerk to the lowest rent re-imagining it is possible to envision of the similar bit in *Pretty Woman*. After I flash some cash, she begrudgingly lets me try on what is the only dress in the whole shop in my size that will do the trick. Luckily, it fits.

As we walk toward David's B&B, he brings up Eligium crap.

'I'm still working on that politically sensitive project I kept trying to tell you about the week before last, in case you're interested.'

'David, just stop. Eligium is gone now. There is no need to follow through with anything you've been working on. Hell, there's no reason to be here right now. Just relax and have fun.'

'OK. But it would be better if I could tell you about it.'

'No! I don't want to know!'

'All right then.'

He gets the message and drops the subject.

The walk to David and Jeremy's B&B is a bit of a trek. After the attempt to bring up the 'politically sensitive project' falls flat, David is eerily silent; I think he doesn't want to say anything else that might upset me and thus make me change my mind about what I'd promised him. When we get into the room and David and I are all alone, he begins to get nervous. He starts to hyperventilate a little. I have to help him to sit down; he manages to start breathing normally within a half a minute.

'Thank you, Charlotte.'

'I wasn't going to have you die on me here in Blackpool.'

'Listen, I find your offer one of the most appealing things that has ever been held out to me in the entirety of my life. However, I think it would be ungentlemanly were I to sit and watch you shower, particularly as it would seem coercive on my part. As wonderful as your offer was, I won't be taking you up on it.'

David is a useless idiot, but it has to be said, a kind and honourable one. There aren't many of those in Westminster. I find myself feeling sorry for him; it's this emotion that makes me decide what I'm going to do next.

'David, you are a nice man. I agree that you watching me in the shower would have been a bit creepy, so thank you for declining the offer. Instead, I want you to stay where you are and keep your eyes on me.'

He nods. I get up to walk toward the bathroom.

'You're not looking at me. I told you to look at me.'

He raises his eyes back in my direction as requested. I then begin to get undressed, removing my clothes until I am in my bra and knickers. I then unclasp my bra and let it fall to the carpet. I pause for a moment to let David get a decent eyeful. Then, I remove my knickers. I pause again to let David take it all in. I slowly turn around, flash my bum at him for a second and then enter the bathroom, closing the door behind me.

The first thing I do once I'm in there, alone, is take the plaster off to have a look at the wound Kostchenko inflicted on my forehead. It seems to have mostly healed. Perhaps it wasn't as deep as it felt like at the time. If I do my hair right, no one will even notice it.

I feel like a new person as the water hits me, like I'm washing away the awfulness of the last twenty-four hours. I think again about killing Bishop; it's going to be very hard without having a personal weapon to hand. I'll have to use whatever's sitting around his hotel room, and it may be that I have to get creative in a hurry.

As I get out of the shower and towel off, I wonder how I'm going to handle getting changed, what with my clothes in the other room and David still there. I don't think he can handle another flash.

'David, I was . . .' I say as I poke my head out of the bathroom, only to stop myself when I realise he's left the room. He has kindly got out of my hair and is probably waiting for me in reception.

I try on the new dress and preen in the mirror a little. I do feel a lot more confident for being clean and well-presented. Outside the hotel stands David, as if we were about to go on a first date together. As we walk back toward the Winter Gardens, it suddenly strikes me that I either have to lose him somehow or tell him some version of the truth that involves at least some explanation of why I'm about to enter a national political conference with fake credentials, something even someone as unobservant as David is going to pick up on if we're there together, particularly if I have to whip out the Russian accent in a hurry. I decide the former is too mean and figure I can get away with the latter.

'Listen, David, there is something I need to tell you. I'm going into the conference with a pass that has the name Oxana Deseroyova on it. I can't explain why I am doing so; it would only put you in danger. I just thought you should know so you weren't confused.'

I can see that he is considering saying something to me and then shakes his head a little and breaks into a semi-smile.

'Thank you, Charlotte. Any secret you ever wish to leave in my care will always be safe, now and for ever.'

Jesus, I've done a number on David. I think if I asked him to saw off an extremity because I needed it for a science experiment, he'd gladly do it for me.

Here we are, the moment of truth. To add to the tension, the security around the perimeter of the conference is more intimidating than I have ever seen it. A metal wall about ten feet high rings half of Blackpool centre, with a cop armed with a machine gun stationed every five to ten feet along. A military helicopter is flying overhead. The scene is dystopian. It's probably always been this bad, every year I've had to attend, and it's only now that I'm noticing.

I try and get into character without having decided what that means. Is Oxana feisty or demure? Smart or thick? I should have thought about this a little more than none at all. I approach the security desk. The guard scans the barcode on my pass. It beeps – first good sign, the pass is real at least. The security guard looks at me, then at the picture that has come up on his screen, then back to me again. A moment later, he waves me through. Whew. Thank you, Oxana, for sharing my likeness so precisely.

I go through the metal scanners without a hitch and I'm in.

'I should go and try to find Jeremy,' David says as he cruises past. 'Have a good conference, Oxana. And thank you.'

I grab a conference calendar and take a look at today's speeches. Bishop isn't due to speak until Tuesday morning, so that's out unless I want to take this down to the wire, which for many reasons I'd rather not. I then scan the fringe events for any sign of him. Yes! He's on a panel talking about Russian manipulation of western elections through social media this afternoon at four p.m. This is unbelievably lucky given one, it is rare that any holder of one of the big four offices of state ever speaks at fringe events at conference and two, the topic is Russia, meaning I have a built-in ice breaker that makes sense both to the event and my persona.

I look at my watch: ten to eleven. I've got five hours to kill at the Tory conference. Thankfully, I have a dodgy Russian fairy godfather connected enough to get me into any room in the building – in theory at least. I aim to have fun testing Mikhailov's claim.

I discover that there is going to be a champagne reception for a select group of Conservative party large donors at midday in a discreet room tucked away at the back of the conference hall after overhearing two wealthy Tories discussing it. I text Sergei Mikhailov: 'NEED ACCESS TO DONORS' RECEPTION, ROOM XX3, STARTS AT 12'. As I approach Room XX3 at the appointed hour, I can hear a scuffle ensuing as one old duffer is turned away.

'I'm terribly sorry, sir, but the party is for invited guests only.'

'I gave half a million pounds to the party last year and you're saying I can't come in and drink some cheap champagne with my friends!'

'Sorry, sir. I can only let in people on the list.'

As the old, posh, very angry rich man walks away shaking his head in disgust, I approach, sure I am about to witness the limits of Mikhailov's supposed soft power.

'Name?'

'Oxana Deseroyova,' I say, trying out the accent for the first time. It needs work, I conclude. The woman in front of me flips through a list on the iPad in front of her and tries to find my pseudonym. She starts shaking her head, about to give me the all too familiar high-end event rejection, when a woman behind her leans over and whispers in her ear. The woman's face registers the intake of information and a second later she smiles at me and says:

'Welcome, Oxana, go on in.'

Here I am, at one of the proper parties at Tory conference, the sort which the plebs like me who toil away in Westminster think tanks never normally get a sniff of. Half the cabinet is here, schmoozing identical-looking men in tweed jackets and mustard-coloured corduroy trousers, all of the ministers managing to look convincingly interested as the rich men drone on and on about how the matriarchy is now in charge of the country and wasn't it so much better when Mrs Thatcher ran the place, never noticing the ironic disconnect between those two prognoses. I grab a glass of champagne and crane my neck, looking round the room for the Foreign Secretary. I conclude that Bishop is not present. Would have been nice to warm him up prior to the four p.m. event, but I've still got that to look forward to.

I don't know anyone here and the real thrill was simply getting in the door; now that the buzz from that has died and there is no practical purpose served by remaining here, I figure I'll down my glass of champagne and then go hang around the exhibition stands, hoping for the best. Just as I am about to put this plan into action, I am approached by Gerald Butler, the MP for West Cornwall as well as Minister of State for Work and Pensions. He and I have never met.

'Hello, are you amongst the hosts then?'

Butler's asking if I'm someone's paid date.

'Yes, this is truth,' I say in my best Russian floozy voice. 'I am with Mr Bishop, he of Foreign Secretary. I cannot find him.'

'Oh, dear, sorry, I haven't seen him today. Listen, while you're here, I was wondering if you could help me a little.'

Into view hovers a Russian-looking bloke.

'This is Anton and he wants desperately to ask me a question about our pension system and I was wondering if you might interpret for us?'

Nightmare situation. My Russian is conversational at best and nowhere near good enough to go into the technicalities of public policy. Here goes nothing.

'Yes, OK. What you want to ask?' I say. Anton and Gerald trade glances in that way two men who don't speak each other's language do when trying to proceed with something practical. After some awkward face pulling and meaningless gesturing, Anton gets the idea that he is now to ask me whatever it is he wanted to ask the Work and Pensions Secretary.

The question sounds long and technical, as expected. I catch more of it than I thought I would; something about how Russia wants to put the pension age up but Cossacks will revolt (?) and then we will have 1917 on our (meaning Russia's, presumably) hands again. Then I lose him completely on the final sentence of the sequence as he asks about something to do with 'philosophy' but that's all I get.

'He want to know how country can raise this pension age but without any potential political problems that come with this. He want to know what "philosophy" could be used,' I say in my Oxana voice to Butler. Along the way, Anton gives me a smile and a nod as I use 'philosophy' in the sentence, which sounds a lot like the Russian word for the same thing.

I worry for a moment that I was too fluent with my English there compared to my initial blurb with the Work and Pensions Secretary, until it occurs to me that Butler hasn't noticed at all. He's already gone into 'I'm about to say something terribly profound' mode – he even strokes his chin as he dictates to me his answer to Anton's supposed question.

'Well, what you need to consider are rate differentials and their relation to the brackets one will put at the end of the period in question . . .'

Gerald drones on like this for about three minutes, completely accepting the premise that even if I was some Russian hostess type for real, I would be a good enough translator to take his policy gobbledygook and make it comprehensible in another language.

'The minister says it depends,' I say to Anton in Russian when Butler is finally finished droning on, which the he grimaces at, knowing that there must surely have been more to it than what I've just translated. By way of retaliation, Anton gives me way more than I can handle back – this time I only understand about twenty percent of what he's saying and not enough to even get the gist of any of it. When he's finished, Gerald looks to me in expectation.

'He says he wonders how a developed country such as the UK can carry on with an outmoded way of paying for people to live in retirement. Wouldn't it make more sense to make the older generation plough the fields like they did in Russia during the days of Brezhnev?'

If you're wondering why I threw in the reference to Brezhnev, it's only because it was one of the only things from the tail end of

146

Anton's spiel that I understood. Butler is now totally baffled; I have started one of the worst games of Chinese whispers in the history of the human race. The Tory MP decides to convey his befuddlement via another long-winded speech filled with jargon, and I know I need to quickly find some way out of this horrid situation. It comes to me: the one area in which my knowledge of Russian excels itself is in what one might wish to describe as the erotic department. Once Butler is finished his latest speech, I turn to Anton and say in Russian:

'I am tired of the Englishman's words. Why don't you and I find a place to have a drink and maybe I'll fuck your brains out afterwards.'

Anton goes beet red and nods his head furiously. I turn to Butler and say:

'He seem to like your proposal, Minister.'

'You know what? That pleases me. Pleases me a lot. Thank you, Anton!' Gerald says with a huge smile on his face. The minister then wanders off and Anton offers me his arm. Once we're outside of the event, I am free to ditch him. He's asking me something about my accent and how it doesn't sound like anything he's heard before and what part of Russia am I from, when I turn to him and tell him in his language that I'm going now and I don't want to see him ever again.

Alone once more, I decide to wander around the exhibition hall a little. This is where corporates, charities, whoever thinks it is worth blowing thirty grand or whatever the Tories are charging now for the privilege, set up a little stand, mostly in order to engage any member of the government who might wander by. Labour conference is no different, particularly when they are in government. Annual conference is a big money-spinner for both of the parties as I suppose it has to be. When you only have a couple thousand members, you need to get your money from somewhere and it can't all come from rich weirdos who want to have dinner at Number 10 now and again.

I approach the Students' Union stand. It is being manned by a young individual who looks like he's still in secondary school and is so obnoxiously un-Tory looking, with his unkempt long hair, poncho, and scruffy trainers, that I just have to speak to him.

'First time at Tory conference?' I ask him.

'No! I've been to the last five!'

'Real Tory enthusiast then?' I say sarcastically. He then gets an earnest look in his eyes that scares me a little. He pauses for a moment before launching into a mini-speech.

'I used to vote Green. I was so sure back then that left-wing ideas were the way of the future. Then I came to my first Conservative party conference. Everything changed for me there. I became a Tory a few days later. Like I say, everything changed.'

'Not enough to get you to dress like a grown-up it seems,' I say. The sartorially challenged young Tory ignores my snarky remark and continues describing his right-wing epiphany.

'I saw the light, I guess you could say. There is a saying that goes, "Reality has a Conservative bias". And reality hit me then. They will have to bury me with my Conservative party membership card in my pocket.'

Ugh, what a bore. I thought at least the leftie-looking guy at the Students' Union stand would be up for a laugh at the whole spectacle. I've never met a born-again Tory before and would be very happy never to encounter one ever again.

I move away from the Students' Union stand without another word to the poncho-clad Conservative. I start to wander aimlessly, eventually finding myself in a wing full of rooms which are mostly empty, clearly on the last stage within the cycle of fringe event-cleanout-nothing happening.

'Charlotte!' I hear a shouty whisper coming from a male voice somewhere nearby say as I walk past several vacant rooms. I look round to see a hand waving out of one of the doors a little behind and to my left. I move toward it, figuring it must be some Tory MP

I know being a nuisance, only to open the door and find myself face to face with the supposedly absconded Freddie D'Hondt.

'I had heard you fled the country,' I say.

'Yes, I did. Didn't go as planned, sadly. The reason for dashing was, well, I was a little bit deeper into the whole Russians giving money to Eligium thing that I may have let on to you when we discussed the matter.'

'Sort of like you neglected to tell me that Lord Duncan was your uncle.'

'A bit like that, yes. You do understand, darling? Had I told you about the whole affair, I would have been getting you into trouble. Even more trouble than you were in already.'

'More trouble than being wanted for murder by the Met and being hunted down by Russian gangsters?'

'It seemed like the right thing at the time is all I can say for myself.'

'By the way, if you're still in the country, where are Smythe and Milding?'

Freddie turns his head to the left and says:

'Come on out, chaps, reveal yourselves.'

From underneath two large heaps of think tank pamphlets emerge both Jerry Smythe and Lawrence Milding.

'Hello, Charlotte,' Lawrence says in a subdued fashion, as if he were a child that had just been scolded for something.

'Charlotte!' shouts Jerry Smythe, as if we were best pals as opposed to having had our last conversation in a toilet in the House of Lords, a chat which involved me holding a knife to his left kidney. 'Wonderful to see you again! We have had the most extraordinary adventures of late!'

'We tried to leave the country in a yacht out of Liverpool harbour. Didn't go as planned,' Lawrence says, still looking chastened.

'Yes, the planning of the whole thing was a little lacklustre, I must say,' Freddie tells me.

'Who was in charge of planning it?' I ask.

'Me, I'm afraid,' Freddie says with no visible shame whatsoever. 'Anyhow, water under the bridge. Sort of literally, as it happens.'

'Can I have a word with you in private?' I ask Freddie. He nods. As we leave the room, the two Tory parliamentarians hide themselves once again under the piles of think tank documents at the back of the room.

As soon as we are in the hallway alone, I don't waste any time.

'The Russians have sent me here to kill Stephen Bishop.'

Freddie doesn't blink.

'Yes, I know. That's why I'm here.'

'How the hell did you know about that?'

'Come now, something like that wouldn't have escaped my purview. Anyhow, I heard about your misfortunes with the Russians and your resultant mission to slay Stephen Bishop and I thought we would pop up here for a visit in the yacht, see if we could be of any help.'

'Do you know Bishop at all?' I ask Freddie.

'Of course. My father and he are old friends. Truth is, he used to babysit me when I was a child and beat me when he did so. Hated the bastard ever since, so whatever you need me to do to help you in this mission, particularly if this takes the heat off of the Russian problem we are all experiencing at present, do let me know.'

'This afternoon, four p.m., Room XX6, be there with me. Bishop is speaking at a fringe on Russian interference in democracy. I just need you to introduce me as Oxana Deseroyova and warm him up a little. I have to assume he won't recognise me from previous encounters but I think we bank that one.'

'Anything else?' Freddie asks.

'When we wrap up the Bishop thing, I want the three of you to come with me to London so I can clear my name.'

I fail to mention that I know that Freddie is suspected of double homicide. Then again, he is supposed to 'know everything' anyhow so I don't feel all that bad about it, particularly after he lied to me and tried to turn me into the cops.

'Of course, Charlotte, by all means,' Freddie says. 'See you this afternoon.'

'In the meantime, keep those two Tory idiots in there on ice. I don't want to lose them.'

'We both have our own reasons for not wanting that to happen, so relax.'

Chapter Thirteen

My plan for how to kill Bishop now in place, I decide I need a break from the conference centre and step outside of the secure zone and into Blackpool proper once again. As I leave through the turnstile, I am approached by a young woman with a placard bearing the legend 'Love Norway, Hate the Bridge' who shouts in my face:

'Tory scum! How many people have you murdered through austerity?'

'None through austerity.'

'What?'

'I'm not a Tory. I'm here on work.'

'Who do you work for then?'

'A green charity.'

Her whole face changes as I say this; I have just announced myself as 'one of the good guys' to her.

'Which one?'

'It's a new one, you won't have heard of it.'

'Try me.'

'It's called the Extinction Imminent Action Group.'

She thinks deeply for a moment.

'You're right, I haven't heard of it. But I love the sound of it! A group of us are going to a café in a few minutes and then we're going to play hacky sack – do you want to join us? I'm Susanna, by the way.'

'Oxana. Sure, that sounds great.'

It's odd that I take Susanna up on her request; I suppose my aversion to Tory conference is greater than I had imagined, and there is nothing else for me to do in Blackpool. I accompany my new friend round the corner, where we see five people who just scream 'left-wing' to me instantly. Two guys and three other gals, all of whom look perfectly dressed to protest outside of Tory autumn conference in Blackpool.

We head to a nearby café that John, one of the leftie blokes, says he got to know intimately during his 'northwest drug days', something I'm rather keen on not finding anything more about. We all order builders' teas which are amazingly low-priced, even for a terrible café in Blackpool. Everything is going smoothly until Jess, the prettiest of the leftie girls, notices that the 'organisation' space on my badge does not read Extinction meltdown rivers of blood whatever I said to Susanna when I met her, but the rather more interesting 'Russian Outreach Service'.

'Oh yeah, that!' I say, as if it were nothing at all. 'We hadn't picked a name for the organisation yet when we were applying for our passes. Someone in the office put the Russian thing down as a joke and the dumb Tories bought it!'

A couple of them laugh and I think that's the end of it. John has other ideas.

'That's a shame. I am fond of Putin and of your country's government in general.'

At first I think he must be joking, but then remember he's so devout a leftie he is protesting outside Tory conference, which is a hell of a litmus test to pass.

'Even though, you know, Putin is homophobic?' I ask him.

'That's just MSM propaganda,' says Jess.

'Yeah, *Russia Today* has debunked that rumour several times and they are the most trusted news source out there,' John says. I want to have this fight with him; I realise quickly it's not worth it.

'I was just kidding, guys,' I say. 'Fuck the MSM!'

153

'Fuck the MSM,' the rest of them chime in, not quite in time with each other.

After the tea-drinking is through, I watch them all play hacky sack with each other under the shadow of Blackpool Tower. For the first five minutes I'm there, I find myself assaulted with vivid memories of the time my father almost threw my mother off the top. It suddenly seems like yesterday, the day trippers from Bolton laughing at us, pointing their fingers at my parents like they were a freak show. The coppers roughing my dad up a little as he resisted arrest, his arms pinned behind his back so hard by the two large policemen I thought they were going to break them. The shame on his face as he looked at me when he was placed in the lift, an ignominy running so deep that his eyes were unable to convey any sense of apology to me, just regret and mortification.

Despite hacky sack being the most boring thing in the world to either play or watch, I find myself oddly content once I'm over my Blackpool Tower flashback. This sadly does not last long, as John decides after a particularly 'wicked move' on his part to try and ineptly chat me up.

'So, Oxana, I was wondering if you wanted to come back to mine tonight and maybe smoke some cheeba, play some video games?'

'I thought you lived in London and are up here to protest the conference.'

'Yeah, but I meant come to my uncle's Lancashire estate. I'm staying there while I'm up north. Only a twenty-minute drive from town.'

'Out of curiosity, how many bedrooms does your uncle's Lancashire estate contain?'

'I don't know. Twenty-five sounds about right.'

'And it's all yours?'

'All mine. For the next couple of days at least.'

'Tell me, do you have family members with large estates in every county in England?'

154

'Most of them, yeah.'

'And you hate the Tories why exactly?'

'Um, you know, because they're Tories.'

'John, I have a serious question for you: are you into left-wing politics strictly for the pussy?'

He laughs as a diversionary tactic. It fails as I continue staring at him. He shrugs.

'Probably a little.'

'Tory girls are harder to get in the sack than the hippies are, right?'

His body language tells me I've pressed a button here. He verbally confirms this.

'They always want so much before they'll even consider sleeping with you! And somehow, you're never posh enough for them! Doesn't matter how many houses your family owns. Meanwhile, these left-wing girls are sold at the first tear shed over a council rent story you've made up off the top of your head.'

'Cute.'

'So, how about it then?'

'Unfortunately, I have things to do with my evening, John, however much I find your rarely found honesty enticing.'

I then lean in close to his ear and say:

'I know Jess is prettier, but Susanna's a much better bet.'

'Why?' he whispers back.

'Way better in bed. Like, by an exponential margin. Trust me.'

I pat him on the shoulder and leave the lefties to get on with their day.

I re-enter the secure zone in need of a BFL and fast. I'm hungry, but beyond that I need a boost to my confidence that can only come from lunching with the elite. After I'm through security, again without a hitch, I look down the list of events, desperate for any Tory MP I might know – and have to settle on one George Spalding, the Honourable Member for East Saddlington. George is an infamous lech and dressed as I am now, I'll end up with eyeball marks all over my cleavage by the time the starters arrive. Again, beggars and choosers and all of that.

I attend the last fifteen minutes of the event as it draws to a close. It is almost completely taken up by a man in the audience giving a speech that begins with him declaring that he is 'somewhere to the right of Genghis Khan' and continues on to become your standard 'when are we going to get a *real* Tory government?' spiel, the sort of thing that is inevitably ubiquitous at Tory conference. I hover by the panellists as George is giving his wrap-up speech on why 'conscription may be necessary once more' (bloody Tories), ready to pounce. He thankfully recognises me, making life a little easier.

'Charlotte! What are you doing here?'

'Putting in a shift, you know, as we all do. Listen, I'm here by myself and I was wondering if we could discuss something over lunch?'

I feel horrible whoring myself out like this, particularly to a non-entity such as Spalding, but I have no choice in the matter. He jumps at the opportunity, as I was almost convinced he would.

'Why of course! Follow me, fair lady.'

I traipse behind him out of the secure zone and back into the teeming life of real Blackpool once again, mission assumedly accomplished. As we emerge, he starts blabbing about some boring shit that I can't stomach, so I decide to ask him where we're going for lunch to assess whether this is all worth it or not.

'There's a little pie and chip shop up the road that is near and dear to me. I go there every time I'm in Blackpool.'

Jesus, pie and chips. I now desperately want to bail on him but it's awkward. Fate then gracefully intervenes.

'Hello, Charlotte.'

It's DCI Murray. I instinctively look round to see if there are any cops behind me.

'It's just me. Apologies to your guest here,' she says before Spalding jumps in.

'I am George, George Spalding. And who might you be, my little black beauty?'

'No one talks like that now, George. Racial relations moved on from there back in the 1970s,' I say.

'I think you and I need to talk urgently,' DCI Murray says to me, ignoring Spalding completely, which is always a wise move. I nod and off we go, leaving poor George to simply shrug and figure that the pie and chips are coming and that is the main thing after all.

'Given you have come alone, I'm guessing I'm not under arrest,' I say.

'For now.'

'I know where Freddie is.'

'I'm sure that you do.'

'I didn't tell him he was a suspect,' I say. 'And further, I wasn't the reason he tried to flee the country.'

'Why are you in Blackpool, Charlotte?'

I need to think fast.

'Freddie did end up getting in touch, out of the blue, but it was after you and I had our last phone conversation. Said he was here for Tory conference and would I meet with him to discuss some way of helping him out.'

'Helping him out with what?'

'He wouldn't say on the phone. I'm meeting him later on this afternoon to talk about it.'

'Where and when?'

'What about this: I'll speak to him and then I promise I'll deliver him to you. Alongside Smythe and Milding.'

'You know where they are too?'

'Not yet. But I'll find out from Freddie and deliver them as well.'

She looks at me, thinking.

'All right, Charlotte. As it happens, while I still want to take him into custody to interview him to find out exactly what he knows about all of this, Freddie is no longer my prime suspect in the double homicide investigation.'

'Really?'

'I now think Lord Snidely was behind everything.'

'Snidely? Why?'

'A lot of it is circumstantial at the moment. Which is why, as soon as you have delivered the three gentlemen you mentioned into my custody, I need you to speak to Lord Snidely as soon as possible while wearing a wire.'

'I'm not the detective here, but Michael Snidely as a murderer? Michael is almost totally useless.'

'All roads lead to him.'

'Fine, I'll wear the wire. When do you want to do this?'

'Thursday evening,. We know that Snidely is booked in to speak at an event in the House of Lords at seven thirty. We were thinking you could ask to meet him immediately beforehand.'

'Thursday evening is fine for me. I assume by doing all this, I'm off the hook for everything?'

'Everything on my end, yes. The Kostchenko thing is more complicated but I will do everything I can.'

'OK then.'

'You'll need to arrange to see Snidely on the parliamentary estate or nearby and then meet us at the southern end of College Green at say, six p.m., get wired up and then go to it.'

'Done. I'll aim to bring Freddie and the other two down to London late this evening.'

'Perfect. Drop me a text when you know when you'll be getting into Euston.'

'Will do.'

She puts her hand on my arm, which temporarily panics me as I fear she is going to flip my conference pass the right way round and see Oxana Deseroyova's name on it, which would result in a lot of uncomfortable questions.

'It's almost over, Charlotte. Once you wear the wire and speak to Snidely, hopefully we'll put an end to all this and your life should return to normal.'

DCI Murray walks off, assumedly to get the hell out of Blackpool as quickly as possible. Once she's gone, I ponder her theory. Snidely murdering Freddie's uncle and Reginald seems far-fetched. Then again, DCI Murray did seem pretty convinced. It would be a shame to have to kill Snidely, but if I have to, I certainly will.

I re-enter the conference hall, this time having a closer call at security. Just when I had let my guard down and convinced myself that there was not going to be a problem with my entering the autumn conference of the governing party, a zone containing the prime minister no less, while posing as a fake Russian, the security guy looks at me funny when the image of Oxana comes onto the screen. He then looks back and forth between the screen and my face before getting up and calling over another guard. Mercifully, this other guy has a couple of glances at each and then says:

'It's fine, let her through.'

Hopefully that should be the last time I need to brave security as Oxana Deseroyova.

As I wander aimlessly, taking a leaflet from the 'Gibraltarians who hate the EU' people along the way, I am half-dreading, half-hoping that someone here will recognise me. I don't know a soul, which again I find half-reliving, half-unnerving. As it turns out, I soon hear a familiar voice emerging from a nearby stall.

'The truth of the matter is, the sooner we move the UK army to an all-robot army, the better, and I think I have some ideas of how we might be able to do that within the next two to three months.'

It is, of course, Chad Cooper. Who else would be lobbying for a droid army at Tory conference? I now have a decision to make. Am I desperate enough for company that I will resort to hanging out with the most annoying man in Westminster? I was willing to go to lunch with George Spalding; I've long since hit rock bottom. I saddle up next to Cooper.

'These robot warriors sound interesting,' I say. He breaks off his little impromptu speech – easily done, as no one was listening or even pretending to listen – and gives me a bear hug.

'It is so amazing to see you . . .' he says before looking down at my badge, 'Oxana Deseroyova . . . You have a secret identity I'm unaware of?'

'I do, as it happens. What brings you to Tory conference this year?'

'Now that Eligium has gone kaput, I need to find a new job.'

'Even though you never worked at Eligium and were paid a grand total of zero pounds for all the times you ever came in, you mean?'

'I need to use every opportunity I can to put myself, you know, in the shop window, as it were.'

'You think you're going to land a job at a Tory conference?' I ask as I laugh at him.

'Stranger things have happened.'

'Yes, seeing you exiting the house of a Russian oligarch/gangster with Lawrence Milding in tow as a random for instance?'

Cooper goes beet-red.

'Look, I was asked by David to go to that particular address at a pre-appointed time,' he says.

'David? Eligium David?'

'It was part of some politically sensitive project he was working on. You know me, anything I can do for the Eligium team and all that.'

I find myself thinking, for the first time, that perhaps I should have listened to David all those times he tried to tell me about his 'politically sensitive' project.

'What is this "politically sensitive" project all about then?' I ask Cooper.

'I still have no idea. And having listened to Kostchenko drone on about his childhood in Volgograd for two hours, I came away none the wiser.'

I ask Chad if he wants to wander around conference with me for a little while. He agrees to the task. We enter the main hall, where one of the junior ministers in the Foreign Office is giving his speech. Tartis? Tarflong? Tartan? I can't seem to remember his surname.

'Who is this speaking?' I ask Cooper. He looks at me like I'm a rank amateur.

'It's Tim Tundall, the Minister for the Commonwealth. Jesus,' Cooper says in as bitchy a manner as he can manage.

'Sorry. Some of us aren't as obsessed with replacing the current military with a robot army as the rest of us.'

'Tundall is big time into my robot army plan, by the way. Big time, big time.'

We sit down and listen to the minster for the Commonwealth give his Tory conference speech for lack of wanting to turn around and leave the hall.

'And what we find is that as Canada's GDP pivots more toward exports, particularly in regard to exploiting their natural resources advantage in a global marketplace that is becoming less American and more Chinese . . .'

The speech is mostly Foreign Office boilerplate and is wearing down the aged audience. About half of them are fast asleep. Then I spot Tundall's face change – he's clearly warming up to pull a rabbit out of his hat.

'That's why it's so important that we build this bridge to Norway,' he says after another wittering or two about Canada's GDP. You can feel the energy in the room rise with this reference to the Norwegian bridge. Several old people awaken from their slumber and instantly re-engage with the speech. Tundall, feeling like the wind is now at his back, then says:

'And if the Labour party think they can stand in the way of building a bridge to freedom, a bridge that will set our people on the road to prosperity after years of oppression and downright carnage, then we must all say to them: no bridge to Norway? No way, Jose!'

161

The crowd, almost to a person, rises to its feet and cheers. Tundall basks in it all, enjoying his rare moment in the spotlight. He then clears his throat and continues.

'New Zealand also has export concerns that we should be engaging with. It, like Canada, is trying to forge a new path in this post-American age.'

As Tundall begins talking about reality again, turning away from the subject of a bridge to Norway that everyone in the crowd all know in their hearts will never, ever be built, the old Tory members fall back to sleep again.

Just while we're here: although it's his own party's conference and so I have to give Tundall some leeway, if anything Labour have been more pro-Norwegian bridge than the Tories. As soon as the country voted for it, the leader of the opposition said we should start building the foundations of the bridge immediately, and various members of the shadow cabinet began talking about how many jobs it would create. MPs on both sides of the House have spoken up about the stupidity of the bridge to Norway, yet it's been drowned out by both front benches being so in favour of the idea.

After listening to a few more minutes of Tundall's speech, Cooper and I wander out of the main hall and back into the exhibition area. We flip through the fringe guide and find out that not only is there an event on a subject no less hallowed than the future of robotics in the defence of the nation, but one that will also feature a person who could be described as Chad Cooper's nemesis, if such a concept wasn't inherently ridiculous: the Parliamentary Under-Secretary for the Armed Forces, Norma Shedding.

Norma is one of the select few former Eligium employees to have gone on to bigger and better things. She was on her way out, on to her Conservative parliamentary party career, when I first started at Eligium. This was during the period when Cooper was still trying to get hired at the think tank and hadn't resorted to pretending that he worked there anyhow.

I have something terrible to admit – Norma is the only person I've ever worked with who intimidated me a little. Just a touch, but I have to own up to the fact that I was somewhat scared of Norma at times. The strangest thing for me was that Cooper clearly didn't have the same reaction at all and always talked down to her. It was amazing how someone so unimpressive and talentless could feel nothing in the presence of the mighty Norma. Probably nothing more complicated than bog-standard sexism, but I still find it stunning when I think back to those days.

Cooper and I decide to attend the Norma event. For me, it's mostly because there will be free food there and I can get the lunch I missed out on; for Cooper, it provides the chance to plot improbable revenge. The fringe is sparsely attended, which means I get to eat a lot of food. They don't manage to even fill half the room; every event organiser's nightmare. I'm wondering what poor bastards put this on, until I see Jeremy standing in the corner under an Eligium banner and have a little laugh. I think about David and asking him about this 'politically sensitive' project at long last but he's not around.

The event has to get all way to the Q&A section, where members of the audience are allowed to ask questions of the panellists, before I realise how the combination of factors in the mix will play out here. Foreshadowing: this isn't going to end well for Chad Cooper.

'You're not going to ask a question in order to get into an argument with Norma that you will lose, are you?' I ask him.

'Are you kidding? That's eighty percent of the reason I'm at this stupid conference in the first place.'

'I thought it was to find a job?'

'*This* is how I'll get my next job. Showing Norma goddamn Shedding a thing or two!'

Cooper's hand goes up. The boy with the roving mike who looks about sixteen and as if he'd emerged from a factory that constructs perfectly Toryish children walks over and hands the device to Cooper.

'I have a question for you, *Ms* Shedding,' says Cooper into the mike as he stands to attention. 'Why hasn't the British Armed Forces made any real attempt to move away from the human army of today and toward the robot army of tomorrow? Could it be due to the obstinacy of certain Parliamentary Under-Secretaries whom shall remain nameless, except to add that their name rhymes with Shorma Shedding. Oh, I mean, sorry, Shorma Bedding.'

Cooper gleams with self-pride, despite having completely fucked up the punchline of his pathetic little speech. Norma smiles, takes a moment to reflect (but only a moment), leans forward and says into her microphone:

'There's no such thing as a robot army. You've been watching too many science fiction films, Chris.'

'That's Chad! Name is Chad,' Cooper says, just before the Tory teen clone takes the mic back off him.

As the session ends, I realise I have another hour to kill before I have to meet Freddie pre-Bishop event. I've decided I'd rather be alone if it comes to it than spend any further time with Chad Cooper. I think about how to do this politely and then decide it isn't worth the mental effort.

'Chad, no offence, but I'd rather be alone now.'

'OK.'

He continues standing and staring at me, as if there was more to say.

'I mean, like, right now. Starting from this moment.'

Finally, Cooper gets it.

'Oh, I see. Right. Well, I'll be off then. Bye. See you next Tuesday, baby!'

He still hasn't moved. This is becoming awkward.

'OK, I'm going to turn around and walk away, Chad, and I am warning you not to follow me under any circumstances.'

I do as I said I would and thankfully don't have to resort to murdering Chad Cooper, in Blackpool at least.

Chapter Fourteen

I find myself so bored in the period between ditching Cooper and meeting Freddie that I almost regret having actioned the former. Almost. I get a drink in the main hotel bar, hoping to find someone I know. I come up empty, so I wander around the exhibition stands a little more with the ambition of running into an acquaintance. I don't even care about having to explain the Oxana name tag at this point, I'm that bored. I find nothing. Party conferences are unbelievably dull when you have nowhere to go and no one to see. Takes me way back to my early days at Eligium; that first Labour conference where I didn't know anyone at all. Ended up wasting about an hour at a stall that had a dartboard with Margaret Thatcher's face in the middle of it, simply because I'm not bad at darts and my constant pelting of Maggie's forehead had made me temporarily popular with the comrades.

I hit the corridor outside of the Bishop event at three forty-five on the nose. Freddie is standing outside already. Given he knows almost everyone in the Conservative party, he appears to be the centre of attention.

'Freddie? Freddie D'Hondt?' a very Toryish-looking woman stops and asks him.

'In the flesh.'

'Didn't I read something about you being dead recently?'

'Probably. The media is always trying to kill me off.'

'I'm sure I'd read you had been murdered.'

'You're thinking of my uncle, Lord Duncan.'

'Oh yes, of course. Poor man. Going to the Bishop event?'

'Wouldn't miss it.'

As the Tory woman moves inside the event, I approach Freddie.

'Right, tell me exactly what you need me to do,' he says, rubbing his hands together.

'As soon as the event ends, you and I saddle up to Bishop. Do a little spiel so that he can locate you on the food chain, then once that's in the bag, you introduce me as Oxana Deseroyova, daughter of a wealthy Russian investor. I can take it from there.'

'Is your plan to say something in a fake Russian accent that will lure him into bed?'

'Yes.'

Freddie thinks for a moment.

'It will probably work,' he says, nodding.

Freddie and I enter the event room, with iterations of the same conversation he just had with the Tory woman outside being done strictly with hand signals. An older man in a country jacket points to Freddie with a confused look and then puts his fingers together into an 'X'. Then the same man holds his hands up, this time giving the international sign for 'what gives?'. Freddie points to himself, smiles, points to the sky and then shrugs.

The Bishop-led fringe event proceeds and it is boring, even by the standard expected of a dull Tory conference fringe event. I load up on free wine as a means of calming my nerves. Even if Freddie and I succeed here, that only means that the start of the hardest kill of my entire life is then dead ahead. I am much more nervous than I have ever been before a set piece, probably because of the severe challenge involved. Alongside Bishop is an MP I've never even heard of and a right-wing journalist. I can't take in anything they say, being as I am totally lost in trying to plan a murder I have no actual way of planning given the numerous unknowable factors at play.

After what feels like eternity, Bishop wraps things up.

'And let me tell you this: if you think we are weak on the Russians and further, that any attempt they might make to subvert our democracy, influence our parliament, or even kill British citizens on British soil will just be idly watched, well, let me tell you something, mister – we are much less weak on that stuff than you would intuitively figure we would be,' Bishop says. This predictably limp-wristed rallying cry gets comically spare applause from the crowd. Here we go, game on. I follow closely behind Freddie, trying to look calm and demure.

'Stephen! How are you? Freddie, Freddie D'Hondt.'

Bishop looks confused for a moment.

'Haven't you been hacked to death recently?' the Foreign Secretary asks, looking confused.

'That was my uncle.'

'Ah. That's what they all say, eh? That comment made no sense at all, sorry about that.'

'You know my father, I believe.'

Bishop smiles as he places Freddie's dad.

'Old D'Hondt is quite the chap. Used to give money to the party but apparently not any longer.'

'He will again when you're leader, I'm sure.'

This gets an even bigger grin out of Bishop.

'I'd like to introduce you to someone,' Freddie says, and I walk forward, toward the Foreign Secretary. 'This is Oxana Deseroyova. Her father is a well-known oligarch who I'm sure you're aware of.'

'Oh yes, of course. Remind me of his name again?'

'Vladimir,' Freddie says, thinking on his feet.

'Vladimir, of course. Old Vlady, how is the boy?'

The latter question is directed at me. I'm in.

'He is good, thank you.'

I start easy, not wanting to seem too eager. Freddie's 'Vladimir' ruse worked because Bishop knows almost nothing about any part of the world beyond Britain, Ireland, and France and is acutely aware of his ignorance and is always looking for ways to mask it. He's blagging it constantly, in other words, which means he is easily fooled.

'I would like to have a drink with your father sometime, if that could be arranged. Look, I'll give you my card,' Bishop says, reaching into his inside jacket pocket. I decide I no longer have any time to waste. I touch the Foreign Secretary lightly on the arm and say, in my bad approximation of a Russian accent:

'We could go for a drink right now if you like and there I could give you his number.'

He looks at his watch and grimaces a little; shit, this plan could be about to fall at the first hurdle. I get a flash of Barbara's bloody corpse which I shove away with great effort.

'That would be wonderful, of course, but I'm on a tight schedule here, I'm afraid,' Bishop says. Here we go: step up, girl. I lean in, showing the maximum amount of cleavage the dress I'm wearing will allow.

'I promise to make the discussion worth your while, Mr Foreign Secretary.'

Bishop gets the same look in his eyes Vladimir Kostchenko did when I invited him into my knickers. He takes the briefest of glances at my breasts and then shifts his eyes around the room to make it seem as if he hadn't. I think I've got him.

'OK then. Why don't we cut to the chase, skip the bar, and head up to my room instead?' Bishop asks. I nod. Thank Christ that worked; for a moment there, failure beckoned. If this whole fringe event set-up with Freddie hadn't worked, I have no idea what Plan B would have looked like. Find out which room he's in and poison his bottled water? I have no supplies to concoct such a thing and no idea how one could get hold of them in Blackpool. As I leave the event, slightly behind Bishop as he charges out of the room, I look back and mouth the words 'thank you' to Freddie. He smiles and gives me a tiny wave.

Bishop and I head out of the conference centre and towards the hotel – it being inside the secure zone as well, so that the politicians can spend all of their time in the zone from the start of conference to the finish if they so choose, which the important ones will do. It's clear he wants to continue to walk a few steps ahead of me to allay any suspicion that we are together, which given what I have planned, suits me to a tee. A lot of people get into the lift in the lobby and I make sure with some effort that Bishop and myself are on the same one. He presses the button for the top floor, the ninth. Everyone apart from Bishop and I has left the lift by the time we get to ours, which makes sense: the top floor is, as always at these things, reserved for ministers of state only. I'm not sure what's going to happen with the cops as I follow Bishop to his room, but I flip my pass over so the front side with the Russian information on it is obscured.

'Oh yes, she's my assistant,' Bishop says to the detail who then smiles. He's seen this all before; the prostitute or young activist who thinks she can get ahead being passed off as someone's 'assistant'. I walk past the men with large guns and follow Bishop into room 98 as he opens it with his card. Once inside, he pounces on me immediately, sticking his tongue down my throat with the urgency of a fifteen-year-old virgin. He withdraws after about ten seconds to have a look at me.

'Good God, you are steaming bloody hot on toast,' he says.

'Thank you,' I say in the ridiculous Russkie accent I've adopted, one that is becoming more and more Moscow prostitute the further I use it. 'Do you mind if I freshen up some little?'

My motivation here is to scout around in the bathroom for possible weaponry given I am completely lacking even my usual accoutrements.

'Do you mind terribly if I use the loo first?' he asks and then dashes into it, not waiting for my response. Fine then: I can see what's available in the greater room, as well as planning my escape route while the Foreign Secretary wrestles with Number One and/

or Number Two out of view. Looking out the window, I realise getting away is going to be tricky; I don't have all that much faith in the drainpipe and it's a bit of a leap to latch on to anyhow. It looks like the only possibility as well. Shit. Well, I'm here now.

I look around for an instrument of death. I quickly identify the corkscrew as being the best bet. Yet it will be hard to kill a man Bishop's size with something so rubbish. I look around the room for anything else to use; there are no other realistic options. I then experience something that has never happened to me before: I don't think I can go through with a murder I have previous set out to commit. I am in the midst of bottling it. Killing Bishop with the corkscrew is going to be messy and difficult. The cops will almost certainly burst in before I've made the vital cut and then I'll be in the worst of all possible worlds: under arrest for attempted murder of the Foreign Secretary, while Tom and his parents will still be executed by the Russians. I am frozen by indecision, moving from feeling like I have to kill Bishop to thinking there's no way I can, every few moments.

In the midst of all of this, I hear what sounds like Bishop collapsing to the floor followed by him screeching in agony. I am about to go and investigate, but the cops burst in through the room's front door a moment later. The bathroom door is then quickly flung open to reveal Bishop with his trousers down, a little semi going that he was clearly working on, one hand clutched to his penis, the other to his chest as evidence that he has just experienced what is almost certainly massive heart failure. His face is blue verging on purple and he is full-on foaming at the mouth. When I first see him after the bathroom door is kicked open by the cops, the hand of Bishop that is at his chest is grasping with all of its apparent might; a few moments later, the same limb seems deprived of all agency. I feel pretty sure that Bishop is either dead already or is past saving at best.

I take stock of the situation as the rest of the police on the floor of the hotel pile in. The first lot to have arrived on the scene are shouting and calling for the paramedics on their mobile phones. No one has seemed to notice me at all as yet. I creep gingerly to the room's front door and look round; no other cops are on the floor, they're all already bundled inside of number ninety-eight now. I dash for the door to the stairwell and make it through without anyone attempting to stop me. I walk down to the reception, through the door of the hotel, and then out of the secure zone. As I make my way towards the train station, I figure that fate has smiled heavily upon me here. Having seen heart failure in several of my victims, after I had caused it to happen via some toxin, I know how serious Bishop's condition was up there. Even if by some miracle he does survive, I figure I can now buy time with the Russians by telling them that I caused the heart attack and he somehow pulled through. Either way, I have to head back to London with Freddie, Smythe, and Milding and hope that I've done enough to save the lives of Tom and his family. And my own, of course.

I have three people to text, which I do once I am at safe remove from the conference area.

'TARGET DEAD. DON'T NEED A RIDE BACK TO LONDON, GETTING THERE MYSELF,' I text Mikhailov.

'GETTING ON A TRAIN BACK TO LONDON. SHOULD BE AT EUSTON IN ABOUT FOUR HOURS HENCE,' I text DCI Murray.

'ON MY WAY TO THE TRAIN STATION. BRING THE TWO TORY BOZOS,' I text Freddie.

To my surprise, the posh trio manage to get to Blackpool station before I do and are waiting for me near the ticket machines. Freddie looks exactly like he did when I last saw him Smythe and Milding meanwhile have decided to dress up for the occasion – as the two ends of a pantomime horse.

'Is that you at the rear, Lawrence?' I ask.

The middle of the horse rises and falls, meaning Milding is telling me my assumption was correct.

'What's with their outfit?' I ask Freddie.

'I couldn't talk them out of it for love nor money. Said they were frightened the Russians would find them otherwise.'

'We look like we're on the world's shittest stag do, with me as the stripper,' I say to them all. 'Come on, let's get back to London.'

There is no direct train from Blackpool to London – we have to go via bloody Manchester. Mercifully however the train to Manchester Piccadilly leaves less than ten minutes after I arrive at Blackpool station; merciful because Blackpool station is one of the worst places in the entire world. The town collects drifters and oddballs, which I've never figured out since if you were going to drop out of society, why go to Blackpool? I mean, surely with a bit of effort you could be bumming around Spain instead. They all seem to get to the rail station, look around, discover they've arrived in Blackpool by accident, and then give up hope and spend the rest of their days there, drinking mouthwash.

We arrive at Manchester Piccadilly and disembark. After Freddie and I grab some sushi and champagne in the station's French quarter while Milding and Smythe stand around the concourse looking like a fake horse, we get on a train to Euston. I text DCI Murray the train's exact arrival time into London.

As England rolls by, I think about Snidely being involved in a plot to frame me and feel weird about it; a slight sense of betrayal that I can't shake off. He was one of the first people of any importance who took an interest in my career. Even better, it became clear that it was not because he wanted to get into my pants, as Snidely's sexual focus is centred mostly on young men. I met him when I was working for a Lib Dem MP named Steve Dorks. He was the only MP who would hire me, which is the only reason why I ended up working for a Lib Dem. I was instructed by Dorks to meet with Snidely as the Lib Dems were trying to get something passed in the Lords and knew there were several Tory peers who were amenable to the Lib Dem side of the argument. I can't recall what the issue was, but given the Lib Dems were all over it, it must have had something to do with either circus animal welfare, legalising weed, and/or changing the electoral system to make it easier for Lib Dems to get elected.

Snidely was the first person to selflessly help me during my Westminster career. After aiding me greatly on the Dorks/Lords problem, he continued doing me favours for no obvious reason. Michael pretty much got me the job at Eligium. It makes me feel sad to think that I may have to kill him if he's the one behind all this. Yet, if he is the person who tried to frame me for double murder, kill him I shall.

'You're sitting on my arm, Lawrence,' says the top half of the pantomime horse to the bottom.

'Sorry, I didn't think it was your arm,' replies the arse end.

'What did you think it was then?'

Long pause.

'Nothing.'

'A bit like it was nothing when you went behind my back and tried to strike a side deal with Kostchenko then, is it?' comes out of the horse's mouth.

'You mean, after you had screwed everything up with the suppliers somehow and brought the Russian Mafia after us? Is that what you're referring to, Jerry?' replies the arse.

I decide to minimise my exposure to Smythe and Milding as much as possible during the ride south, so I head to the buffet car for some booze. I'm almost there when I notice that Freddie is following close behind me.

'What are you doing?' I ask him.

'The same thing you are, I suspect.'

Freddie gets them in at least: two gin and tonics. I think about slipping some poison into his drink as revenge but think better of it; Freddie is too useful to playfully bump off. We take a seat in the buffet car without either of us having to explicitly say we have no desire to hurry back to the pantomime horse. As we do, the fallout from Bishop's death is hitting the news, which I catch coming from a radio playing behind the buffet car's bar – sounds like they have completely shut down Blackpool for all intents and purposes. The police have no idea whether there was any foul play involved in the Foreign Secretary's death at this stage. Freddie and I are all alone in the buffet car, except for the man serving behind the bar, who is out of earshot.

'From the sounds of things, the mission was a success,' he says.

I nod.

'How did you do it then?' Freddie asks me.

'I got lucky. The bastard had a heart attack on the loo, Elvis-style.'

Freddie laughs and claps his hands together.

'Jesus! That is one hell of a stroke of luck, Heard.'

'It's a good thing too. I don't think I could have done it. As in, there was no way I could have killed Bishop with what I had to hand and got out of there quickly enough.'

'Everyone needs a bit of luck in life now and again.'

Given the strange situation and the alcohol flowing in my veins, I decide to be bold with Freddie.

'How did you know I kill people?'

He laughs at the directness of the question.

'Same way I know everything else that happens in Westminster, darling.'

'Did you sell me to Jerry Smythe as an assassin?'

'No. Well, not intentionally anyhow. He was going on at me about how Ken Bromley was standing in his way of some perceived glory and I said something to the effect that you would be perfect for fixing such a problem.'

'Do a lot of people know about my extracurricular activities?'

He shakes his head.

'Hardly anyone. Don't worry unduly on that front.'

'Anyone else at Eligium know?'

'I don't think so, no.'

I decide to take the conversation up a further notch.

'Were you involved in framing me for the murders of your uncle and Reginald?'

He seems taken aback by this one.

'Of course I bloody wasn't! What made you think that was possible?'

'The cops figure you might be involved.'

'Right. That's inconvenient.'

'Why did you help me get close to Bishop?'

Freddie turns to face me and says:

'Because I like you. A lot.'

'Like me as in, you'd like to sleep with me?'

'Like you, as in, I'd like to be your boyfriend.'

'Boyfriend? That's a word I'd never thought I would ever hear you use in any context. I also never pictured you as the settled type.'

'One day, every man has to settle down. You're the only woman I've ever met that I would contemplate that with.'

'Why me?'

'You are the most beautiful woman in the world, which isn't a bad start. You not only have the heart of a serial killer, you are in fact a serial killer. You're perfect.'

I don't have to tell Freddie the truth here. But I do anyway because I figure this isn't exactly sensitive information I'm about to disclose.

'Thing is, I think I'm in love with Tom.'

'Tom? From the office? Really?'

'When you were trying to flee from killer Russians on a yacht, I was at Tom's parents' house in Buckinghamshire, hiding out. We slept together while I was staying there.'

'And you think you love him now because you two slept together?'

'It's a lot more than just the sex. I've never been in love before but I'm pretty sure that's what it is.'

Freddie takes a moment to absorb the news.

175

'Well, bugger. I'm happy for you, Charlotte.'

'Sure you are.'

'No, I am. There must be another razor-tongued, stunningly gorgeous, serial-killing female walking the streets of London somewhere.'

'I'm sure you'll make her very happy.'

With this, we seem to reach a dead end in the conversation.

'I guess we'd best get back to the pantomime horse,' Freddie says, and we finish off our G&Ts simultaneously, each take a deep breath, and brave the Smythe/Milding situation. Which, in our absence, has greatly deteriorated. Smythe and Milding are engaged in a fist fight with one another, all while still wearing the stupid costume they are sharing, meaning the pantomime horse looks like it's flopping about in its death throes, ready to explode. They are bouncing all over the carriage, spilling people's drinks, bumping into bystanders, and causing everyone to flee for their lives.

'Hey, hey, hey!' I shout at them, as loudly as my voice will carry. They stop fighting immediately, causing the previously bouncing off the walls pantomime horse to come to a sudden halt. I walk over to them and rip the costume in half, exposing Milding's upper body and face to public scrutiny. He does the weirdest thing in response: he slaps his hand over his face so hard, it causes him to let out a little 'ow'.

'Right, you're sitting apart from one another!' I say in my most motherly voice.

'But everyone will recognise me!' Milding whines.

'One, you're an obscure Parliamentary Under-Secretary of something or other – no one on this train will have any idea who the fuck you are. And even if they did, they aren't going to pick up the Russian gangster hotline and turn you in. Understand?'

'OK,' Milding says, and then takes a seat a few rows away, immediately burying his head in his hands like a five-year-old boy who's just been told off for eating Play-Doh.

The rest of the journey south is uneventful. When we get to Euston station, we all trudge outside with the intent of everyone finding cabs home. I see DCI Murray coming toward us before Freddie does.

'Frederick D'Hondt, you are under arrest on suspicion of conspiracy to murder as well as conspiracy to pervert the course of justice.'

As DCI Murray reads out the rest of the standard spiel, Freddie looks at me with a strange expression: part admiration, part devastation. He is handcuffed and goes along with the police with no fanfare.

'What about these two?' I ask DCI Murray, pointing at Milding and Smythe.

'They can remain at large for the time being,' she says, both to me and them. 'They both had a chance at police protection and decided instead to get on a yacht in Liverpool, so we're not extending that favour to either of them again. Thanks, Charlotte.'

DCI Murray walks away without another word.

'Gosh, that was a spot of bad luck for Freddie, wasn't it?' Milding says. We continue walking toward the cab stand. However, when we get there, we find someone waiting for us already.

'Hello, Charlotte Heard.'

It's Sergei Mikhailov.

'Didn't I deliver?' I ask, spreading my arms.

'You did. Nicely done.'

I then realise that I have two men behind me that both assume the Russians want them dead and are now exposing the fact that they are in easy reach. At least, Lawrence is; Jerry Smythe's face is still obscured by the top half of the pantomime horse costume. As if reading my mind, Sergei looks behind me and says:

'Who are these friends of yours?'

'Just some random guys I was talking to on the train. You know, a girl gets lonely.'

He looks at them again. Mikhailov starts to get a quizzical look, pointing at them as he thinks further about who they might be. Following a tense moment, the Russian smiles.

'Aren't you the Parliamentary Under-Secretary for the Pacific Rim?' Mikhailov asks, pointing directly at Lawrence.

'Yes,' Milding says, completely forgetting all about potential execution at the hands of Death's Soldiers now that someone has recognised him and remembered his job title correctly. Smythe hits him in the arm.

'Shut up, Lawrence,' Jerry snarls in terror, thinking the two of them are about to get whacked. Instead, Mikhailov shrugs and turns back to me as Smythe and Milding start hitting each other like children again.

'Good work. I want to say as well . . .I would like to say . . .'

Lawrence and Jerry fighting has distracted him and the Russian is now annoyed at them both.

'You've had your fun with the lady, or all the fun you are going to have! Get lost, you two, before I get upset with you, and you don't want to see what happens then!'

The two Tories walk away. Within a few seconds, they are in a cab and are gone. Once they are off, I feel I can't let this opportunity slip by.

'You weren't looking for those two?' I ask Mikhailov.

'No, why?'

He seems to be telling the truth.

'Jerry Smythe, Lawrence Milding. You didn't try and kill them?'

He laughs.

'Why would I want to kill those two idiots?'

'I don't know, the whole Eligium money-laundering thing?'

Mikhailov waves his hand and lets out a puff of air from his teeth.

'That was Vladimir's business. To tell you the truth, we thought little of his affairs and wanted no involvement. I don't even know the basics of the whole affair and do not want to know them now that Vladimir is dead.'

Interesting. This seems to add to the supposition that the Russians didn't have anything to do with any of the killings designed to frame me. That brings me back to why they happened and who is behind them all. I believed Freddie when he said he wasn't involved. Snidely on his own? It just doesn't seem plausible somehow.

'Let's take a drive,' Mikhailov says in a way that is impossible to interpret. We walk, flanked by several large Russian gentlemen, to a black Mercedes parked illegally on Eversholt Street. I get in the back seat where Mikhailov joins me.

'I don't know how you did it, but you managed to have it look like natural causes. This was beyond what we had hoped to achieve.'

'You wanted the best, you got the best.'

'You, your boyfriend, and his parents are now, as you might say in English, off the hook.'

It becomes clear that I am being driven to my flat, which is awfully nice of them to do for a single girl in London at this hour of the night. As we pull up in front, Mikhailov says his farewells.

'Thank you for your work.'

'No problem.'

'If you are ever looking for freelance opportunities, you have my card.'

'I'll keep it in mind, thanks.'

I watch the Mercedes drive off down the road, turn right and disappear from view. I grab my phone to text Freddie.

'SORRY,' is all I send him.

I unlock my front door and step into my flat. I've been away for almost a week. It feels so nice to be home, I find myself only having the energy to throw my clothes off, chuck them into the corner, and then pass out on top of my bed.

Chapter Fifteen

I wake up after twelve hours of sleep feeling much less refreshed than one should feel after twelve hours of sleep. I had pushed myself to the physical limit over the past few days. I now have three whole days to kill, with no job nor even a prospect of employment. Everyone I might possibly know is at Tory conference until Wednesday. Except Charlie's Angels. I text them the latest – notably, that they can now come out of hiding. I let them know about the Snidely meeting on Thursday and to be near Parliament on alert from six onwards that evening. I want to ask them if they will hang out, but that would be me sinking far too low. As bored as I am, appearances must be kept up.

I try and gather the energy to go and do something with all this free time. I fail. I end up mostly hanging around the flat by myself and watching sappy movies.

I text Snidely, asking to meet him at six in the Lords on Thursday night. He texts me back straight away to say, sounds great, I'll put your name at the peers' entrance. I text DCI Murray to confirm it's on with Snidely.

Bishop's death is all over the news. Thankfully, the police have now declared it a heart attack with no foul play involved. I still have to shut the television off between sappy films as the airwaves are filled with glowing tributes to a man everyone in Westminster knows was a total prick. His wife has been wheeled out several times; I wonder if she was aware of just how much her newly deceased husband cheated on her when he was alive. She must have known.

'He was a decent man. People say of politicians that they are unfaithful and untruthful. Many are. Stephen was one of the good ones,' she says on one of the news channels with a completely straight face.

Tuesday afternoon, just as I'm throwing some clothes on to pop to the shops, my phone rings. I'm thinking that it must be DCI Murray checking in, yet my display informs me that it's Tom. I think briefly about dodging the call before realising I can't bring myself to do it. I haven't made any contact with him at all since I was taken away from his parents' home by Russian mobsters who might possibly have been escorting me into the woods to blow my brains out, so this is hardly smothering behaviour on Tom's part.

'Just wanted to make sure you were OK. I left it for a couple of days as I didn't want to be pushy or anything.'

'Yes, thanks for that. Been busy.'

'You escaped from the Russians without injury?'

'That I did. Listen, about what happened at your parents' place, you know, between you and me . . .'

'Don't feel in a rush to talk about it. Given what's going on in your life at the moment I don't want to add to your burdens.'

'Thanks for taking me in. I appreciate it.'

'Any time, Charlotte. And I mean that. If you need to hide out at my parents' place again, just let me know. Under whatever ground rules are required as well.'

'You're saying I don't need to bang you if I ever need an alternative roof over my head.'

'I would have put it much more delicately than that, but yes, that was one of the major implications of what I was trying to communicate to you.'

I now feel the urge to get off the phone before I say something I'll regret.

'Thanks for calling, Tom.'

'My pleasure. What are you up to this evening?'

'I have a meeting with a prospective employer,' I lie. Somehow, I don't feel like I can see Tom before this Snidely thing has played out.

'Right. What about Thursday?'

'I have to go the House of Lords and meet with Lord Snidely while wearing a police wire.'

'Snidely? Why Snidely?'

'They think he's behind the murders of John Duncan and Reginald. Or one of the chief conspirators in the whole ordeal at least.'

Tom laughs.

'OK, interesting theory,' he says. 'Snidely is harmless.'

'The cops are convinced he's faux harmless.'

'I'm no criminologist, but if Snidely is a murderer, I'm Napoleon Bonaparte.'

'I'll call you tomorrow. Let's get together this weekend.'

I can hear his smile over the phone.

'OK, sure. Look forward to it.'

'Bye, Tom.'

'Goodbye, Charlotte.'

Hanging up is painful. What should I do about this unfortunate mental blip that has led me to declare love for the man who answers the phone at Eligium? The answer is thankfully obvious: get some food in me and then stop watching sappy movies that activate the girly gland in my brain.

Wednesday is empty and sheer torment. My only joy all day is watching a news piece on the BBC about how angry parliamentarians are to be called back from recess early. Normally, there would be a break until the Monday following Conservative party conference. This year, the prime minister has recalled the House for an extra two days in order to debate the bridge to Norway debacle. Even better, Lawrence Milding pops up on my screen out of nowhere to discuss the matter.

'I believe that it is wrong to recall Parliament in these circumstances, pulling away from the single-minded concentration my own party needs to have in regard to its own conference,' he says. Cleared of the fear of assassination by dodgy Russians, Milding is right back at it. 'I have no complaint to direct toward the prime minister, who has clearly been pushed into this position by the official opposition, who simply will not let us all have the bridge that the people overwhelmingly voted for.'

By Thursday, I cannot wait to get this Snidely showdown done and dusted. I can practically feel the minutes tick by until I can't take it any longer. I tube it into town and go to the National Gallery, spending a lot of time looking at the pre-Renaissance stuff. I like it better somehow than the paintings that came after; I enjoy the simplicity of them. Like I say, I don't really understand art, but I like the way looking at it makes me feel. Perhaps that's the whole point and I'm not missing anything at all.

When the time comes, I walk down Whitehall toward Parliament. Finding the undercover police van parked next to College Green isn't tricky – a large, blocky, white number with the words 'Phone Company' stencilled on the side is clearly the badger. Another tick for the Met in this department; way to master subterfuge, chaps. I knock on the back door. Nothing. Again. Nothing. On the third attempt, some teamaker type opens it a tiny fraction.

'Charlotte Heard, looking for DCI Murray,' I say.

He holds his index finger up to me and then closes the backdoor again. A couple of seconds later, he reappears and waves me in.

'Hello, Charlotte,' says DCI Murray as she takes off a pair of headphones to greet me.

'Am I getting wired up in this closet on wheels?' I ask.

'Afraid so. Let's quickly go over what we're looking for you to get Snidely to say this evening.'

DCI Murray runs me through the basic script. She wants me to start on the new think tank and then ask questions about the funding and from there get onto the Russians and their involvement with Eligium. Then I'm supposed to move from that to questions about Freddie's involvement with the Russians. I somehow have to use all this to get Snidely to stand up in the middle of the tearoom in the Lords and shout, 'I did it!' like a character in an Agatha Christie novel, following which he'll tell me the intricacies of the way he pulled it all off.

'This seems unthought-through, if I'm being honest,' I tell her as the techs put the finishing touches on my wire.

'It is. This is fishing more than anything. I've worked out that all roads lead to Michael Snidely and I don't know what else to do other than get a wire in there and hope for the best.'

Great. An evening spent trying to coax out of a man who could make a rock look sociable a confession to multiple murders, with nothing solid in terms of evidence to put in his face to even hope to get him to crack.

'Shame about the Foreign Secretary, isn't it?' Murray asks me in a way that seems leading.

'I'd say he was a good man, Stephen Bishop, but he was kind of a scumbag.'

'Police say there was talk of a woman fitting your description leaving the floor immediately after he died.'

'Perhaps it's the latest woman Michael Snidely has made up to look like me, eh?'

'Perhaps.'

I exit the 'Phone Company' van and go to the peers' entrance where I give my name to the police officer stationed there. He says I'm not on the list. What an ignominious start: doughnut-head Snidely forgot to have someone put my name at the door, forcing me to have to call the stupid Lord while standing there at the entrance.

'Hello?' he answers, sounding like he's still in bed.

'Hi, Lord Snidely, it's Charlotte. I'm at the entrance and they don't seem to have my name here.'

'Oh, Charlotte, I am so sorry about that. Hand the phone over to the nearest policeman.'

I do so and after watching one end of an annoying three-minute phone conversation which consists of the poor cop saying little else except 'Uh huh' and 'I see' over and over again, he finally hands me back my phone and says, 'Go on in.'

I'm greeted at the coat racks by a dishevelled and completely pissed Lord Snidely. This strikes me as odd: whatever I can say in the negative about Michael, he's always impeccably attired and is a light drinker.

'Jesus, what's up?' I ask as we kiss cheeks.

'Oh, Charlotte, I am in such a state. I apologise both for my appearance and my dipsomaniacal state. However, just wait until I tell you what I have to tell you about the week I have just had!'

Perhaps this is going to be more promising than I thought. Trying to get something out of an already well-oiled Snidely is going to be a lot easier than trying to get him to open up dry. He sounds full of surprises already.

We head to the Lords bar – apparently, Snidely hasn't had enough of a snootful just yet. He orders me a white wine and himself a treble gin and tonic.

'You are a sight for sore eyes! And just the person to talk to, as you need to hear a lot of what I am about to say, for your own good as much as anything else.'

He pauses, taking a huge slug off his boozy G&T, polishing off about half of it in one go before he speaks again.

'First of all, the job we discussed. Truth is, I have no idea where we are now. Both Jerry Smythe and Lawrence Milding have stopped returning my calls. I don't know what to tell you and given the chaos that surrounds everything, perhaps you should seek other work. So sorry to have to tell you that.'

I briefly think about telling him everything I know about the Russians putting money into Eligium and how I am aware that the new, proposed think tank that seems to have hit the skids was just going to be a continuation of that. I hold off for now, preferring to see where Snidely is going to take the conversation on his own steam.

'That's not why you're three sheets to the wind, on account of my vocational troubles, is it?'

'I have some things I have to tell you. Things I'm not at all proud of.'

I get a little excited. It's starting to look like this could be an easy night's work after all.

'I have done some bad things. Very bad things indeed,' Snidely continues. 'I allowed myself to get involved in something that was not only illegal but looking back on it, immoral. As a trustee of Eligium, I allowed large amounts of money from a Russian donor to flow through the charity's bank account. Jerry, Lawrence, and I took money ourselves out of the whole scheme, all while knowing beyond a doubt that it had been illegally obtained in some manner or other. To be clear, Lawrence, Jerry, and I were each personally financially enriched by this same Russian donor.'

And then, Snidely begins to cry.

'Oh, Charlotte! What have I done! If it were a matter of me going to prison, I should happily take it. But look what they've done to Reginald! To poor John Duncan!'

I jump at this reference.

'How was Lord Duncan in involved in all of this?'

'Oh, that's how it became so complicated! He gave Eligium some money to do a project on – get this – undo Russian influence in UK politics! Reginald, the silly bugger, thought it would be good to accept as it might keep the charity commission clear of what we were doing. Not thinking of course about how our Russian donor would respond to such a thing. Rather badly, as it turned out, leading to what appears to be a total clear out!'

'Clear out?'

'First, John is murdered. Reginald is murdered next. Kostchenko, the Russian donor, gets murdered himself as well. It looks like the Russians are killing us all off one by one before we can tell the police anything at all!'

Snidely continues crying.

'Hold on: you think the Russians are killing everyone?' I ask, sounding as naïve about all this as I can manage.

'Of course they are! They think we, in league with John Duncan, set the cops after them and their money! I mean, who the hell else would have the manpower and the ruthlessness to kill us all? I know I'm next to get it. It's only a matter of days now, I'm sure of it.'

'Jesus, Michael, if you think they're coming for you, why don't you skip the country?'

'That wouldn't do any good. The Russians can find you anywhere you go. If I flee, they'll make my eventual death more barbaric. No, I will sit here, in the House of Lords, drinking my final hours away.'

I'm trying to take this all in. Clearly, Snidely isn't the killer, that much must be obvious even to DCI Murray, who is conveniently listening in to this whole conversation. Yet I'm no nearer to understanding who killed Duncan and Reginald, given I'm still almost certain it wasn't the Russians.

'Look, I want to help you here,' I say to Snidely. 'I think I might be able to save your life so long as you are totally honest with me. Can you do that?'

He nods like a small child accepting he's been a bad boy.

'OK then,' I continue. 'Who at Eligium knew about the whole deal with the Russians? I need to know everyone who was in on the scam.'

'We kept it tight. I knew Kostchenko, who as I say was the Russian donor. We agreed that Reginald would have to know at least the basics of what was going on given how much money was going to be sloshing through the accounts that he would see going in and out. All those clearly dodgy suppliers – we knew it wouldn't work unless Reginald was squared off.'

I'm getting impatient – Snidely isn't telling me anything I don't already know here.

'OK, so who else at the think tank was involved?'

'Freddie D'Hondt found out about it somehow and we shut him up with a small cut. That's it.'

'Not even anyone else on the board knew about it?'

'God, no! Them especially. We knew that none of them ever look at the accounts, and particularly as the money was going in and out reasonably quickly, there was no need for them to know anyhow. They would have either wanted to put a stop to it or wanted a slice of the cake, and being greedy, we weren't going to do that.'

'Was anyone on the Eligium staff other than Reginald and Freddie in the loop?'

'No, no, definitely not.'

He thinks for a moment and then a light bulb goes off, which I pick up by his change in expression.

'Well, other than Reginald's assistant, I suppose.'

'Reginald's assistant?'

'Yes, you know the chap. What was his name?'

I feel a cold draught come over me. The next question is one that is hard for me to ask.

'Tom?'

Snidely laughs, which makes me instantly feel better.

'That nice chap who answers the phone? No, not him.'

I can't think of who else he could mean. And then it comes to me.

'Chad Cooper?'

Snidely shakes his head.

'That name rings no bells. Not him.'

'Think, Michael, think.'

Snidely seems tortured as he wracks his sozzled brain for the information he's after.

'It was just some chap who worked at the think tank. I don't know. It doesn't matter anyhow. Now, you said you had a way of protecting me from the Russians?'

Reginald never had any assistants; we couldn't keep hold of the interns he verbally assaulted, never mind him having one all to himself full-time.

'I need to know everyone who might have known anything about this at the think tank, so I need you to remember the name of this "assistant" of Reginald's,' I say insistently to Michael. 'The closest Reginald had to an assistant around the office was Tom and you've said it wasn't him.'

Snidely thinks again. Suddenly, his eyes light up.

'David! That was the chap's name!'

Finally, a real clue. I then recall David's 'politically sensitive' project and now know I need to understand it, as soon as possible. There is no point in carrying on this conversation with Snidely and so I thank him for the drink and then depart the Lords bar before anything more can be said. As soon as I am out of earshot, I call David. As expected, he answers after one ring.

'Charlotte! How nice of you to call!'

'Hi, David. I realise you never told me about that "politically sensitive" project you have been working on and now, I'm all ears.'

'Oh yes, of course! Well, I just thought some of it might interest you, particularly in light of the fact that two of the main people managing it were subsequently murdered!'

'What are you talking about?'

'Reginald assigned me the project and then I had to work on it with Lord Duncan, who was the project's benefactor. Strange how they both then got killed a few days later, right? Or well, I thought so anyhow.'

'What was the project about, David?'

'Russian interference with western democracy. Spicy stuff, yes? The big problem with it was that Jeremy had been working on it for a while before Reginald took it off him and gave it to me. Jeremy

189

was upset about that, which gave me no end of grief. In the end, I felt I had to secretly let him help me with it. That's why he was with me the night we all staked out the Russian's place in my car. That was one of the reasons I was so keen to talk to you about it; I was disobeying Reginald's orders in allowing Jeremy to continuing working on the Russian project. I wanted you to give me the all clear on that front, as it were.'

'Why didn't you mention the fact that you were working on something Russian-related that night given who we were staking out?'

'I tried several times to talk to you about my politically sensitive project, Charlotte, but you always shut me down.'

David has a valid point there.

'What did Jeremy do on the project after you agreed to continue letting him work on it?' I ask.

'He mostly handled Lord Duncan, who was a tricky character. In fact, it was rather odd: the night Lord Duncan was killed, Jeremy had conducted a meeting with him.'

I start to think about Jeremy being involved in all of this, something that had never previously occurred to me. If he'd met with Duncan the night the peer was killed, that would instantly bring Jeremy into suspicion. That still doesn't explain the Russian connection – of which there again seems to be one, given the project Duncan was funding.

I thank David and end the conversation. I'm now lost in thought considering all of this, walking down one of the House of Lords corridors, when someone directly behind manages to shove me into one of the dining rooms in a way that is effective without causing a scene. I am in the room and the door is shut behind me before I can take it all in. And then, there I am: face to face with Jeremy himself.

He looks different. For a start, he is dressed in an expensive-looking black suit, white shirt, and black tie; his hair is slicked back, shiny and tight. But it's Jeremy's eyes that make him seem like someone else: alive and intelligent, in sharp contrast to their usual deadness.

'How long have you been following me?' I ask.

'I have been shadowing you everywhere since you got back into town from Blackpool. I see you managed to satisfy Sergei enough for him not to execute you, well done. He's not an easy man to please.'

I decide to try and take advantage of the wire I'm wearing.

'Why did you kill Lord Duncan and Reginald?'

'What you want to ask me is why I tried to frame you for the whole thing.'

'I was coming to that, yes.'

Jeremy begins to pace. Like everything else about him now, the way he moves is different. He looks like a panther, fluid in movement and ready to strike.

'I was told by Reginald three months ago that I was out unless I brought in a paid project. I went to everyone I knew in town and could get no one to put any money up for an Eligium project. Desperation set in. There was one card I had left to play that I had resisted up until then. I called my estranged father, Lord Duncan.'

'Duncan was your father? You're Freddie's cousin?'

'And Freddie doesn't even know it. My father had me out of wedlock with my mother, who was a call girl. My mother and Lord Duncan came to an arrangement: that he would pay for my education and then give me an allowance that would last for the rest of my life, so long as no one ever found out I was his son. I was to be his dirty little secret. I only went to him for favours twice during the rest of his life – once was to get me the job at Eligium, which he did through Freddie; the second time was a couple of months ago when I was desperate to bring a paid project into Eligium. He agreed to fund a project around Russian interference in western democracy. At first, Reginald was pleased. Then, he suddenly went cold on the whole thing. He gave it to David as a way of killing it. Then he said that he was going to sack me anyhow, even though I had fulfilled my end of the bargain. I needed to know why he wanted to kill my project and subsequently found out about the Russian money flooding into Eligium from David.

'I thought alerting my father to the fact that dodgy Russian money was flowing into the think tank he was helping to fund would gain me his favour, but he reacted in the opposite way. He became furious with me for getting him involved in the organisation in the first place and told me our deal was off; that he was cutting me off from my allowance as soon as possible, consequences be damned. His wife had died a few months previously and so his main reason for wanting to keep me a secret had vanished. I developed a plan to kill my father before he could cut off my allowance.

'Then came Reginald. After the Charity Commission started to cause the organisation problems due to the fact that my father had made a complaint to them about Eligium based on what I'd told him, Reginald blamed me for "ruining a good thing" and told me he would do everything he could to destroy my career within Westminster. So, you can imagine the rest.'

'Why frame me for the murders?'

Jeremy laughs.

'That was a last-minute detail. I knew of your handiwork, of course, and had watched it with some degree of admiration over the past few years. Yet you always treated me with contempt. Just like you did in the Two Chairmen the day of my father's murder. I saw the plan to frame you for the murders as the revenge of, as you might have put it yourself that afternoon, "the white, over-educated, middle-aged has-been who should retire to some coastal town". You, the gorgeous ice-queen, infamous for having got away scot-free with a string of murders, was going to be sent down for a couple of homicides you had nothing to do with! Poetic justice at its finest!'

He paces away from me. I think about bolting for the door but decide I want to hear the rest of what Jeremy has to say and further, have it all be on police record via my wire. As well as Jeremy's unfortunate reveal about me as a murderer, but I instantly remember that I can pin all that on Svetlana. Jeremy continues talking.

'I had Svetlana follow you the evening of my father's murder. Meanwhile, I had a pre-planned meeting with Lord Duncan himself at the Eligium office. I got him to come along as I told him that I had new information about Eligium's sources of funding that might affect him personally and that I would only discuss it in person. He was predictably furious with my ruse and said although he hadn't actioned the end of my allowance as yet, he was now determined to do it the following morning.

'I drugged my father at that meeting and kept him in the Eligium boardroom awaiting further instructions from Svetlana. She called to say that you were in Vauxhall – I took advantage of the geographical convenience and put my father in a cab across the river, telling the driver his passenger was drunk and could he drop him at Vauxhall bus station. I then told Svetlana to disengage from following you and prepare to do her worst to Lord Duncan, whom I knew she would recognise from photos of my him I had shown her.'

'How the hell did you find a woman who looks exactly like me?' I ask him.

'That was a stroke of good fortune. Your ex-boyfriend, that James fellow, had a period about six months ago where he approached all of your Eligium colleagues, the male ones at least, and asked for any information on your dating status. David, Freddie, all the rest refused to answer his questions, but I spotted an opportunity at the time to find out more about you. In doing so, I discovered that following your unfortunate break-up, which James says you did via smashing a guitar over his skull . . .'

'He was playing "Purple Rain" on it at the time, just to be clear.'

'He took to ordering women from an online service that will send you girls from Russia with their faces cut into any shape you wish for. James had a penchant for ordering one of these poor unfortunates made to look like you via pictures he would supply, only to get sick of them and dump them after a few months. He'd then get itchy for another hit of the same and order another Charlotte lookalike.'

'There are more than one that looks like me?'

'There are three that I know of. Svetlana, Katerina, and, of course, Oxana. All sisters, as it happens. James really was obsessed with you. He spent most of his healthy inheritance on this little project.'

'All right, but how did you convince one of these Russian lookalikes to pose as me and kill Lord Duncan and Reginald?'

'Wasn't difficult. After poor Svetlana had been dumped by James, she wanted nothing more than to get revenge upon the woman whose likeness she was surgically made to resemble in what turned out to be a mostly fruitless venture from her perspective. And as luck would have it, Svetlana and her siblings also had training in the art of murder.'

'Did James know about the homicides?'

'No. I convinced him that you had killed my father, which is the reason he began stalking you again, I believe. I also convinced him at the same time that he had introduced you to the peer in the first place, making him believe that the murder of Lord Duncan was something that he was partially responsible for. This all seems to have set him off, leading to his unfortunate suicide in your flat several days later. Collateral damage, that one was.'

'What about killing Reginald in the pub?'

'That turned out to be a piece of piss. I rented the pub out for the day and gave the staff a thousand pounds each to clear off, using Svetlana and Oxana as the only people that had any contact with anyone connected to the place. I called Reginald and told him that I had information about what the Russians were up to and that his life could be in danger – all too believable after the Duncan murder, of course. He was reluctant at first as he was still blaming me for everything going wrong with the Russians in the first place, but after I told him I knew what I knew because I was actually Lord

Duncan's son, that convinced him to come along. Poor bastard showed up to find just me and Svetlana, her holding a gun to his head the moment he walked in.'

'And then you got him to call me while he was at gunpoint.'

'Indeed.'

'How was Freddie involved in all of this?'

'Hardly at all. Poor Freddie was terrified of being killed by the Russians given it appeared that they were cleaning house. He worked for the think tank, had been taking a small cut of the profits from the laundering exercise, and it was his uncle that had alerted the Charity Commission to what they were up to. I might have pushed him toward greater alarm in this respect myself. The yacht ploy was impressively terrible. But no, he wasn't involved in framing you, if that's what you're digging for. He didn't even know about the Deseroyova sisters, at least as far as I'm aware.'

Jeremy continues to pace around as he speaks, looking like he's preparing for battle. He's clearly going to kill me inside of this room. It's the only thing that makes any sense. I realise I have one card left to play.

'I'm wearing a live police wire,' I say.

'I know,' he replies, still calm.

'What now then?'

'I want to achieve the proper denouement to my meisterwerk, which is what we're both here for, with you to be my final, ultimate victim. I will have to hurry up a little.'

Then, to punctuate his last statement, Jeremy removes a gun from his inside jacket and points it at me.

'Any final words, Charlotte Heard?' Jeremy asks. He cocks the gun. I need to buy time in the hopes the cops figure out where I am via the wire.

'Plenty. Plenty of final words. Can you really stand to kill me? Think about all the things I could teach you. Oh, the things you still have to learn about mass murder . . .'

'Goodbye, Charlotte.'

I hear a loud noise that makes me scream. I close my eyes; I figure out quickly that I have not been shot and look up to find Jeremy knocked to the ground, the gun several feet away from him on the carpet. Standing between Jeremy and me are Charlie's Angels, who have intervened on my behalf at the last moment. They must have descended from the ceiling.

'Sorry that was so last second,' Kate says while keeping her eyes trained on Jeremy, who is up again and trying to get to his weapon. 'We just wanted to make sure he got through the whole story before we pounced.'

'Good thinking,' I say.

Violet kicks Jeremy's arm away just as he's about to pick up the gun. He then manages to kick her as he quickly gets back to his feet. Kate and Aashi attempt to incapacitate him, but Jeremy is fleeter of foot than I could have ever imagined. He dodges a particularly nasty-looking roundhouse from Kate, getting hold of the gun off the floor as he does. He tries to shoot Aashi but the gun jams.

The three Charlie's Angels look briefly to one another, nodding as they do so. Clearly they have cooked up a Plan B and are about to activate it. Violet jumps up onto Aashi's shoulders, rising to stand erect upon them. Kate then jumps up onto one of the tables, instantly leaping from there into Violet's arms. Aashi moves forward towards Jeremy, who looks a little freaked out by whatever is about to come his way. Violet brandishes Kate's body like a weapon, swinging her toward Jeremy as if she were a baton. Jeremy figures out a way to defeat this strange beast: he ducks to the floor and then kicks Aashi's legs as hard as he can. It works, with Aashi falling to the ground, taking the other two girls with her.

I use this opportunity of bodies lying around in a heap to run out of the dining room Jeremy had forced me into. I turn to look back and see that he has noticed my exit and escaped from the room himself, presumably with the gun back in his jacket.

I realise I am at an advantage here. I can run while presumably Jeremy will avoid this in order to not draw attention to himself. Turns out I am wrong, as I see Jeremy jogging pretty quickly toward me. I figure my best bet is to try and get to Central Lobby as quickly as I can, where at least I will have the cover of police officers.

I manage to take a few shortcuts and soon enough I'm in Central Lobby, the little square that sits between the House of Commons and the House of Lords. As it happens, it is packed full of MPs.

'What are we voting on?' I ask one of the thicker-looking Labour MPs, figuring he won't know that I'm not a fellow PLP member. I'm doing this mostly to blend in somewhere to make it more difficult for Jeremy to find me.

'Nothing, I don't think,' he says with a northern accent so thick I struggle to understand him. 'The speaker has cleared the House is all.'

It's worked. I am now encased in a hive of Labour MPs, a few of the ones that have actual brain cells, looking at me strangely, clearly wondering who the hell I am. I realise that this trick will reach its natural end in a best-case scenario when I reach the chamber itself, if not well before then, and so when the chance arises, I remove myself from the pack of MPs and try to blend in with the journos who are assembled in a pack.

'Hey there,' I say to a *Telegraph* journalist I know a little.

'Charlotte. How are you? What are you doing here?'

'I traded in the think tank world for your fine profession.'

'Really? I hadn't heard! When did this all happen?'

'It's my first week.'

'Jesus, first week and all of this shit to write about, good luck. Who are you writing for then?'

'*Mail on Sunday.*'

'Nice work. Listen, I have to go and try and strangle a quote out of one the stupider Labour MPs.'

'There's a very thick one standing over there, with the red and gold tie.'

197

I point to the MP I had first spoken to. The *Telegraph* journalist spots him and gives me a thumbs up.

'Thanks! We should catch up over a drink sometime soon,' he says.

'Indeed!'

Off he goes. I stick close to several of the others, all of whom are absorbed in their phones. I try and do the same to blend in. I'm starting to feel relaxed, like the cops must have grabbed hold of Jeremy in some other part of the estate, when I get that unmistakable feeling of a gun at my back.

'Don't move or I'll kill you right here.'

'In the House of Commons corridor?'

'Where better?'

I start to panic; I can tell he's serious and that my life is on the edge here.

'You'll never be able to escape if you kill me here.'

'I'm either going to prison for the rest of my life or I'm dying here, tonight. I haven't yet decided which I prefer.'

Jeremy sneezes – and I take the chance it affords me. I elbow him in the guts and twirl out of range. By the time he recovers a couple of seconds later, I'm in the fray amongst the Labour MPs again.

'Excuse me, I haven't seen you before in the lobby, but going into the chamber itself isn't allowed if you're not a Member of Parliament. I hate to ruin your attempt at a "scoop" here,' says a well-known Labour MP whose husband was also an MP until he lost to a woman who had a job stacking shelves in the constituency. He later went on to star in his own cooking programme on ITV.

'There is a man several paces behind with a gun who is determined to murder me.'

The Labour MP looks for signs I am joking or insane; when these are not present, it's clear she doesn't know what to do with the information I've just given her and decides to walk toward her usual spot on the opposition green benches. I'm in the chamber now, so I follow closely behind the Labour MP and sit down immediately next to her. She desperately wants to say something to me and almost does; yet she decides at the last moment to simply stare straight ahead of herself instead.

I see the speaker of the House walk back to his chair just as Jeremy enters the chamber. My ex-Eligium workmate looks around for me; I duck behind the MP with the cooking show husband in order to obscure my face.

'Order! Order!' the speaker says. As all of the MPs rush back to their places on the green benches, Jeremy takes a seat on the government side of the House. As he does so he draws stares from those nearby, followed by shrugs when they come to the conclusion that Jeremy must be someone who has won a by-election recently that they hadn't noticed.

'Point of order,' the speaker says. 'Now, I cleared the House as certain members – and I'm looking to avoid calling on names specifically here – were watching softcore pornography in the chamber. If this happens again I shall not cease to clear the chamber once more. The Leader of the House!'

The Leader of the House rises to the dispatch box. At this moment in time, the position is being taken by Shirley Hasetol, who is the worst. Her nickname isn't 'Hateful' for nothing – she tried to run for leader of the Conservative party a few years back and was rejected, even by members of the Conservative party, who usually look past that sort of thing, for being particularly nasty. She got caught out planting fake stories in the newspapers about several of her opponents, a ruse which only failed because the stories she tried to leak were so obviously bogus. She accused one of them of having an affair with a woman when everyone in the lobby knows he's a closet homosexual, to name only the most idiotic.

'Thank you, Mr Speaker. The next order of business is another debate on what to do about the proposed bridge to Norway that, as everyone in the House knows, was put to the people in a referendum a year or so ago. A referendum in which the people voted for their bridge to Norway and should therefore get their bridge to Norway. Unfortunately, Mr Speaker, if we built this bridge, some of those in this House, particularly on the opposition benches, claim it would bankrupt the country and we'd have to instantly shut down the NHS. Since the government cannot come to a resolution that can carry a majority of the members of this House, we intend to hold a series of indicative votes on the matter. I give way to my honourable friend.'

Bradley Sheldon rises to weigh in on the matter. A particularly stupid backbench Tory MP, this ought to be fun.

'Thank you, Mrs Leader of the House. I would like to remind her that the British public overwhelmingly voted for the bridge to Norway, fully knowing what they were voting for. The government's plan for a bridge to Norway is clearly for something that would not qualify as a bridge and therefore has been rejected. These indicative votes are therefore nothing more than a way to avoid building the bridge the people of this country so overwhelmingly voted to have built!'

There are plenty of cheers from the knuckle-dragging section of the Tory backbenches for this little slice of polemic nonsense. The Leader of the House rises again.

'I would like to remind the honourable gentleman that the government is committed to the will of the British people; we would simply like to find a way to do so that does not reduce the entire country to what may turn out to be literal smouldering ruins. I give way to the Right Honourable lady.'

The Labour MP I've been hiding behind rises and begins giving a speech about what a terrible idea the bridge to Norway is, all while trying to sound like she isn't calling more than half of the British public idiots in the process. As she's in full flow, it occurs to me that I had forgotten for the past couple of minutes that I am on the run from a madman who wants to take my life. The joy of being in the

House of Commons and sitting on the green benches has been enough to do that. Would I want to spend an evening in here, debating a bridge to Norway? The answer is: of course I bloody would. Never before has my dream of being an MP crystallised in such a profound way. More than ever before, I know that being a member of parliament is what I was put on this Earth to do.

This pleasant thought is snuffed out when I look up to see that Jeremy has found me now that my camouflage has risen to speak in the House. He is furiously pointing at me. I shrug back at him thinking, 'what the hell is he going to do? Shoot me in the House of Commons?' Turns out, this is precisely what he has in mind. He takes his gun out of his pocket and points it at me. Bereft of other options, I duck behind the bench in front of me and scream:

'A man with a gun on the Tory benches!'

This causes temporary confusion, with the Labour MP cutting her speech short to look round in order to understand what's happening. There is a lot of murmuring going on in the House now. A few MPs then spot Jeremy holding his pistol and begin to shout in terror. The speaker of the House steps in.

'Order! Order! What is going on? The Right Honourable lady will be heard! Order!'

Then, Jeremy points his gun in the air and fires it. The sound is punishingly loud within the confines of the chamber. MPs are now in a panic, some running for the exits, some taking cover just as I am doing behind the green benches; some are clearly unable to move, standing still like deer in the proverbial headlights. In the midst of all of this, the Speaker of the House remains glued to his chair, his facial expression unchanging in spite of the chaos that surrounds him. The fact that a deadly weapon has just been fired in the House by a man who is clearly not an MP, yet has somehow inveigled his way into the Commons, does not seem to be denting his mood in the slightest.

Jeremy stands with his gun pointed in my direction again as I continue to take shelter behind the Commons bench in front of me, peering up only a little to get the lay of the land. There are only about fifteen or so MPs remaining in the chamber at a rough guess.

'Charlotte Heard, the ripper of Westminster, scourge of the sexual harasser, reduced to cowering behind the benches she hopes in vain to one day occupy. How sad. How truly sad,' Jeremy says in a kind of mad roar. At this point, the cops storm in, one of them armed with a machine gun that he points at Jeremy.

'Put down your weapon! Now!' shouts one of the policemen.

Jeremy seems completely unfazed by the armed cops.

'I am armed with a military grade pistol, Mr Police Officer. As you well know, I could tear through the bench and easily kill Ms Heard with it. Point the barrel of your gun down now or I will shoot her.'

The policeman thinks for a moment and then does what Jeremy asks. The Speaker of the House decides to get involved at this stage.

'Mr Gunman, if I could intervene here.'

'No, shut up,' Jeremy says to the Speaker of the House of Commons.

'Order! Order! I will not be talked to like that in this chamber! Does the man with the military grade pistol understand?'

Jeremy seems weirdly cowed a little by this. He keeps his gun aimed at me but his eyes droop a little.

'I understand, Mr Speaker.'

'Now, it seems to me you have a limited range of options staring at you here. You can drop your weapon and be immediately incarcerated. That is the most sensible of the options available. The other is that you can try and kill this woman here, a Miss Heard I believe is her name. You will either succeed in this or fail but either way, in pursuing that goal you will be killed by the police. Lastly, there is a third option.'

'Which is?' Jeremy asks, now agitated.

'You can try and kill me.'

'Why would I try and kill you?' Jeremy asks, confused.

'Because I am going to annoy the bejesus out of you until you attempt it. How I intend to do so is by arguing with you that trying to kill me is your only logical course of action. I shall begin now: by trying to kill me, you shall achieve much greater notoriety than if you murder Miss Heard, who is not someone of any national importance. I sincerely hope I do not cause Miss Heard any offence with that last statement.'

'None taken,' I shout.

'Whereas, if you were to kill the Speaker of the House, you would be famous for ever,' the Speaker continues. Jeremy wants to dismiss this argument, but instead finds himself bizarrely taken in by it. The Speaker notices.

'Ah-hah! I can see you contemplating my words very deeply, sir,' the speaker continues. 'Yes, you want fame, that much is obvious. Who else but one seeking notoriety would enter the House of Commons with a view to shooting someone whilst in this hallowed chamber, am I right?'

Jeremy wants to say something but can't think of a cogent counterargument against the Speaker. Meanwhile, his gun is still pointed unmistakably at me. All of a sudden, he gets himself together.

'There is more to my motivation than mere fame-chasing, Mr Speaker,' Jeremy says.

'Wounded vanity, perhaps? Did the lady reject your amorous advances?'

This gets to Jeremy and knocks him mentally off balance once again. The hand that is holding the gun starts to shake a little now.

'No, this is not about such trifling things,' Jeremy says, panic just starting to edge into his voice. The Speaker of the House has got to him.

'If this is not about a love quarrel, then I still say you are much better off shooting me than Ms Heard for all of the reasons I have already given. And I will give you another: you clearly hate me.'

This comment catches Jeremy completely off guard.

'What? I don't hate you!'

'Clearly you do, sir. Clearly you do. I see it in your body language. You are the type of person who has absorbed all of the anger the right-wing tabloids have foisted in my direction over the past few years and wish to do me in as a result. Am I right?'

'No! Look, I'm centre-left in my political leanings if you must know!'

Jeremy is now shaking a great deal. I start to get afraid that the gun which is pointed in my direction is going to go off accidentally.

'I don't believe it. You are UKIP if you're anything, sir. Believe you me, I have seen them all in this chamber, sitting in this chair, and you are UKIP to the core.'

'Take that back!' Jeremy yelps, his gun hand now trembling a great deal.

'I shan't, sir. As it is very clearly true.'

Jeremy swivels to point the gun at the Speaker of the House. This makes the Speaker break out in a large grin.

'Ah, ha! I knew that you hated me, sir!'

'I don't hate you, Mr Speaker. I just need you to be quiet.'

'Point of order here, sir. You see, in this House . . .'

The Speaker starts to go off on a long rant that is mostly nonsense. This causes me to take a moment to look up at the ceiling of the chamber – where I notice something that allows me to understand the Speaker's plan. Dangling dangerously, looking to fall to the floor any moment, is a large chunk of the stone masonry just clinging onto the roof of the chamber. Jeremy must have loosened it when he fired his gun into the air.

'Shut up! Shut up!' Jeremy shouts, unable to take any more of the Speaker's ramblings.

'Shut up, Mr Speaker, please,' the Speaker says.

'Fine, please shut up, Mr Speaker!'

'Any last words?'

'What?'

'I said, any last words? This is the standard question asked of the condemned man, is it not?'

'What are you playing at?'

'Look up.'

Jeremy shakes his head, thinking this is a diversionary tactic by the Speaker. This means he does not see the gigantic piece of masonry that strikes him on the head a moment later, knocking him to the ground and then crushing his skull almost completely as both Jeremy's noggin and the piece of masonry hit the floor with an almighty racket.

The gun, the military grade pistol, lies still in Jeremy's dead hand as his face lies in pieces beneath the broken stone.

Chapter Sixteen

One year following the death of Jeremy by falling masonry in the House of Commons and life is sweet. Tom and I got back from our honeymoon only a few weeks ago; now I'm having to juggle work and my new life as an MP candidate, standing for the Conservative party.

After the predictable press clippings following that tumultuous evening in the Commons, I had job offers thrown at me from all directions. I ended up taking the CEO role at Policy Stage, one of the two biggest think tanks in the UK. I decided to go with the Tories in terms of trying to become an MP for a load of fairly straightforward reasons. One, they asked me and Labour didn't. Two, it fits with my new think tank role, it being centre-right-leaning. Three, I think I like the Tories more than Labour. At least, I feel more comfortable in the Conservative party than in the Labour party. I guess I should have added a number four in there: it looks like the Tories are going to be in power for a while, and so my chances of being in government are much higher. All this added up to running as a Tory candidate. The seat I'm trying to take is held by Labour, but with a majority of less than 500, so gettable.

Despite all danger for me evaporating reasonably quickly, the immediate aftermath of the House of Commons incident involving Jeremy was messy and convoluted. I was taken into custody briefly for questioning by the Met, the investigation led by DCI Murray, which centred mostly on the death of Kostchenko and my plea of self-defence. I was also questioned about some other murders the Met had on file, some of which I had committed but most of which I had nothing to do with. DCI Murray was particularly interested in the portion of Jeremy's confession caught on wire in which he seemed to intimate that I am a well-known murderer, as well as a point in the conversation in which I seem to confirm this fact to him. Thankfully, it was all turned around within hours, and I was then free to get on with my life, no longer pursued by the police, Russian mobsters, and/or homicidal ex-workmates.

I'm in the campaign office today. The phone rings – Tom answers.

'Good morning, Charlotte Heard's campaign headquarters?'

He rolls his eyes in a way that tells me he must be talking to Conservative Party Headquarters. They have recently taken offence at some of my more aggressive campaigning techniques.

'They are asking if you will withdraw the leaflet we circulated earlier this week about Julia Damen being a former Satanist.'

Damen is the Labour candidate I'll be running against in the next general election. Although it isn't for another four months, we are in non-stop campaign mode given the marginality of the seat.

'I'll get back to them on that one sometime when I'm not washing my hair.'

'Do you want me to say that verbatim to CCHQ?'

'Give me the phone.'

I grab the receiver off my husband perhaps a little more aggressively than absolutely necessary.

'Listen, if you have any suggestions on how you might win this marginal seat while avoiding playing dirty, let me know and I'll take it under consideration. In the meantime, my local party is au fait with the leaflet, so you can shove it up your over-centralising arses.'

I then hang up the phone. Confession time: I'd wanted the leaflet to highlight the fact that Damen used to be a *Stalinist* – but as soon as I saw the misprint, I knew it was much better. Fate and all of that.

'Listen, I have to be back in London to speak at an event – would you mind calling everyone and telling them tonight's door knocking is off? Oh, I forgot to say: I might have to spend the night in London,' I tell Tom as I begin to head out the door.

'Why don't I come to London with you?'

'You're going to pick up the next batch of "Julia Damen was a Satanist" leaflets from the printers tonight, remember?'

'Of course, of course. Sorry, on it. See you tomorrow?'

'Probably. Thanks, dear.'

I kiss my husband on the cheek. I then depart the campaign office, intending to walk down to the railway station. It's a long ramble, about half an hour, but I like the peace and quiet of it, particularly as a pre-London exercise. As I walk past the fields I think back to my wedding. Tom looked great in the suit I picked out for him. Barbara and John were an unbelievable help with everything; we got married in the church village about three miles down the road from their house in Buckinghamshire. Barbara said I had done wonders for Tom, John, and herself. Been a real lifesaver I had, she even said to me at one point. Little did she know how unconsciously literal she was being.

Tom and I started seeing each other in a normal human fashion about two weeks after the Jeremy in the Commons incident. After three months of dating, Tom popped the question. I was tempted to say no before I realised that would have been a stupid move. Tom is the perfect man for me: he is smart, funny, good-looking, great in bed, of limited ambition himself and thus happy for me to be the breadwinner in the family. To have let him pass me by when he was offering himself for ever in that way, just because part of me would have liked to have got to know him a little better before getting engaged, suddenly seemed an error of life-defining proportions I was not prepared to make.

The wedding itself was amazing. I refused beforehand to get swept away with all that 'best day of your life' horseshit – but I have

208

to admit, it was the best day of my life. Charlie's Angels were my bridesmaids and all surviving ex-Eligium staff were present. David got us a lovely present. Can't remember what it was now, but I recall thinking at the time he'd gone above and beyond the call of duty. Freddie had seemingly forgiven me for handing him into the cops – he was released shortly after the Jeremy's head being crushed incident, which I suppose helped – and got us a priceless chandelier as a wedding present. Lawrence Milding, who had recently become the Foreign Secretary replacing the late Stephen Bishop, gave us a set of FCO coasters as a present, the cheap bastard.

Jerry Smythe and Michael Snidely could not be present due to their incarceration. A large-scale investigation into the Eligium money-laundering scheme was carried out, with those two going down for it. Lawrence escaped scot free, as you may have guessed from his promotion into the Cabinet.

For the honeymoon, Tom and I went to Laos. We saw some temples here and there but to be honest, we mostly stayed at the hotel where we drank and shagged. Thinking about it, we could have saved the airfare and just honeymooned in Cornwall for all we got up to.

'Charlotte Heard,' comes a voice nearby, breaking me out of my reverie. I know who it is before I turn around and see his mug glaring out at me from the back seat of a black Mercedes.

'Sergei Mikhailov. How lovely to see you again.'

'Where are you walking to? We can give you a lift.'

'Just the train station and I'd prefer to walk, thanks.'

'I think you should get in the car,' he says, implying heavily that he is not offering me a ride out of the goodness of his heart. I stop walking, the car halts its crawl, I open the same door Mikhailov's face appeared out of and climb into the Mercedes.

'How is your feeling on the ground here? Will you win the seat?' is the Russian's unexpected opener.

'Could go either way but I'm quietly confident.'

'We could help push it in your direction, if you'd like.'

'Thanks, but no thanks.'

'Suit yourself. I have a job for you.'

I laugh.

'I'm out of that game. Wouldn't be a good look to be caught for murder while running for office, if you take my point.'

'I can make it worth your while.'

'I'm certain your offer will be generous, but like I say, I'm out of that line of work permanently.'

'Five hundred thousand pounds.'

I have to pause to take that number in.

'Jesus, whose life is worth that much?'

'I will only tell you if you change your mind and decide you are "back in the game" now.'

Half a million quid is a hell of a lot of money. All for seducing some Russian bloke and putting a little of the old powder in his vodka? Perhaps I should tell Mikhailov I'm interested – but no, I have too much to lose now.

'No thanks, Sergei. But thanks for thinking of me anyhow.'

The Mercedes pulls up in front of the train station.

'Suit yourself, Charlotte Heard. I have only this to say: you might well make a fine politician. But you are one of the best assassins I have ever come across. If you went pro, you could take over the world. I would be happy to help you as much as I could with such a career change.'

'Again, thanks for the offer.'

'Scoff if you will, but tell me this: why do something you will only ever be so-so at when instead, you could be the best in the world at something much more lucrative?'

It bothers me that Mikhailov has a point here. I say my goodbyes and promise to have a think about it.

I arrive at the station is nine minutes before the next train to London is due to depart. Perfect: just enough time to get myself a coffee. The train pulls up as scheduled and I clamber on board. As we roll out of the station, into view hovers DCI Murray. It is the first time I've seen her since I was released from custody with all charges dropped shortly after the Jeremy incident. She takes a seat across the table from me.

'This is an odd coincidence,' I say sarcastically to her.

'I went by your office and the chap there said you were on your way to London.'

'That's my husband, Tom.'

She gives me a 'you go, girl!' face alongside a thumbs up.

'Anyhow, I came to the station in hope more than expectation and then saw you board,' she says.

'What in particular did you want to discuss with me, DCI Murray?'

She slides a picture across the table. It is of a woman's corpse, beaten badly, bloodied, with multiple stab wounds in the abdomen.

'I have a couple of murders on my hands which I think were committed by the same perpetrator. I thought you might be able to help me with the case.'

'How exactly would I be able to help you?'

'I have a lot of partial evidence, much of it circumstantial, and I thought going over it with you might help me get into the mindset of the murderer.'

'Why would I be able to get inside the mind of a murderer?'

'You've spent more time up close and personal to one of them than anyone I know.'

She smiles at me in a way that reveals the intended ambiguity of her last statement.

'As flattered as I am by this offer, I don't have the time. In addition to my full-time job running one of the largest think tanks in the United Kingdom, I also have a campaign to run in a marginal seat I might be the MP for in a few months' time. Thanks for thinking of me, but . . .'

'There are two big local church groups I believe you've been trying to get to support your campaign, if I'm not mistaken.'

'Go on.'

'With one of them, I'm on good personal terms with the pastor. He's not really political and normally supports the Labour candidate in the area. I'm sure I could convince him to do otherwise. Most of his flock, as I'm sure you already know, vote in the direction he points to.'

'And the other one?'

'My cousin Ethel runs the office in that particular parish.'

'How convenient.'

'I have a large family.'

I have to smile at DCI Murray's skills.

'All right then, you've got me,' I tell her. 'So long as it doesn't take up too much of my time.'

'Can you come by my office on Friday at ten?'

'Make it eleven and you're on. Same place?'

'Same place.'

'Right then,' DCI Murray says as she gets up out of her seat. 'I'll leave you in peace. See you Friday.'

As she walks down the corridor, toward the carriage door, I find myself wanting to know the answer to a question that has nagged at me recently.

'DCI Murray?'

She stops and then turns around to face me again.

'What's your first name?' I ask her.

She smiles.

'It's Sheila.'

She then disappears into the next carriage. I think about the interaction between the policewoman and me for a few minutes as Surrey speeds by and conclude I feel a bit chuffed by it all. Look at me: wanted as an accomplice by both sides of the law.

When I get into the office, Sabine, my personal assistant at the think tank, is flustered.

212

'That Chad Cooper guy is here again!' she squeals at me.

'Where is he?' I ask, deadpan.

'In the boardroom talking to one of the interns.'

I collect my thoughts and then decide how to handle this situation. I walk over to Kate's desk.

'Are Aashi and Violet in?'

'Of course,' Kate says. 'Aashi is over at Mark's desk discussing the housing paper and Violet is in the kitchen.'

'Gather the two of them and meet me in the board room in three minutes.'

'Will do.'

I walk to the boardroom, open the door and walk in.

'The thing about this project is its personal nature to me,' Cooper is droning on about to some young-looking female intern we've clearly taken on recently.

'Right, Chad, why are you here?' I shout.

'That's very metaphysical of you, Charlotte. Why are any of us here?'

'Reginald may have put up with your shit at Eligium. And I'll admit, I haven't been around enough lately, what with my campaigning, to let you know that this crap isn't going to be tolerated in my back garden.'

I turn to the intern.

'Sorry, my dear, what is your name?' I ask her.

'Doreen.'

'Right, Doreen. I think you should leave the room now before things get messy.'

She nods and scampers away in a manner that is most impressive, as if she were a lizard.

'I was just about finished with Doreen there, you know,' Cooper says to me, irritated. 'Now I'm going to have to pick it all up with her again.'

'No, Chad. You are not picking up anything again, not round here.'

Right on cue, Charlie's Angels appear behind me, all of them bringing the fierce along for the ride. I am about to order the girls to pick up Cooper and throw him down the stairs when another thought suddenly strikes me. While it is tempting to be mean to Cooper here and now, it won't get rid of my problem long-term. He'll just be back here soon enough, annoying another intern.

'Girls, would you mind leaving Mr Cooper and I alone for a moment?'

They all look at each other confused, but then quickly turn around and leave Cooper and me in the boardroom alone together.

'Thinking about it a little more, I'm glad you're here,' I say. 'I realise I haven't given you enough of my time recently.'

'Well, I can't say I'm not annoyed about it. But I understand you have a campaign to run, so I can cut you some slack. Now that I've got your attention at last, I have a few ideas I want to run past you. I have a brand-new angle on the robot army . . .'

I place my index finger onto his mouth, causing Cooper's eyes to almost bulge out of their sockets.

'Why don't you tell me about it tonight – at my place.'

'Of course,' Cooper says, trying to keep himself together. He does that thing blokes often do when they are flustered, pulling down on his jacket as if suddenly embarrassed by his legs. 'What time will you be expecting me?'

'Seven, sharp.'

'See you then, then.'

For a moment, I think Cooper is going to play this relatively cool and walk out without another word. But no – Chad Cooper is as Chad Cooper does.

'Can I just say that I knew this moment would come. Looking back on it, I should have known your wedding was all a tease for my benefit and that the day would come when you and I would . . .'

'Just shut up and get out of here before you blow it, Cooper!' I shout. He thankfully takes the hint and scarpers. I text Kate:

'FULL-ON BATEMAN RED ALERT. BE IN THE AREA OF HQ FROM SEVEN TONIGHT.'

A few seconds later, Kate bursts into the boardroom.

'Can I just say, this is long, long overdue. Anything extra you need on this one, please let any of us know.'

'Will do. Thanks.'

'With great pleasure.'

Jesus, I knew Kate was no fan of Cooper's, but I didn't think her hatred of the guy was that heartfelt. She shuts the door, leaving me in the boardroom by myself once again. I decide to stay there for another few minutes by myself as it has a nice view of the Houses of Parliament from the far window. I walk over and stare out at the estate, thinking about how wonderful it will be in a few months' time when I walk into it for the first time as an MP.